OUTLAW
JUSTICE

Overdrive: Book Two

ADAM KNIGHT

BIG NOW // Too long But // Always BROTHERS!

JK Jeff

Reader's Praise for COWBOY ENDING available in Print or E-Book Format.

"I really loved this book, so instead of waiting for a mail from Amazon to ask me to review this, I logged on and started writing this review. A first for me."

Dec 11, 2013

"This book is urban fantasy, but much to my enjoyment there are no vampires, werewolves, or demons in it. I liked the book for its sincerity and the older (presumably wiser) main character..."

Jan 27, 2014

"Knight's main character and hero of the book is rough around the edges but in an approachable, personable, relatable way. He's a down-to-earth, tell it like it is kind of guy and it's hard not to like him."

April 3, 2014

Customer Reviews truly are the lifeblood to an independent authors' success. Thank you to everyone who took the time to read and recommend COWBOY ENDING to others.

COWBOY ENDING: Book 1 of OVERDRIVE

Available for Purchase via:

AMAZON
SMASHWORDS
BARNES & NOBLE
APPLE BOOKS
KOBO
And Select Stores

As a proud, full time resident of the City of Winnipeg it seemed only appropriate to begin my literary journey in my hometown and display pieces of it prominently as set pieces in this novel. The axiom "write what you know" has been essential for me in this process and I am hopeful that this tale becomes a fun read for other citizens of Winnipeg, whether current, former or future.

If you have enjoyed this book I invite you to join the Official OVERDRIVE Facebook Page and start a conversation. I will be visiting as often as I can to provide insights and updates for future stories and answer any questions you might have.

Thank you very much for taking a chance on my work. Writing has been a passion of mine for as long as I can remember.

You can also follow me on Twitter (@OutlawAK) .
though I warn you in advance I also use this forum to
talk about my upcoming Pro Wrestling dates, workout
routines and various other entertainments that make me
laugh.

Regards,

Adam Knight
Twitter - @OutlawAK
https://www.facebook.com/OverdriveSeries

"Outlaw Justice" is the second book in the "Overdrive" series and the first series published by the author. Look for Book Three late in 2016.

For Merida.

My life. My laughter. My little girl..

I love you.

Prologue

Jennifer Klassen disappeared without a trace.

Well, that's not precisely true. No one disappears without a trace.

Someone, somewhere saw something.

Jennifer was last seen leaving her downtown office at the usual time, approximately four-thirty P.M. Co-workers reported nothing out of the ordinary to the police. She did not appear distressed or upset in any way, at least no more so than anyone did coming back to work from a vacation that is.

Jennifer Klassen was a dental hygienist who worked out of the Medical Arts Building on Graham and Edmonton. Her employer, Dr. McCarthy described her as being in good spirits despite the sweltering late summer heat. She waved good-bye and shared jokes with her coworkers and the receptionist on her way to the elevators. She waited at her usual bus stop with familiar faces, people who recognized her as a regular rider of the number eleven through North Kildonan.

The four-forty-seven arrived right on time at four-fifty-one, as usual a victim of evening rush hour.

Jennifer got on the bus with the crush of people heading home.

She didn't get off at her usual stop near the Chief Peguis Trail.

No one remembered where she got off.

The digital camera set to record passenger movements for their own safety in case of an emergency was inoperable and had been for weeks without being reported. Winnipeg Transit was conducting an internal investigation into equipment maintenance processes.

Regardless, no one could confirm when she had gotten off the bus.

At first Norman Klassen didn't panic. It wasn't uncommon for his wife to be late coming home from work. Once in a while she stopped for coffee or made a quick shopping trip to the mall on Portage Avenue, especially on very hot days to avoid discomfort on crowded buses. It also wasn't uncommon for her to not return text messages in a timely fashion. Jennifer was horrible for letting her smartphone's battery die or leaving it on airplane mode.

By nine o'clock. he started to get worried.

By ten he was working the phone. Calling friends, family and the co-workers he had numbers for.

By ten-thirty he was speaking to the police.

By eleven the Police were building a file on Jennifer and adding her name to the ever growing case file assigned to the Missing Women Task Force.

The case file was twenty-seven names deep.

*

Cristal stood out in the side street with one hip thrust forward provocatively as she waved at the oncoming headlights. Well, head*light* really. Only one of them was working.

She hoped the look on her face was "helpless and friendly." What she felt was "tired and irritated." Cristal was sick of being the bait for Jim and Otto's carjacking scheme.

For weeks they'd been working in different areas of Winnipeg, usually near shopping malls or similar complexes with later business hours. Looking for those charitable folks who were tired and not thinking too clearly, but honest enough to offer help in boosting another person's ride.

Honest people who were then ambushed, left tied up and had their car stolen. Along with their belongings.

The press had been following the case that the police were building, sending warnings out to the general public. Sketches of the perpetrators had been circulated, though all of them were wrong. People were lousy at giving proper descriptions especially during times of stress and duress.

At least that's what Otto said. Cristal was hungry and didn't care. But helping these two dimwits out was still a step up from giving lap-dances at private house parties or waiting tables.

So she smiled helplessly and waved at the oncoming headlight.

The van slowed. Cristal's smile wavered, taking in the battered old Ford. Cracked windshield. Rust becoming more dominant than the paint job along most of the siding. Front bumper missing a mooring and hanging low on the left side.

Fuck. This piece of crap ain't worth the effort.

But it's hard to wave a guy off after you've gotten his attention.

A man's head leaned slightly out the driver's side window. All Cristal could make out in the dim light was a shock of unruly hair and a pair of bright eyes.

"What's up?"

Showtime.

"Hey, sorry to bother." Winsome and nervous, plus a bit of eyelash fluttering. *Brings out the chivalry in every sucker.* "My boyfriend's truck won't start. He thinks it just needs a boost."

The man peered at her quietly for a moment..

Cristal fought down a touch of nerves. *This would be the one guy who still reads newspapers.*

"Where's the truck?" he asked, surprising Cristal.

She motioned with her head off to the alley behind her, hoping her winsome-turned-grateful smile hadn't slipped. "We backed it out of the road, over behind the Bulk Barn."

The man's eyes tracked her motion. Following the usual plan Otto stepped out of the shadows and waved, smiling widely.

The man said nothing a moment for a moment.

"That your boyfriend?"

"Yeah."

"Who's that with him?"

"His brother, Jim."

More silence.

"Heading to a party or something?"

Cristal sighed heavily, with an exaggerated up and down bosom movement. The distraction worked, as the man's gaze came back to her.

"We're just coming back from the casino. The truck died over there," she pointed vaguely in the direction of the main road. "So we pushed it outta the way. Didn't want to block traffic."

The man grunted. "Considerate of you. Lots of traffic at three a.m. Tough to flag down help though." He flicked his eyes back to Otto and Jim, considering in the darkness.

Cristal started to get nervous.

"If it's too much trouble we can wait for CAA."

He made up his mind.

"No problem. I'll take a look."

Cristal breathed a quiet sigh of relief and stepped aside, allowing the beat up whale of a van to pull ahead to the darkened alley until it was nose to nose with Otto's truck. Cristal hurried to catch up, hard to pull off in high-heeled boots but doable.

The man who stepped out of the truck wasn't what she expected. Both Otto and Jim's faces became suddenly strained as a guy who could've been a CFL linebacker stepped into the humid air, placed a black cowboy hat onto his head went to pop the hood of his van.

"Need cables?" he asked.

Otto coughed slightly, visibly reconsidering things. "I got some if you'd rather."

"Fine."

Otto motioned to Jim who went around and climbed into the back of the truck, ostensibly searching for booster cables.

Cristal stood off to one side and casually leaned against the wall of the Bulk Barn, a lone bulb in the establishment's sign flickering to life intermittently and adding more shadows to the alley.

She narrowed her eyes against the flickering.

I hate this part.

"You gonna pop your hood?"

"What?"

The big man motioned with the brim of his hat to Jim's fumbling. "Buddy's searching for cables, let's pop your hood and get ready."

"You in a rush?"

"It's three in the morning and I still need to grab groceries from Wal-Mart and snag a burger before finally going to bed. So yeah, kinda."

Otto nodded calmly, all nervous smiles. "Cool man, no worries. I appreciate the help." He went over to the driver's door, reached through the window and popped the hood while glowering at Jim. "What's taking so long?" Not a real question, part of the usual script.

Jim followed up with his line. "Cables're buried under your pressure washer."

"Oh okay." Otto's found the catch and lifted the hood, securing it in place. He turned to the big man, asking the question designed to throw him off his guard."You wanna buy a pressure washer?"

"What?"

"It works good. I just got a new one for my job and can let this one go cheap."

""Why the fuck would I want to buy a pressure washer?"

"They're about three hundred bucks new. I could give you mine for... "

"There's nothing wrong with your battery."

Cristal blinked in surprise.

That's not how this works.

Otto choked on his words, sputtering a few times as he stared up at the big man who was in turn peering intently at the truck's open engine.

"Wh-what?"

"Your battery's fine. Almost fully charged I figure."

"How do you... What're you..."

The big man adjusted his stance and directed his next sentence to Jim who was still fumbling in the back of the truck though his eyes never left the engine. "If you're going to jump me, now's the time."

Oh fuck.

Otto blinked for another moment, and began to stammer out a denial of some sort. Stalling for time as he fumbled at the inside of the engine casing, feeling for the pipe he kept hidden there.

Cristal felt the hair on the back of her neck and all along her arms suddenly stand on end.

Otto's expression changed in an instant, snarling openly as he brandished the hidden pipe and took a step forward.

The flickering light from the Bulk Barn's sign buzzed loudly in the stillness before erupting with a loud crack. Hot glass shards burst into the night, showering Cristal's head and the pavement around her. Her eyes burned from the sudden light that flared into the darkness, blinding her as she dropped to her knees.

Noise drew her attention. Metal slamming. An engine roaring. Otto screaming.

Her eyes cleared.

The truck had fired to life which was impossible. Cristal could see the truck keys dangling from the chain attached to Otto's belt.

The big man's eyes seemed to blaze in the night as he pressed the truck's hood down hard on the back of Otto's head while the engine roared in his face. Otto's hands and feet flailed uselessly, his screams pitching higher with the revving of the eight cylinder Dodge.

Jim finally appeared out of the alleyway, climbing over the back of the truck and onto off the roof of the cab. He brandished a tire iron in one hand as he leapt through the air in a frenzy.

Jim wasn't a large man, but he wasn't small enough to explain what Cristal saw next.

As Jim came flying down, the big man contemptuously swung his free arm and swatted him into the brick wall of the Bulk

Barn. Jim staggered drunkenly on his feet, crying out in pain but still standing.

Then the big man grabbed Jim firmly by the ear and slammed his face to the hood of the truck. Otto screamed from the impact as Jim finally crumbled to the ground.

Cristal whimpered in fright, cowering in a ball on the pavement.

The big man turned his gaze towards her briefly. He paused in his actions, seemingly lost in thought.

Then he tossed the truck's hood up. It creaked loudly as it reached the end of it's restraints. Otto heaved himself away from the engine, his face a mess of burns and blood. Otto's voice never dropped below a scream as he turned back towards the big man with fists raised.

Sparks streamed out from the truck's engine, shooting like fireworks into the air. The truck's abruptly went silent, as did Otto's scream as he flinched back from the sight.

The big man stood before Otto lit now only by the single headlight from his van.

"Now you need a boost," he growled.

Otto sputtered wordlessly for a moment.

Then a vicious punch knocked him senseless, leaving him laying in a heap.

Cristal trembled wordlessly, clutching at her arms and shying away from the sight. She barely noticed as the big man knelt down and began searching through Otto and Jim's clothes.

He found Otto's wallet and quickly rifled through it, pulling out a few meagre bills.

"Wh–what are you... Are you stealing their money?"

The big man's eyes focused on her. "Seems like buying dinner is the least these clowns can do."

Something clattered at Cristal's feet making her flinch.

Jim's cell phone.

"Wh-what …"

"Dial nine-one-one. Get some cops down here." The big man stood up and dusted himself off, walking back towards his van. He paused at the door glowering down at her from under the brim of his black hat. "Well, get to it. I'm hungry and don't wanna miss Whopper Wednesday at Burger King."

Cristal's fingers trembled as she started to dial.

Shoulda been a waitress.

Chapter 1

"I need a favour, Joe."

I paused mid sip, glancing at Cathy over the brim of my coffee mug.

"A favour?"

"Yeah."

I took a moment to respond.

"I'm allergic to cats."

"What?"

"A favour is asking someone to watch their cat while they're away." I finished my sip and put down the ceramic mug with a small smile. "And since I'm allergic to cats I can't help you."

Cathy leaned back in her chair and crossed her arms under her not insignificant breasts and peered at me with lips pursed and one eyebrow cocked.

"I don't have a cat."

"So you're asking me to watch the Captain's cat? What, he

doesn't have friends? Besides, I'm not sure how appropriate that is."

"Of course he has friends. That's not... Max doesn't have a cat either."

"Oh good. 'Cause I'm allergic."

Cathy pinched the bridge of her nose with the well manicured fingers of her left hand and sighed.

I chuckled softly behind my small smile and sipped more coffee.

We must've made quite a sight in the small cafe in Old St. Boniface. Though the new evening co-anchor and lead investigative reporter for Winnipeg's highest rated evening newscast Cathy Greenburg would stand out in any crowd. Especially dressed in her high fashion, news-cast sponsored finery. The dichotomy of seeing her sitting across the tiny diner table from a scruffy, near three hundred pound man dressed in shabby blue jeans, a rumpled white tee-shirt that was way too tight across the shoulders would've been enough. Especially with a battered, black cowboy hat resting on the table between them.

But since we were surrounded on all sides by sweaty construction workers on break and groups of elderly folks from the nearby apartment buildings and retirement homes there were a lot of eyes checking us out as we talked.

They say opposites attract.

Those people are full of shit.

The matriarch of the French-Canadian family who ran the cafe topped up my coffee and smiled warmly at me as she took our orders.

Once she left Cathy recovered her composure and was once again pursing her lips at me.

"It's been a while since you've done that."

"Done what?"

Her eyes narrowed dangerously for a moment.

"Driven me crazy with distracted prattling. You did that to me all the time in college."

"Did I?"

"You did."

"Huh." I sipped coffee. "Old habits, I guess."

"It's irritating."

"So is being asked to a friendly lunch when you really want to guilt me into a favour."

Cathy's face reddened slightly, eyes flickering down to her own cup.

"Sure, it's nice to hear from you and all," I continued, my tone wistful. "It's been what, three months since you've called? Still, that's better than the previous twelve year gap in communication we had after I left school. And I'll take any excuse to take an extended lunch break from my shitty job at *Canada-Pharm.*"

"Joe, I wasn't... I didn't mean to..."

I shook my head gently. "Hey, it's okay. I know you've been busy The promotion at work. The highly visible moving in with your boyfriend that somehow made the papers. New responsibilities. New life. I get it."

"You don't have to make me feel bad about it."

"You don't have to lie to get me to meet you for lunch."

Cathy reached across the small table and gripped my free hand tightly. "I didn't lie to you. I *do* want to talk, hear how things are going. Like I said to your mother when I left the message, it's been too long."

"Huh," I grunted, trying to ignore how good her cool and soft fingers felt over my battered knuckles. "Wonder how long it woulda been if you didn't need a favour?"

She took her hand away sullenly and stared at me from across the table. The sharp movement drawing eyes from a few of the curious patrons.

I ignored them all. I'm good at that.

"You want me to leave?"

"You want to go?"

"Just answer the question, Joe. I don't want to argue. I want to talk."

A million spiteful things bubbled just at the tip of my tongue for a long moment. All of them inexcusable to say to a friend at the worst of times, never mind to a friend who'd had my back more than once during the crazy shit I managed to find myself in back in the spring.

Besides, Cathy was a good person who genuinely cared. And those type of people never deserve to be berated by selfish assholes who didn't get enough sleep the night before.

Plus the judgemental looks I was getting from a table of grandmothers over in the corner was making me feel bad.

I cleared my throat and straightened up wearily in my chair, putting down my mug and forced myself to meet her eyes gently.

"I'm sorry. Please stay."

Cathy's eyes softened.

"I'm sorry too. I wanted to check in more often."

"I'm sure. Life. It gets busy."

Cathy's eyebrow arched again, this time mockingly.

"Would be easier if you had a cell phone and I could text you."

"Pfft. Texting. That'll never catch on."

Cathy laughed softly. "Seriously, Joe. You're going to have to join the twentieth century eventually. I can't leave messages with your mother forever."

The cheap halogen lights in the cafe's suspended ceiling flickered once in time with the painful twisting in my guts. I quickly shut my eyes and calmed the tingling sensation that had started up at the back of my neck. The lights immediately resumed their normal humming cadence and I opened my eyes again.

Cathy's expression was pained.

"I'm sorry. I wasn't thinking."

I shrugged. "S'okay."

"How is she doing?"

I shrugged again. "Good days and bad. Docs put her on new meds, took her off some others."

"Is there any progress?"

"Some. We're moving her into a facility on Sunday."

"Wow. Really?"

I nodded.

"How do you feel about that?"

"It sucks. But it might be the best thing for her. She's starting to need more regular attention from doctors and the like, more than I can provide her at home anyway." I took a breath to clear my head and attempted to lighten the mood. "More'n likely she's just sick of my cooking."

Cathy smiled gently.

"You cook?"

"Best soup and sandwich you'll even have. Outside of this place, of course." I indicated the cafe with a short motion of my head just as the establishment's matriarch passed by. Her smile lit up the room and earned me another top up on my coffee.

Cathy's smile stayed in place but her eyes got inquisitive as she peered at me.

Made me uncomfortable.

"What?" I gave my tee shirt a glance. "Did I spill coffee?"

Her dark eyes kept peering.

"You've changed."

"I have?"

"Yeah."

"Well, this is a new-ish shirt. Only a couple weeks old. For real, I didn't spill on it did I?"

Cathy ignored my deflection and pointed at my chest almost accusingly. "You're confident."

I blinked at her in confusion.

"Confident?"

"With me. With the wait staff. Most importantly with yourself." Cathy gave me the once over from her seat and pursed her lips. "And why the hell not? Things have changed for both of us since *Cowboy Shotz*."

Mental images flashed behind my eyes at the mention of my

former place of employment.

Fire.

People screaming.

Blood.

A burned out body buried in the wreckage of the DeeJay booth.

Parise's chest bursting from gunshot wounds.

Candace Cleghorn's smiling face from an old picture hanging in the basement of the house she shared with her brother.

Pain.

I shook my head and rubbed my calloused fingers over my eyes to shove the images away. It had only been a few months since the bar had burned to the ground so it shouldn't surprise me that the images wouldn't go away that quickly. But a part of me knew they'd never go away. I would remember that horrific night in minute detail for the rest of my life.

Which makes sense I suppose. Life changing moments should stick with you, shouldn't they?

"You okay?" Cathy asked, her voice concerned and suddenly more hushed. Realizing that we had some nosy neighbours here in the cafe.

I forced my eyes open and took a quick look around, noting that none of the light bulbs or machinery had malfunctioned in the last few moments. I took a small pride in that, thinking I'd started to get a grip on my little issues.

"Sure. I'm fine." Coffee cured everything so I took a big sip, letting the prairie farm cream and Columbian goodness wash away the memories. "Just been... It's tough to think about that night. About the stuff leading to that night."

Cathy took a look around the cafe herself hesitantly. Once certain that no one was listening she lowered her voice even more. "You mean the human trafficking with Korean officials or the you getting shot part?"

Phantom pain flared in the faded scars on my chest and abdomen.

Gunshots suck, just in case you were curious.

"All of it really," I answered carefully, also keeping my voice low. "Did you hear anything else about... Well, the stuff that you weren't allowed to broadcast."

Cathy grimaced and shook her head. "Everything I've heard is public record as far as I know. Officials like to play things close to their vest when they're involved in things, but in this case the Canadian Government has been an open book. The South Korean Ambassador has been cleared of implications while his sub-ordinate has been assigned with all the blame and planning. The assistant was the point person that Parise's crew got in contact with, allowing them to expand on the prostitution ring they were already running out of the nightclub. Whether he really was acting without the Ambassador's knowledge is impossible to determine without breaking international laws. Immunity and all that."

My mouth twisted bitterly. Kicking myself in the ass mentally once again for being too wrapped up in my own head to see the blatant signs of wrong doing happening right under my fool nose.

"So that's the end of it?" I asked. "People have been arrested that they could arrest. Case closed?"

Cathy nodded. "As far as the police are concerned the mystery surrounding women disappearing from *Cowboy Shotz* and the involvement of Officer Parise and his group is closed. There was enough evidence leftover via bank transactions and other documentation to close all the loops there."

My stomach fluttered briefly in both relief and guilt. "So... That's it?"

"More or less." Cathy's eyes flickered oddly. Her fingers fiddled nervously with the paper napkin in front of her. "Officially the police are claiming the nightclub fire was an accident, that eyewitness reports of a large man starting a brawl with staff members and the disgraced police officers are misconstrued and unrelated."

Shit.

"But unofficially they're keeping an eye out for... For someone?"

She shook her head. "The police are too busy to care about you, Joe. As far as they're concerned, one of the bar's crew members got greedy and started a fight. Things escalated out of control. Other people got involved and the place caught on fire."

"Huh." I grunted before muttering. "Actually not too far off the mark."

Cathy went silent for a long moment. I filled the awkward seeming silence with coffee and introspective looks. The last thing I wanted was for this lunch to turn into a Q and A session about what got into me, why I didn't call the police directly and what really happened inside the club that night.

Though that day was coming. Likely sooner than later.

"As I was saying," Cathy began again, breaking our reverie. "The police have been working overtime on lots of ongoing issues. Which is why they're more or less satisfied with... Well. With that issue. Between the recent car jackings and seemingly random assaults, the streets of Winnipeg aren't the safest place to be anymore."

I started to get a sinking feeling in my stomach, and I doubted it was about the early morning arrest of two former car jackers found unconscious next to their truck. "You were saying something about a favour?"

Cathy took a deep breath and placed both hands on the table before her. "Since we know that the women going missing from *Cowboy Shotz* were not part of the ongoing case of disappearances the police are back to square one with their original investigation."

My stomach sank a bit further. "How many is it now?"

"Twenty-seven women are reported missing as of last week."

"Huh," I grunted. "And this relates to your favour how?"

"I'm going out on the streets tonight. And tomorrow night. And every night I can make time to do so."

"Going out where?"

"Downtown. Different places. Public places. I'm going to be the bait in the trap that catches this sick bastard."

My stomach dropped all the way down, somewhere between my boots.

"And I need you to watch my back while I do.

Chapter 2

"You *did* tell her what a stupid idea that was didn't you?" Tamara asked from behind the fitness desk at the downtown YMCA.

I scowled darkly at her.

What was I gonna say?

"And you're *still* going to shadow her? While she what, conducts a sting operation?" Tamara shook her tiny head, sending her little bob-cut of hair bouncing and readjusting those librarian style glasses she always wore. "It's not like this abductor even has a type if what the papers are reporting is true."

"It is, apparently."

"So what? One night she'll wander around like a helpless businesswoman? The next as a frayed grandmother?"

My scowl got even darker if that was possible. "We're going to be hanging with the hookers on Higgins tonight actually."

Tamara's snort was loaded with disdain. "No wonder you agreed to help."

I woulda been lying if I said anything to deny her.

It was later than I cared to train at the Downtown Y. But since

I'd taken an extra half-hour for my lunch with Cathy the time bandits over at *Canada-Pharm* insisted I make it up past my usual quit. Frustrating but what can you do? The post business crowd rush had just started to trickle into the gym and within minutes the cardio floor would be a complete shit show of people hogging treadmills and the like.

Thankfully it took a bit longer for the weight pit to fill up.

Tamara continued muttering darkly to herself as she led the way up the spiral staircase to my home away from Mom's Basement. I didn't catch all of it but the words "thinking with the wrong head" seemed prevalent for some reason.

I sighed.

"Should I have left Cathy hanging? Off to do this on her own?"

"This is her plan, not yours." Tamara retorted over one shoulder as she threaded her way between the weight trees and various Hammer Strength brand machines over to the lonely, old school squat rack that she knew I preferred. "If she wants to go lollygagging around the seedier parts of Winnipeg in the hopes of attracting a dangerous abductor that sounds like her business and not yours."

"Lollygagging?"

"What?"

"Lollygagging?" I repeated with my small smile.

Tamara rolled her eyes expansively as she reached the far wall and turned to rest her shapely backside against the railing there. She made a quick note on the clipboard she carried with her to keep records of my daily improvements and difficulties encountered during my workouts while I slowly went through my usual warm up routine. Rolling my neck, wrists and other joints in slow circles while taking slow, even breaths.

The now familiar tingle at the back of my neck began to buzz slightly in anticipation of the efforts I was about to begin while my stomach began to rumble ever so faintly. Lunch had been four hours behind me by this point and my head was just starting to ache.

After twenty minutes I had worked my way up to the maximum poundage the YMCA's weightlifting bars would safely hold. I could've gotten there faster, but Tamara was very careful to make certain I didn't rush through the motions on every lift. She took the time after each set to check my pulse, have me feel for strains or tears in my ligaments and joints and to make certain I took in enough water.

The crowd in the weight pit was getting hard to ignore as they surreptitiously eyed my little corner of the gym. Apparently it wasn't every day that a dude did Olympic strongman calibre lifts on the clean-and-press. For reps.

I stared at my sweaty reflection in the mirror as Tamara held my wrist and kept her eyes on her stopwatch.

It was no longer possible for me to think of myself as a fat man.

My whole life leading up to the night I got shot had been a constant struggle with my belly and my diet. I'd tried every workout plan, gone to several nutritionists and was a workout fanatic. But no matter how hard I trained, the eating bug kept kicking me in the ass. Nothing says "waste of time" more than a Burger King run right after a 2 hour powerlifting session.

No matter what the ads will try to tell you, at the end of the day you truly are what you eat.

I could feel the small smile on my lips trying to turn into a smirk. Manfully I restrained that urge. I might've been getting a bit cocky about my appearance, but I'll never be the kind of douchebag that smirks at himself in the mirror.

I hope.

"Remarkable," Tamara muttered, releasing my wrist and making notes on her clipboard. "Every day you come in here and every day it's remarkable."

The tingle at the back of my neck flared as I caught my breath, eager to have me push myself for a tenth set. I was eager to oblige.

"One more?"

"If you like. Though if you'd rather we can move on to seated military press, since you've got a date tonight."

"Har har," I muttered, bending down and deadlifting the overloaded Olympic bar to the reinforced iron pegs on the squat rack with a grunt. The crowd began to disperse once I started stripping the bar down.

Tamara was leaning against the wall again and staring at her clipboard as I re-racked the plates, her eyes unfocused. Clearly distracted.

"Everything okay?" I asked.

She blinked, refocusing on me. "Yeah. I mean... Yeah. I'm fine. Just have a few things on my mind."

"Clearly." I finished racking the plates and towelled my face with the hem of my tee shirt. "Anything I can do?"

Tamara laughed and motioned to her notes. "Apparently there's a lot you can do."

"I also listen."

She blinked her eyes again and broke contact. "I know. Just... It's nothing you need to worry about."

Her tone of voice called her words a lie.

"But I know you're there if I need you. I promise."

I stared down at Tamara's tiny form for a long moment, fighting the conflicting emotions in my head trying to tell me what to do or say next. Words to convince her to open up. I was her friend after all. A damned good friend too. One that trusted her implicitly with all of the craziness in my life since getting shot. All of the headaches, the hunger pangs, the impossible feats of strength and speed. Getting shot, did I mention that? That last night at the club.

She knew all of my biggest secrets.

Which meant I could trust her to tell me hers when she was ready.

I grunted. "Okay. Shoulder press?"

Tamara sighed slightly, her lips turning into a tired smile. "You know it."

"Cool."

Being six-and-a-half feet tall has a lot of benefits, but it sure sucks when the rest of the world is designed for the average person. It took me a full minute to readjust the seat on the overhead press bench with out accidentally tearing the knobs off and leaving me stuck with an equipment repair bill. However once I'd managed to drop the seat right down I squeezed my shoulders past the support bars and began my warm up sets.

"Oh, I think I've figured out why you keep getting headaches."

Tamara mentioned off-handedly.

I nearly lost my grip on the bar as it came down, just barely avoiding an embarrassing forehead to iron collision.

"You're just telling me this now?"

"I wanted to get your workout going first. And besides, it's only a theory."

I grunted in response, standing up to load the bar with more Joe-sized weights.

"I'll take the theory of the top scoring kinesiologist in her University class any day. Sure would be more informative than anything I've been able to figure out."

Tamara's cheeks coloured slightly as she readjusted her glasses unnecessarily. "Well I did have a little help."

My heart skipped a beat. "Help?"

"Yeah. I asked my Professor some questions and..."

"Wait, what kind of questions were you asking?"

She arched one eyebrow mockingly at me. "I promise you that none of the questions involved details like improbable strength gains, remarkable recovery time from injuries, oh and by the way my friend's name is Joe."

It was my turn for the cheeks to redden slightly. I hid it by scowling mock-fiercely and shaking one fist at her face.

Tamara stuck out her tongue impishly, completing my belief that she'd never grow up either. "They were general questions about the concept of metabolism and its effects on the human body in more than just the commonplace athletes."

"You think I qualify as a commonplace athlete?" I could feel the self-conscious thirteen-year-old boy's chest deep within me puffing up with pride.

Tamara blinked again, her eyes flickering from her clipboard and back to me. She visibly discarded what she was about to say next before continuing. "What we spent most of our time debating were the invisible effects that the human body suffered after extreme exertions."

I finished loading the bar and sat down, settling my grip and lifted off. "So what'd your Prof' say?"

"We discussed how peak athletes, and I mean the absolute top one percent of people on Planet Earth have different issues they need to deal with in order to maintain a normal standard of life. How because their bodies are performing at a level above and beyond that of everyone else that the demands their body places upon them in order to fully recover from their exertions are almost alien to others."

I racked the bar gently and grabbed for my water bottle. "What kind of demands?"

Tamara made a brief note on her clipboard, tracking my set before flipping pages and reading. "In extreme cases where peak athletes pushed their bodies to the edge – which of course they need to do in order to remain at the very top of their field – there have been recorded cases of people suffering from intense stomach cramps, nausea and the stress headache that comes along with all that."

"Sounds familiar."

"Joint pain. Muscle strain and weariness. The need for ten hours sleep a night at a minimum."

I thought back over the past few days, trying to figure out if I'd even slept for ten hours in the past week.

"Basically," Tamara went on, breaking into my reverie. "It all amounts to the same thing, which is the heightened metabolism of these peak athletes requires more input to the bodies in order to maintain that level of output."

"Huh?"

Tamara's eyes narrowed as she looked at me. "You know what I'm talking about. Marathon runners the day before a big race make sure to eat double or triple the amount of carbohydrates they normally consume in order to have the strength to finish a five hour run. Professional football players who eat everything they can get their hands on in order to maintain the extra muscle mass required to be effective on the offensive line."

I could feel my familiar headache beginning to increase as the tingle at the back of my neck started getting sharper.

"So what're you saying? I need to eat more than most people?" It was my turn to narrow my eyes and quirk a brow. "Hello? Not exactly breaking news. Look at the size of me."

Tamara stepped in closer, her voice dropping to a near whisper. "Joe. I'm trying to tell you that the rate of calorie output you're experiencing is significantly greater than anything I can find recorded anywhere in the University's records."

"Uh... Pardon?"

She nodded fractionally. "Joe, you've lost over thirty-five percent of your body fat in under four months while maintaining the same body-mass-index. That means for every pound of fat you've lost you've converted it into muscle. It takes years for people to make that kind of an extreme turnaround, even with illegal methods that type of conversion is nearly impossible."

My eyes started to go dry from lack of blinking as the headache began to pulse in time with the tingling sensation.

Tamara's eyes turned serious. "If you keep experiencing this kind of growth in strength and endurance, if you keep pushing yourself with these super human workouts - I'm worried you might get to the point where you can't consume enough food on a daily basis to keep up with your metabolism."

I was out of funny things to say.

"And that's bad?"

"Joe, it might kill you."

Chapter 3

"Joseph, tell me you are not going out dressed like that."

"Uhm..."

My mom leaned wearily against the counter in our kitchen, frowning darkly at me with her tiny arms crossed in a classic pose of parental disapproval.

Seriously, how does a sickly woman pushing sixty manage to look down at you with such disdain while having to crane her gaze a foot over her head to look you in the eyes?

Self-consciously I glanced down at the clothes I had pulled out from the very back of my closet. In the last few months it had gotten more and more difficult to find items that fit appropriately as my body changed in time with the weirdness I was living with. As such I often came out with a mismatched selection at the best of times.

"Really?" I asked sceptically. Hitching at the waist of my overly big jeans and trying to tuck in my too-short black tee shirt. "I figure once I throw the coat on it'll be okay."

Mom blinked at me. "A coat? Joseph, we're in the middle of a heat wave."

I shrugged. "I'll be out late. Won't be too bad."

"Joseph..."

"Mom, it's fine." I tried to cut off any further conversation by slinging the old black leather coat I'd picked up at a thrift store on and settling it firmly in place. It was too snug in the shoulders, but almost everything I owned was those days.

At least the length was right.

"See?"

Mom's lips pursed. Clearly she disagreed but wasn't going to press the issue.

"Do you have a belt?"

"Yeah. It's in the van."

"Where did you say you were going again?"

I hadn't said.

"Cathy's asked me to help with a story." The best fibs to your mother are the ones that start out with the truth before getting completely glossed over with a lack of facts. "Met me for lunch today. Needs my help meeting some people to interview."

Mom blinked.

"Your help?"

"Yeah."

Mom glanced at the old fashioned analog clock hanging on the mantle overtop the kitchen sink.

"It's getting a bit late to be conducting television interviews, isn't it?"

"Twenty-four hour news cycle."

"Did you get a job as a cameraman?"

"Mom, you know where I work."

"So then why are *you* the one helping her with these interviews?"

I sighed.

Mothers. They hate gloss.

Her eyes got worried.

"Are you doing something dangerous, Joseph? Like... Like in the spring?"

Cowboy Shotz. Fire. People screaming. Gunfire. Parise's blood spattering my face. Fleeing the burning building one step ahead of the authorities and the media.

I shivered.

"No Mom," I replied, my fingers firmly crossed as I shoved both hands deep into the pockets of my jeans. "Nothing dangerous."

"Are you sure?"

No.

"Yeah, Mom. I'm sure."

Mom stared at me blankly for a few more moments before giving up.

Ignorance can truly be bliss, another parental truth. It helped keep her sane through my brother Donald's teenaged years.

My dead brother, Donald.

Of course she's worried, moron. How could she be anything else?

Shit.

I crossed the tiny kitchen floor and gave her as gentle a hug as I could manage.

And then I quietly told her what Cathy wanted from me. All of it.

"Well, that makes more sense than her wandering the streets by herself at this time of night." Mom was a fan of Cathy's, loved seeing her in the CTV Anchor's chair and also enjoyed her infrequent visits for coffee. Mom smiled up at me wearily and squeezed. "Good for you for helping your friend."

It was my turn to blink.

Well. That went better than I expected.

"So... You're okay with this?"

"Okay is a relative term, Joseph." She stepped out from my arms and leaned against the counter again fishing in the sleeve of her fluffy robe for a stored tissue. After coughing wetly and wiping her mouth she continued. "But I told you before, I know that look in your eyes. The one where you're committed to something. Something you know is right. It's what drives you."

My cheeks felt hot. "Mom... I'm just driving her around. Keeping an eye out."

"And if she comes across something important? Something she can take to the authorities? You'll make sure she gets that information out. Because that's what you do, Joseph." Her smile was tremulous but more than a little proud. "You were meant for more than what you set yourself up for in life. For what I set you up for."

Guilt punched me in the gut with her words.

"Mom, it's okay. I'd never want..."

She cut me off. "I want more for you. I want you to feel and look this determined more often in your life." Her smile became slightly ironic. "I'd wish you found more determination in a more practical field, like pipe-fitting or welding."

I smiled sadly, pushing away the guilt and reaching for comedy. "Me too. Those guys're unionized."

And that ended the conversation.

For now.

"Are you still hungry?"

My stomach growled an affirmative, but it almost never stopped doing that anymore. So I shook my head slightly, fumbling through my coat pockets. I settled my keys and wallet more comfortably and ignored the faint stirrings of a headache along with Tamara's concerns that echoed in the back of my skull.

"What time are you expecting the real estate agent tomorrow?"

Mom sighed again, fatigue screaming in her every gesture. "I'm not sure. I was hoping to have the house tidied before he came. I'm sure he'll want to take pictures. Put them up on the listing."

"Make a list and I'll get to it first thing."

"Don't you work in the morning?"

"I work every morning. But I can take a day off if I have to. This is important."

Mom shook her head and started to walk out in to the living room. Without thinking about it I got in step with her, took one arm and guided her back to the couch. Her blankets and pillows were in slight disarray so I made certain to straighten and fluff them up how she liked before helping her to settle in.

As I tucked the blanket up to her chin, Mom's weary eyes locked on mine again. All weariness gone.

"Be safe, Joseph."

I smiled as reassuringly as I could. "I'm always safe."

One hand pressed up against my chest, her fingers touching the scars beneath my shirt from the gunshots that changed my life.

"Be safer."

Her eyes closed. Within moments her breathing evened out and she fell into a medication heavy sleep.

I stood up and stared down at her for a long moment. Then my eyes scanned away, taking in the entire room. Memories flooded, flickering like an old-tyme projector in my head. Dad in the big corner chair, loading his pipe with the ball game on TV. Donald going over his homework with Mom in the far corner. Me reading *The Black Cauldron* on the couch where Mom now slept. Donald and I wrestling on the floor after watching a tape of the Warrior beating Hogan in the SkyDome. Hours of flashcards as Mom drilled basic math into both of our skulls. Dad standing tall over the both of us, his face stern as a deserving scolding for our mishaps began.

Dozens of memories.

Hundreds of them.

Soon, the memories would be all we had.

Mom had finally taken her doctor up on his suggestion to relocate into a medical care facility. Not exactly a nursing home, but a middle of the road location where she'd have regular helpers on hand to check her vitals. A place where she'd have help with the cleaning and cooking. Basically a place to have assistance available whenever she needed it.

Assistance not named Joe Donovan.

Guilt racked my gut again. Guilt at not being enough to take care of her all by myself. Guilt at the relief I felt knowing I no longer would have to care for her all by myself.

I turned in a circle, examining the room again.

This house was the only home I'd ever known. After Dad and Donald... After that I'd been carrying the load. Making the mortgage payments. The medical bills. Cooking. Cleaning. Working two, occasionally three jobs to keep everything together so that Mom would be safe. So she would have a comfortable place to rest. To recover. To feel like home.

The real estate agents wanted to put the house on the market in a week. Given the state of the neighbourhood they predicted a quick sale. Possibly a bidding war.

I closed my eyes.

This is a good thing, right?

No answer.

I sighed again and turned away, pulling the keys out of my pocket and grabbing my cowboy hat off the kitchen counter.

Time to go to work.

Chapter 4

You know all of those movies and TV shows where cops go on stakeouts? How there's always a lot of witty banter quickly followed by wild action, foul language, some bad attitudes and then the inevitable fisticuffs-and-or-gunfight?

Real stakeouts suck ass somewhere after the second hour of nothing happening.

I love my van. I really do. Three hundred and fifty thousand kilometres of bad road on the odometer. Cracked windshield. One headlight out. A steel plate over a back window covering the spot where some punks made the mistake of breaking into her. An old cassette player for music. Dirty, dusty and smelling more than a bit like sweaty gym clothes.

All of these points give her character.

None of them make her comfortable for prolonged sitting in the dark.

Which I had been doing for nearly two hours.

'Course, I doubt a Jaguar woulda been much better.

I stretched my cramping back as best I could and tried to ignore the sweaty-balls feeling I was getting in my jeans as I absently fanned at my face with the brim of my beat up felt hat. Mom's voice nagged at the back of my head, making me rethink the logic of my black leather coat in the middle of a late summer heatwave.

After picking Cathy up from the TV station downtown we'd made our way over to Higgins Street to where it met up with Waterfront Drive. Back in the day this was a very popular spot for... uhm... "Short-term Relationship Consultants" to set up shop as it were. Since the completion of the new Disraeli Overpass directly overhead it was less popular for that type of company, but it was as good a place to start as any though. Plus there was plenty of space for me to park my van where it was well hidden under the cover of darkness while still giving me a clear view to the street.

Which I needed since Cathy's plan to have me use the "hidden microphone" she'd borrowed from the station didn't want to work when she handed me the receiver. Static. White noise. And a bit of a shock for Cathy from the microphone which was more than a bit uncomfortable for her since it was stuck so deeply between her... In her bra.

I silently blamed myself for the malfunction. Lately I'd gotten very good at controlling the way electronic equipment functioned when I was around. The microphone was the first thing to die near me in weeks.

Well, the first thing to die by accident. Those fools carjacking people got what was coming to them.

It had been beyond trippy to understand that the correlation between the tingling at my neck and the electricity in the air around me were connected. And by "trippy" I mean "completely fucking terrifying."

One day you figure you're a normal dude, then next you're recovering from a triple gunshot wound to the chest in under two weeks and benching like a strongman competitor on TSN the week after.

I adjusted in my seat again and peered out to the street where Cathy was stalking along the sidewalk provocatively in a pair of high heeled leather boots that stretched up past her knees but still well short of her mini skirt.

Okay. She's hot. And dressed in a complete *Pretty Woman* outfit minus the big eighties-style hair.

So basically, she looked the part if you had absolutely no idea what most street walkers wore these days.

Might as well be wearing a sandwich board with the words "undercover hooker" written in big bold letters on it.

At the same time, I didn't have an issue with Cathy's costume – not just because I'm a pervert, thank you very much. In the back of my head where all of my unvoiced concerns remained unvoiced I approved of her decision to look obvious, because it made her that much less likely to actually *be* abducted.

Don't get me wrong, the thought of some crazy person kidnapping women off the streets of Winnipeg made my blood boil. There's a demolished building near the corner of Portage and Main that went up in flames as a testament to my dislike for such activities.

But that same building scarred me in return and has made me very wary about going off on some hair brained comic book vendetta. There are consequences to all of one's actions. Three men died in front of me that night, one of them by my own hand (and by the hand of the power centre behind the flaming DeeJay booth to be specific).

Things like that haunt a guy.

Or at least they should.

It was weird thinking about that last night at *Cowboy Shotz*. The violence. The fire. The intensity. The smell of smoke, burning liquor and blood.

Tamara had suggested I go see a counsellor, see if I was dealing with any sort of PTSD. My mind whirled at the idea of trying to explain to a shrink everything I was dealing with. Dude would have the loony bin trying to lock me up before I left his office.

That night... The way it made me feel... I don't know if I can ever truly explain...

Noise from the street.

Voices. Shouting.

I blinked my eyes, focusing my vision away from my memories and to the road in front of me.

A small crowd had gathered at the entrance to the overpass, just out from under the streetlights leaving everyone in silhouette. Looked like three men and a few women. One of the woman was being dragged forcibly by her arm into the shadows.

Shit.

Cathy.

I was out of the van and stalking towards the small crowd with my hat firmly settled in place before the decision to do so had fully formed. The tingle at the back of my neck exploded and sent shivers of energy racing along my nervous system, pulsing in time with the ache in my skull and the hunger pangs in my belly. But those annoyances were minor as I took in the situation, my eyebrows narrowed in dangerous focus.

Showtime.

Definitely three men, all dressed in your typical street thug apparel. Pants a few sizes too large to better expose their boxer shorts. One of them sporting an old-school Jordan basketball jersey over his wifebeater and bandanna look. The other two were unremarkable. All three of them had tattoos high on their necks indicating allegiance to one street gang or another. It was hard to keep up with them all.

The ladies in question were hanging back a bit. Definitely what I would call the "modern working girl" type. Crop tops with denims or cheap yoga pants. Hair loose but quick to tie back. Definitely not escort material, but the type you find working for the drugs that gangs provided them.

My knuckles cracked audibly as I continued my Terminator-walk, the opening strains of the classic flicks' theme song beating loudly in my head: Dun-dun-dun DA-dun!

Yes. I'm a geek. We've covered this.

I was making no effort to sneak towards the crowd. In my long experience of breaking up scrums in nightclubs I've rarely found an approach that worked less effectively when shit was about to hit the fan than the quiet, rational tactic. Some people can pull it off but those people aren't me. When you're six and a half feet tall and as big as a defensive lineman you gotta play to your strengths.

Cathy's face was determined. The benefit of having been in trouble with gangs before was showing as I approached. Don't misunderstand, she was still clearly terrified. But there's a difference between terrified and incapacitated by fear. Her eyes were wide but registering everything; faces, locations of people and so on.

Huge turn on.

Okay. Fine. I've got it bad for her. I admit it. Stop judging me, dammit.

One of the girls stopped her caterwauling at Cathy and pointed at me, her tone and pitch changing to something higher and more grating if that was possible. If my head wasn't already sore this alone would've pushed me over the edge.

All three thugs turned and gave me the eye. None of them were a physical presence but all of them looked very familiar with violence and being in control of dangerous situations. They began to bluster and raise their voices at me. Their words didn't reach my brain. Oh my ears heard the sounds but I was too far gone. The Neanderthal in my belly was beating his war drum and demanding action.

I obliged.

The first thug stepped ahead of the pack while reaching behind his back for what was undoubtedly a weapon. Fear surged in my heart as the old scars on my chest flared with phantom pain. The tingling at the back of my neck became a surge, rushing from my fingertips to toenails. I was immersed in energy. The world seemed sharper. Details crystallized in my eyes. Everything seemed to slow down.

People like to talk about adrenaline causing this affect naturally in people. And while they're right to a certain degree, Lord knows I've been in enough scrapes to have experienced that testosterone fight or flight rush of pure fire, that experience is nothing compared to what I felt.

Before the thug's hand cleared his body I had closed the remaining gap in two huge strides, eating up the distance in a burst of energy. I transferred that energy and momentum to the size fifteen steel toed boot that drove heavily into the cartoon bull logo with a vicious flat footed kick. There was an audible crack under the rush of air exploding from the man's lungs before he was launched off his feet and into the crowd of people behind him. One other man and two of the girls were knocked sprawling like so many bowling pins.

Cathy seized her moment and picked up the spare.

As the man holding her flinched back in alarm, Cathy twisted free of his grip and drove her pointy knee right into his balls in a sharp and ruthless motion. Cries of surprise turned to soprano singing as he slowly toppled to the pavement.

The third thug was pushing his way up from the pile, his face awash with fear and rage. Gripping a pistol he'd fished out from somewhere in one hand as he made it up to his knees.

One stride closed the distance between us in a flash, allowing me to kick the pistol away. Another crack suggested I might've broken his wrist in the process. His scream of pain confirmed my suspicion. My right fist silenced his screaming.

"Joe!" Cathy cried out from behind me.

I pivoted on one heel with both hands up in a defensive posture, electricity firing down from the back of my neck to the very tips of my toes.

Cathy stood where I'd last seen her, overtop the writhing punk holding his kneed groin and looking like he wanted to vomit. Cathy's expression was flushed from excitement and still showing fear. But it was different now.

Plus, her hands were up in the air like you see on every cop show ever.

I turned my gaze to the right. The third streetwalker stood a safe distance from us both. Her feet were planted firmly with shoulders squared. One hand gripped a semi-automatic pistol with the business end pointed squarely at my chest. Her other hand was holding a cell phone up to one ear.

"Get your hands up!" she demanded in a no-nonsense, expecting to be obeyed voice.

I blinked, the energy still surging through me though I could feel its strength fading as my stomach cramps and headache began to reassert themselves.

Still. She isn't that far away. I might be able to fuck with her phone. Keep her from calling more gang-bangers

I took a step forward, my scowl deepening as I concentrated through the headache on the tingling at the back of my neck.

The woman made a show of flicking a tab on her pistol with her thumb while its point never wavered from my chest.

"Joe!"

"I said don't move, big man!

I took the hint. I even raised my hands slightly, though I kept concentrating and striving for control of that electric sensation. This wasn't something I'd really practiced. Honestly I spent most of my time trying to figure out how to keep things from blowing up around me. This was different. And way harder.

The woman's authoritative voice broke my introspection as she barked into her phone. "Yes this is Officer Melissa Swan with City Vice. I am requesting immediate backup at Waterfront and Higgins just under the Disraeli Overpass. I have several people to bring into custody."

The tingling sensation vanished as realization hit me like a blast of cold water.

Shit.

Chapter 5

Interrogation rooms are everything you figure they might be.

Cold.

Damp.

Basically as uncomfortable as possible without being torturous.

Which was a good thing, seeing as how the pain in my stomach and head were doing enough torturing already.

The sharp halogen bulbs flickered irritatingly overhead along with the familiar persistent humming that everyone hates. I couldn't tell if I was causing the flickering or if it was just the usual crappy connection those types of bulbs often seemed to have.

Either way, it did nothing for my mood.

I leaned forward onto the cold metallic table, grinding the palms of my hands into my closed eyes in a vain attempt to dull the pounding at the back of my skull. My stomach had gone from cramping in hunger to completely sour making my mouth dry and tacky.

Shoulda let Mom pack me a sandwich.

Though that wouldn't have helped much.

I'd been waiting in the cold, concrete walled room upwards of forty-five minutes. It had taken a very short time for Officer Swan's backup to arrive, which wasn't too surprising given the Police Service's headquarters were only about ten blocks away.

Two squad cars and the inevitable paddy wagon made their way over. Rough hands processed and cuffed everyone there. The three gang-bangers, the ladies of the night, Cathy and finally myself. Rights were read, heads were tucked into backseats. Gang members were placed into the wagon while Cathy and I were separated, one into each squad car.

Probably just as well. Not sure I had anything to say to help the obviously panicking Cathy out as we pulled away.

The rooms' steel door finally squealed open accompanied by two sets of sharp footsteps. I waited until the door squealed shut again before moving my hands and cracking open my dry eyes.

Officer Swan had changed into a respectable pantsuit. Discarding her undercover hooker gear in exchange for something more appropriate for interrogating suspects. Her badge and pistol were clearly visible and clipped to her belt. She'd even taken the time to clean up her face, removing the slightly garish makeup and tying back her shoulder length hair. Her expression was serious and her notepad was yellow. She took the seat across from me, its legs squeaking painfully loud as she positioned it for sitting.

The man who entered the room with her was not what I was expecting. Clearly a complete gym rat given the way his button up dress shirt seemed ready to pop at every seam. The top button was undone underneath his black tie. With an intentionally shaved head and a serious expression the indigenous man crossed his arms and leaned away in the corner beneath the security camera. No badge was visible next to his pistol.

Bad cop.

Good to know.

I leaned back in the hard wooden chair and placed my calloused hands carefully in my lap as I faced Officer Swan. It was a struggle to keep a pained expression off my face, but I figured I had one chance of getting out of this mess without a charge on my personal record.

Time to be as calm and professional as possible.

I stifled an exhausted yawn and waited.

Officer Swan eyed me cautiously from across the metallic table. Her fingers fiddled with the notepad as her lips pursed in thought. In retrospect I don't know how I didn't see her as an undercover officer right away, especially given how self possessed and confident she played things. It was clear that underneath her pantsuit was the physique of an athlete. Someone who had to train endlessly to keep her reflexes sharp. Something that was probably essential not just for her undercover work but to maintain her status within the Old Boys Club that was the police force.

In my defence, it was dark out and I was busy being all introspective. That can distract anyone.

"You're in a lot of trouble, Mr. Donovan." Swan's voice was deeper than I expected. Distinctive for a woman. She glanced down at her notepad briefly, collecting her thoughts. "Do you often hang out in dangerous parts of town looking for hookers to save or was this a special occasion?"

My Dad's voice resonated in my head, cutting through the ice pick stabbing behind my eye. *Never answer a rhetorical question, son. That's how people who think they're smarter than you try to confuse the issue.*

In my thirty-three years on the planet, it was rare that saying nothing had gotten me into trouble.

I blinked my eyes carefully, trying to get some moisture back behind the lids and kept the rest of my face neutral.

Swan let the silence hang for a few moments.

"Nothing to say?" she asked, smirking slightly. She made a show of writing on her notepad.

The man over the corner adjusted slightly.

I ignored him.

"I will say, Mr. Donovan that you have a remarkably clean file." Swan flipped a page and started skimming along points with her finger. "No arrest record, prior to tonight. A few traffic violations. A few comments about statements given from your time working nightclubs when Police were called in for the more violent partygoers." She shook her head slightly and met my eyes. "If it wasn't for the victim report filed after you got shot back in April I would say you were the most unremarkable man I've ever arrested."

I blinked some more but made no other reaction.

Swan smiled. I'm sure she thought it was genuine.

"Nothing to say?" she asked again.

I shrugged.

"Why not?"

"You haven't asked me a question yet."

Swan's smile broadened, turning her head to the man in the corner. "Look at that, his tongue works."

Too many one-liners tumbled to the tip of said tongue right then, but I managed to keep them to myself.

Officer Swan turned back again, picking up her pen and settling in for note taking.

"What were you doing out under the Disraeli Bridge tonight Mr. Donovan."

I shrugged.

"Were you looking for trouble?"

Shrug.

"Are you a racist?"

That made me blink.

"What?"

"Racist. Out on the town, looking for Indian punks to beat up." Swan waved a hand at me, as if encouraging me to spill my guts. "It's okay, we see that sort of thing from time to time."

I grimaced as the idiocy of that statement rattled behind the pain in my head.

"Something troubling you?"

I shook my head as minimally as possible and resumed my I'm-bluffing-you-with-a-pair-of-eights Poker Face.

"You sure?"

"Is this going to take much longer?" I asked calmly.

Swan blinked.

"Excuse me?"

"It's getting late and I need to work in a few hours."

Swan's smile turned into more of a smirk. "Well you should've thought of that before you got into trouble tonight Mr. Donovan. I have a lot of questions to ask that..."

"You know why I was out there. You already spoke with Cathy and she's already told you everything."

"Did we now? What makes you so..."

"Cathy Greenburg is a local celebrity. The anchor for CTV's nightly newscast and also a media darling for her relationship with Max Poulin, Captain of the Winnipeg Jets." That fact didn't do anything for my headache. Despite myself I pinched at the bridge of my nose trying to relieve some pressure. I had middling success.

"So you think that we showed her special treatment?"

"Of course you did. The WPS needs all the positive coverage you can get. Also the hockey team is one of the highest profile sponsors for the annual Police Officer's Ball. You don't have much choice other than to treat her with kid gloves and to make sure she's been taken care of."

Officer Swan crossed her arms and looked like she wanted to scowl through her professional smile.

"You seem pretty sure of yourself."

I shrugged again. "I'm betting she's sitting in the Officer's Lounge sipping on coffee with a few gentlemen, telling stories while they keep an eye on her for you in a more comfortable setting while you and Franco Columbu over here give me the grilling you wanted to give her."

The man in the corner managed to suppress a smile while Officer Swan completely lost hers.

"You think yourself a smart man, Mr. Donovan?"

I sighed. "I think I'm tired. I think I did an old friend a favour tonight and it got me arrested and interrogated."

"If you cooperated and answered my questions you'd be out of here sooner."

"You already have the answers from Cathy. You want my corroboration? Fine. Cathy's digging for information on the continuing disappearances of women in Winnipeg. You've provided no more information to her or the rest of the media. She asked me to watch her back tonight as she – against my wishes – pulled a Vice routine and got all whored up as bait. She ran into trouble with actual street people and I stepped in until you arrested us." I coughed briefly as my dry throat reared its ugly head. "Did I miss anything?"

Swan's eyes looked like she wanted to leap across the table at me despite the calm, self-possessed front the rest of her body showed.

"What's your interest in the missing women?"

I turned my gaze to the man in the corner. His voice was crazy deep, though given the size of his chest cavity that wasn't terribly astonishing. His dark eyes were piercing and all trace of humour was gone from his expression.

I shrugged.

"No interest?" he pressed.

"No more than anyone else in Winnipeg."

"How so?"

I shrugged again. "I got friends. A mom. They could be a target for all I know."

"Is this a personal vendetta for you?"

"Nope."

"Really?"

"Yup."

"Most people don't go all Batman when a friend asks them to."

"Most friends aren't like Cathy."

He nodded slightly. Knowingly.

Shit.

Dammit poker face, what happened to you there?

"Still," the man continued. "Given your history I would have thought this was a more personal issue for you."

I blinked, flicking my eyes over to Swan who had gone stone faced herself.

"She read off my record. I'm clean. Why would this be personal for me?"

"Well for starters, your old bosses at *Cowboy Shotz* were tied to this case for a while. Stands to reason you'd have an interest in what happened next."

Chapter 6

Somehow I managed not to panic.

It was a near thing.

What does he know?

I cleared my throat carefully.

Nothing. No one knows anything. If they did you'd have been arrested months ago. Be cool.

"May I have a glass of water?"

The man smiled and motioned to Officer Swan. After a moment where I thought for certain she was going to protest loudly, she stoically got up and left the room.

"Good guess, by the way." The big man continued genially once the door had closed. "Your friend Miss Greenburg is keeping a few of the Winnipeg Police Service's rookie blue shirts happy with that smile and her outfit as we speak."

Don't let him distract you.

"Why would you think I have anything to do with what happened at *Cowboy Shotz*?"

"Did you?"

"Did I what?"

"Have anything to do with what happened there? I merely asked about your previous employers. Were you there the night of the fire?"

I could feel my heart rate increase ever so slightly. Normally this would've been accompanied by the tingle at the back of my neck flaring up and making the overhead halogens flicker spasmodically. All it did this time was twist my guts more sharply and send an extra spike into my skull.

Ow.

Despite my pained expression I managed to keep any of the panic from my face. I think. Honestly I have no idea what my face looked like anymore. Maybe dirty and unshaven. I got nothing.

"Mr. Donovan?"

"Who are you?"

"Hmm?"

I managed to shrug my shoulders again without wanting to dry heave onto the table. Seriously, my whole body was starting to seize up on me. "You know me. I know her," Officer Swan returned at that moment holding a glass filled with ice and water that couldn't have been as cold as the expression on her face. Not used to being sent on errands I guess. My head moved fractionally - we can call it a nod - towards the officer as she placed the glass on the table before me. My hand barely trembled at all as I reached for it. "Seems like if you get to ask me questions I get to know who's asking them.

The man's lips pursed slightly. Might've been hiding a smile. Might've been working a loose tooth. "Lieutenant Cliff Connell. RCMP Special Crimes Division."

Water.

My God, water.

The first sip turned into a gulp and felt like a wash of clean hitting my system. The grit and dry mouth I was experiencing dissipated almost instantly and the cramp in my belly eased as every drop hit it. I sighed with relief, my headache receding from blind agony to its normal manageably painful state.

"Better?" Officer Swan asked neutrally.

My small smile made an appearance. I nodded again. "Yeah."

She grunted.

"So. Special Crimes." I rolled my head around, feeling the vertebrae crack and pop. "Kinda vague."

Lieutenant Connell shrugged, straining the seams of his dress shirt. "Serial kidnappings are thankfully not a regular occurrence in Canada. No point in having a team only focusing on that."

"So that's confirmed then?"

"Hmm?"

I motioned with my head to Swan. "WPS is investigating this as a serial kidnapping?"

"We're not at liberty to discuss..."

Connell cut off her automatic cop reply. "There's not enough evidence to upgrade the case to homicide. There are too many instances for it to be women choosing to walk away from their lives, though a few of the missing might fit that category." He shrugged again. "Kidnapping seems the best fit until we know more."

"What do you know?" my lips asked before my brain could stop them.

"Thought you didn't care."

Yeah, dipshit. I thought you didn't care.

I scowled slightly, though mostly at myself.

"Call me curious. I don't like people who prey on others."

"Again," Swan said loudly, overriding Connell who looked ready to say more. "We are not at liberty to discuss an ongoing investigation." Her eyes stared a hole at the overly muscular man in the corner, challenging him to gainsay her. Connell conceded quietly, making a small gesture with one hand.

Swan nodded sharply and resumed her seat across from me, trying to regain some composure to her obviously frazzled expression.

I popped a few ice cubes into my mouth and chewed them loudly, hoping the sound was louder than the growling in my belly.

"Okay then, let's start at the beginning." Swan rearranged her notepad and made a few quick scribbles with her pen to loosen the ballpoint. "What were you doing tonight under the Disraeli Overpass?"

Really?

I eyed Lieutenant Connell over in the corner briefly. His expression went full on cop face.

No help there.

"Mr. Donovan?" Swan's pen tapped repeated on the pad. "Are you going to answer my question or am I going to have to detain you?"

"Detain me for what?" I spat, my temper starting to get the

better of me. What? It had been another long bloody day at work. My headache made it hard to sleep. Mom had still needed lots of care when I got home, no matter what favour Cathy needed me to do. And it's not like my workouts with Tamara aren't taxing either. Factor in the need throw some hurt on a bunch of admittedly deserving fools and then getting arrested, no one should be surprised that I was getting frustrated.

Swan put down her pen and assumed a stern expression. "Mr. Donovan, your actions compromised an undercover sting operation. An operation in which I spent months trying to work my way into the *Native Posse's* street crew, posing as a down on my luck single mother willing to do anything to feed her children." Her dark eyes smouldered dangerously. "Nearly all of that work is now wasted thanks to you and your girlfriend wanting to play detective."

Guilt. Just in case I didn't feel lousy enough already. Now I was getting hit with a heavy dose of guilt.

She probably really was a mother at that. Only moms can lay a guilt trip with no lead time and make it stick.

My temper faded and my headache began to resume its' intensity. I leaned my forearms on the cold metallic table.

"She's not my girlfriend."

"What?"

"We covered this. Don't you read the newspapers?"

"Mr. Donovan, if you don't cooperate I will be given no choice but to press charges."

"Go ahead."

Swan blinked.

"What?"

I shrugged. "Press charges. Fill out the forms. And I'll call Cathy using my one phone call that you told me I have when you Mirandized me..."

"We don't call it that," Connell interrupted.

I paused. My eye brow quirking at him over in the corner.

He motioned with one hand vaguely. "We read you your rights under the Charter of Rights and Freedoms in Canada."

Apparently I watch too much *CSI Miami*.

"Really?"

He nodded.

"That's a real mouthful."

"Gets the job done."

Swan was getting aggravated. "Lieutenant Connell, if you don't mind..."

"Fine," I broke in. "You read me my rights, one of them is a phone call. So I'll call Cathy and she's call her boss. Her boss'll call the CTV lawyers. And while you're still trying to get the paperwork done to work out a charge that I'm guessing the CTV lawyer will get pleaded down to a misdemeanour given my – as you pointed out – clean record, you'll then have to deal with the blowback of any media attention that Cathy and her boss decide to throw on this incident." I met her glare as calmly as I possibly could. "And I am certain you've got better cases to build against the three gang-bangers who not only do you *know* are involved in street prostitution but now have witnessed attempting to assault and possibly murder two citizens of Winnipeg."

Silence.

Which was fine by me. I hate talking. I think I wore out my vocal chords with all that chatter.

Officer Swan was beyond words, staring at me with vicious intent. All sense of her professional demeanour began to fray at the seams.

Lieutenant Connell stepped away from the wall, coming up beside her. His voice was soft but I managed to overhear a few of the more pertinent details.

"He's clean."

"But he's involved with..."

"You can't make this stick."

"I've spent months..."

"I'll smooth it over with your boss. This one's on me, Melissa. It's on me."

Swan's expression softened faintly. Her hand gripped part of Connell's bicep and she nodded, turning to gather up her notepad.

I should've left well enough alone.

But...

"For what it's worth, I'm sorry."

Her eyes snapped to mine once again.

I grimaced sheepishly. "I didn't want to see Cathy get hurt and she would've gone without me. Once the punks grabbed her, I didn't know what else to do."

Swan closed her notepad sharply and stared down at me for a moment.

"Now you know what pretending to be a hero costs the people whose job it is to hunt these criminals." Her voice was cold. Unrelenting. "Your actions cost me months of my life."

Saying sorry again felt redundant so I followed Dad's advice and kept my mouth shut.

Swan's breath exploded in a huff as she turned to the door. "You're free to go. Don't let me catch you pulling this kind of bullshit ever again."

Chapter 7

The door slammed shut, echoing in the cold room and my cavernous head painfully.

"You okay?" Connell asked, peering down at me.

I rubbed at my temples and closed my eyes.

"Not really," I muttered as I stood up gratefully, my legs and back cramped from a long night of sitting and picked up my battered cowboy hat, settling it carefully in place.

"We've got Tylenol."

I waved a hand minutely, muttering. "Waste of time." I looked at the door just over the head of the RCMP strongman. He was giving me the eye - not like *that* people, settle down – and clearly trying to figure something out. "Problem?" I asked.

He pursed his lips. "How much ya bench?"

A laugh escaped my lips. "Seriously?"

His eyebrows rose to the ceiling. "About weightlifting? Always."

"I figured. What's your best? Three-sixty? Three sixty-five?"

Connell actually smirked. The smirk I work my ass off not to have when I'm in the gym. Though to be fair all dudes who lift get that look now and again.

"Four-oh-five for reps."

I whistled appropriately. And legitimately. That's a good number.

"How about you?" He asked heading towards the door and opening it for me, the metallic squeal making me wince again. "You gotta be near four bills yourself."

It was my turn to smirk, but I kept it off my face.

"I do all right. Don't go for personal bests too often these days. Lots of Olympic lifts and cardio."

Connell nodded and led me down the hallway. "Well looks like you're doing good with that. Diet's nice and dialled in too I figure. You competing?"

"Is there a powerlifting meet coming up?" I asked.

Connell laughed. "Not that I am aware of. But the Manitoba Amateur Bodybuilding Association has their big event every April. You should think about entering."

I blinked in astonishment. While my physique had changed significantly in the last couple of months no one had ever accused me of being an actual bodybuilder before.

"Uh... no thanks. I'm just trying to lose the beer belly."

Connell snorted. "You should consider it. The Manitoba roster is pretty thin for dudes in your weight class."

I had the brief mental image of myself standing in front of a crowded auditorium with all of my body hair shaved off, sporting a spray on tan and covered in baby oil while wearing a bright yellow banana hammock.

Apparently it's possible to flush with embarrassment when your mind wanders.

I shook my head to clear it and followed Connell down the hallway.

We rounded another corner into the main room. Several officers were at desks filling out reports on their computers with suspects seated and restrained in front of them. Off to one side I saw Officer Swan gathering up a large folder crammed with notes before heading off down a separate hallway. Another door slammed moments later.

Shit.

"I appreciate you cutting me slack, Lieutenant." My voice was low but I meant every word. Yes, I do have a problem with authority figures, but not the ones who use their power with regard for others. Those are the people you *want* to have that kind of position after all. "I know what Cathy and I were doing was stupid, but she's... Well..."

Connell sighed. "She's a reporter. And she's used to getting her way." Connell's eyes flickered to the hallway Swan went down and lingered there briefly. "I know how that can be to deal with."

"Still... If I've done something to fuck up her case I'm going to feel like shit."

He shook his head. "She's got plenty on that crew of fools. By the time the case ever gets to trial they might even serve some time. Nothing you've done is likely to trump what she's got. Odds are her C.O. Was going to pull her from U.C. Duty within the next week or so anyway. Her case is solid."

Relief seeped into my gut. Not as satisfying as a midnight pizza would have felt, but it was a start.

"That said," Connell continued his eyes narrowing. "The WPS and the RCMP has a very firm stance on outlaw justice and vigilantism. Not only does it only cause more harm than good, more often than not innocent bystanders who just want to be left alone get pulled into trouble along with the wannabe heroes."

"Ain't that the truth," I muttered sourly.

A sharp female laugh that I would've recognized anywhere reached my ears. My eyes tracked across the floor to what I presumed was the officer's lunchroom. The window on the door was hazy but it was clear to see a feminine shape and two males having what appeared to be an amusing conversation.

"Coffee room?" I asked.

"Coffee room."

"Mind if I grab a cup on the way out?"

"I think I've done you enough favours already tonight."

"So, that's a no?"

Connell smirked again and fished around in his pocket before handing me his business card. I took it with a raised eyebrow.

"In case you feel like talking."

"About gym stuff?"

"About missing women."

My stomach lurched again.

I made a show of looking at the card disinterestedly before replying with the obvious question; "What makes you think I know anything about missing women?"

Connell's eyes were calm but serious. "Because your old bosses got involved with the trafficking of Canadian Women into the Korean sex trade and got killed by rivals after a bomb was set off in their club."

That was sorta the official story.

I wasn't going to correct him.

Not that I was there or anything.

I cleared my throat carefully. "Doesn't really answer my question."

Connell eyed me carefully before motioning me to follow. He was heading away from the coffee room, away from Cathy. But it seemed impolite to just ditch him given that whole getting-charges-dropped thing.

We stopped at Swan's desk. I knew it was hers from the old-fashioned name plate holding down an errant stack of paper. I was surprised to see how many actual files filled with actual paper were resting there. Apparently despite the computer age having hard copies of information was still useful.

Connell picked up two file folders. One was remarkably slender while the second needed that old-fashioned string binding to hold it together. Connell flipped open the smaller folder first.

"Joseph Alan Donovan," he read aloud while skimming down the file. "Early thirties. No criminal record. A few minor traffic violations, however nothing outstanding at this time. Permanent resident of Winnipeg with one dependant, your ailing mother. Held a variety of entry-level office or manual labour jobs over the past decade. Nothing seems to stick for you save for your extensive work in the nightclub industry. Most notably with the crew over at the venue previously known as *Cowboy Shotz*. A venue where you got shot by a member of the *Native Posse* while protecting fellow staff members and your patrons." Connell looked up from the folder with an approving glance. "Aside from that one shining example of selfless heroism, you appear to be a completely unremarkable yet upstanding Citizen of Winnipeg"

It's chilling to think that somewhere it is possible for persons in authority to be able to compile a list of your whole life and negligently throw it together for the world to read. I could feel my hackles rising slightly. Made me want to disappear off the grid and just... Shit, I don't know what it made me wanna do. But dammit, that's creepy.

Connell hefted the second file and unwound the string. With great care to not mix up the order papers were in he began to sift through them.

"This here details in short form what we have learned about the events leading up to that fateful night at your old place of employment." He paused at one page and held it up so I could see it.

It was an official police photograph of the late Officer Chris Parise in full dress uniform, smiling his million dollar shit-eating smile and fooling the world. The image of a man loving his role as the city's top cop who could in no way be involved in any illegal undertakings.

Lightning flashed in my brain. Memories.

I could feel his blood spattering my face again. Could see the life disappear from his eyes.

It made my skin crawl.

My expression didn't change however.

"This man's involvement," Connell continued his voice hard. "Correction, the involvement of himself and his two law enforcement partners is what brought the RCMP into this matter. Prior to this we had no jurisdiction to apply resources to a missing persons case in the city with so many similar cases happening out in the countryside."

"Wait," I cut in. Surprised and concerned. "This is happening all over?

Connell shrugged. "Yes and no. Canada's land mass is impossible to keep track of for any force. In rural areas - which is the obviously the focus of our national jurisdiction - it isn't uncommon for someone to go missing and be missing for weeks without us getting a report on it." Connell shook his head sadly. "Been that way since the dawn of the Mounties. We do our best, but..."

"But you're fighting a hopeless war."

Connell nodded. "We pick our battles. And once the WPS members were proven to be involved here in Winnipeg we were given the authority to partner with Internal Affairs to root out any others who might've been involved and get this case put to bed."

"Were there?" I asked as casually as possible.

"Were there what?"

How do you look only mildly curious when you know the answer to the question you're asking? See, this is why I couldn't be a lawyer. "Were there other officers involved?"

Connell glanced down to the file, flipping through it carefully again. "While the details involving the fire and human trafficking out of *Cowboy Shotz* are buttoned down and resolved, until it is proven conclusively that this case is not related to the ongoing missing women operation I am not able to discuss many actual details. But unofficially, I feel safe in saying that the only dirty cops involved in this case are the ones who perished in that inferno."

My poker face didn't fail me. If I was feeling better I might've gone to the casino and seen how far the thirty bucks in my pocket would've gotten me at the tables.

Time to change the subject.

"I still don't see what this has to do with me."

Connell flipped through to near the end of the case file and stopped on one page in particular. His gaze fixated on it for a moment before he continued.

"Mr. Donovan, your record portrays you as you are. A fine, law abiding citizen. Your care for your mother and your extensive work in the security industry shows that you have an interest in protecting other people, even if only by protecting them from themselves." He peered at me carefully. "In the weeks leading up to this event you were hospitalized in the line of duty. Protecting people who ultimately were involved in a series of horrible crimes, including murder. Going by your record and what I can figure about you, you're not the type of guy who likes the idea of having worked for that kind of criminal. Or any kind of criminal."

I grimaced, not enjoying the head-shrinking process. "Man, I just worked there. I worked a lot of clubs. Most of the guys running those clubs were some kinda crook too. It's the nature of that industry, attracting scumbags" I shrugged dismissively. "Bills pile up though. And bouncing's a gig I can always get."

"Maybe so. But I think maybe you saw something. Maybe you heard something. Maybe you don't even know what you saw or heard. But I believe when you take the time to think about it all and go over things, if you can remember a connection - any connection – between your old bosses and the ongoing investigation of missing women..." Connell's eyes went back to the page in the case file. "I think if you remember something you'll want to give me a call."

This conversation was hitting me too close to home. Time to get flippant.

"Right. My old bosses talked about their illegal behaviour in front of their bouncers." I scoffed loudly and stared at Connell even as the old-tyme film projector began to warm up in the back of my mind, starting to sift through all the conversations I could remember having and overhearing Parise and Aaron have. "What makes you so damned sure I'll want to give you a call even if I remember anything?"

Connell blinked wordlessly and held up the page he was focused on.

It was a picture. The image was hazy, a blurred extreme close up in black and white. Smoke seemed to fill every inch of the frame where white fire didn't distort the visual.

However what was clear as day was the shadowed outline of a very large man wearing a cowboy hat carrying an unconscious female form out of what appeared to be a burning building.

Connell's eyes never wavered from mine. "Because you care, Mr. Donovan."

Chapter 8

Despite feeling gut punched I was fairly sure the poker face hadn't disappeared.

Time to bluff.

"Who's that?" I asked. Don't think my voice trembled but I wouldn't have bet on it.

To his credit Connell didn't call me a liar to my face. "We don't know who this is for certain. Reports at the time from patrons in the bar were sketchy at best. The Koreans arrested for their involvement weren't overflowing with cooperation and none of the staff members we spoke to could remember seeing this man in the building." I almost sighed with relief as he put the photo back in the file and sealed it up again.

"But I have my suspicions," Connell continued.

So much for relief.

"Huh." I grunted noncommittally. "And this relates to me because?"

Connell looked back at me with an innocent expression. "Who said it had anything to do with you?"

"Well, you were implying something..."

"Was I?"

My head was hurting again.

"Okay, fuck it. Whatever." I held up his card, made a show of tucking it into the back pocket of my faded denims. "It's late, I'm starving and I'm supposed to work in the morning. Are we done?"

Connell nodded.

I turned away and settled my jacket as I headed to the coffee room.

"Stay out of trouble, Mr. Donovan," Connell called after me. "People who play with matches sometimes get caught in burning buildings."

I froze in place, my heart pounding in time with my headache again.

I looked back over my shoulder. But Connell was already on his way to join Officer Swan in processing the gang-bangers

Leaving me standing there in the middle of the police station frozen like an awkward teenager at the high school dance.

He knows.

I shook my head.

He suspects. That's all.

My heart rate slowed and I started walking again. My nose caught the scent of stale donuts as I passed a filing cabinet. A *Tim Horton's* box rested there. Three lonely pastries were rapidly becoming day-olds as I stared at them.

I had a powdered lemon filled morsel jammed into my pie hole before I remembered that I hate lemon filled morsels. But my stomach was enflamed with hunger and I couldn't be bothered with little things like flavours and preferences.

Moments later I was finishing off a dutchie and prepping my system for the dry honey cruller I was carrying on my way to the coffee room. The influx of simple sugary calories brightened my mood immediately.

Fuck that guy. There's no evidence or footage of me at the club. He's fishing. Yeah. What the fuck does he know?

My renewed sense of confidence lasted until I stepped into the coffee room and nearly bumped into Myron Sampson.

He was in uniform. Badge and service revolver in plain sight. Flak jacket slung over one shoulder. He was short for a cop, with close cropped hair and a pair of steel rimmed spectacles. His salt and pepper goatee was as precisely trimmed as I remembered. His eyes were cold and dark. That I hadn't remembered. In truth, I can't remember ever having had a conversation with him before.

What I did remember was his crew of associates.

Parise. Miller. Mackie.

Sampson was the fourth member of the police officer crew that had gone in as "business partners" with Aaron at *Cowboy Shotz*.

He was the only one not at the club when I walked in the front door and knocked their whole operation apart.

At least, not until he arrived with the rest of the WPS SWAT Team and assassinated Parise right in front of me.

Not that I could prove that of course. And according to Connell's own words, Sampson had managed to pass scrutiny with not only Internal Affairs but an independent RCMP investigation as well.

And now he was in the coffee room where he'd been chatting up Cathy for the better part of half an hour and staring me dead in the face.

The very same face that was covered in donut powder and a stunned expression.

Great.

"Joe!" Cathy exclaimed, standing up from the cheap vinyl chair she was occupying. She looked tired but more or less unharmed. Even comfortable with an empty mug on the table in front of her and a borrowed policeman's coat hung over her shoulders. The coat somehow gave her provocative outfit a sense of vulnerability. "Are you okay? I was getting worried."

I took in the rest of the room quickly as I ran the sleeve of my leather coat over my pastry powdered lips. Nothing out of the ordinary here. TV in one corner. Vending machines near the door. Coffee percolating away near a small sink and fridge. One other policeman was in the room but no one I recognized. Young guy, probably a rookie.

Whatever.

"Joe?" Cathy asked again, her voice worried.

"All good," I replied quietly giving her my small smile. "Just some forms and routine questions. Nothing weird."

"Seems like you two had quite the night," that was Sampson, peering up at me with his all-seeing, detail oriented eyes. "I don't suppose I need to warn you about the consequences of sticking your nose into police business do I, Mr. Donovan?"

Yeah. No subtext there at all.

I peered down at Officer Sampson steadily. My head was still aching fiercely but the bit of water and sugary donut carbs had actually eased the agony in my belly. My blood was up and I knew that if things had to happen right now that I would be good to go. The hairs at the back of my neck began to rise just as a faint thread of the tingle started up.

Sampson was a small man but no pushover. Wiry. Strong.

Quick and well-trained. Specifically his training as a SWAT member plus his on-the-job combat experience made my years of tossing drunks out of nightclubs look as amateurish as they were.

I didn't want a fight.

At least I didn't want one here.

"Mr. Donovan?" Sampson repeated, his feet adjusting slightly in front of me.

Now or never, Joe. You gonna gamble on this? Make an accusation you have no way of backing up? What happens to you if you do? Do you admit to being at the club? Do people find out about you? About what you can do?

Consequences.

Actions have consequences.

Dammit.

"People should always worry, Officer," I finally replied, my small smile firmly in place even though I couldn't keep my eyes from going cold. "The world can be a dangerous place after all."

Sampson didn't smile. His face gave nothing away.

"Yes it can. Which is why we encourage citizens to leave the police work to the professionals."

"As I was telling you, Officer Sampson," Cathy broke in, seeing the tension rising and stepping forward to get in between the two of us. That tiny feminine barrier slid in place and most of the tension instantly broke.

Neither of us wanted to rumble.

Again. Consequences.

"As I was saying," Cathy repeated. "This is just a misunderstanding. Joe was helping me do some research on a story for the Crime Beat on CTV. I have the utmost respect for the WPS and was just trying to find the best angle to showcase the work you all do."

Sampson turned his expression to her, a small smile of his own appearing. "Of course, Miss Greenburg. Hopefully we won't see you again under these circumstances." His eyes included me in the conversation again. "Either of you."

Cathy's professional TV personality laugh was working overtime. "Oh, I have no doubt. Thank you so much for your hospitality, officers." She shrugged her way out of the borrowed coat, the second officer retrieved it with a smile and a none-too-subtle glance down her exposed cleavage. "But it's way past my bedtime. Ready, Joe?"

My small smile widened very slightly. My eyes didn't leave

Sampson's.

"I'm always ready. Let's go."

Chapter 9

"What the *hell* was that about, Joe?" Cathy's voice was hushed but still heated as we hustled down Princess Street away from the Public Safety Building. "I had to spend half an hour answering questions and then even more time making nice with those officers while waiting for you. I used up all of my best talking points to keep things light and to take heat off of ourselves. And then you..." She was too pretty to look like she wanted to spit but I swear to God that's what her face looked like. "I thought you were going to knock Officer Sampson out!"

I shrugged, glancing back over my shoulder. No one following. Not that I would really notice unless they were like ten feet behind me or anything.

Stealthy shit. Not my thing.

"I thought about it," I admittedly quietly.

Cathy's eyes were incredulous. "What is the matter with you?"

"What?"

Cathy made another disgusted noise and stared at me.

"Are you incapable of respecting authority? Why would you be so stupid as to get belligerent with the police after they agreed to drop charges?"

Stupid.

I hate being called stupid.

Sure. I'm a big guy. Despite the advantages of being bigger than most people the disadvantages seem disproportionately offensive when they crop up. One of the disadvantages? People assume big equals dumb. Now to be fair, stereotypes exist for a reason and I've worked with a ton of large dudes whose collective IQ wouldn't have enough knowledge to write a cohesive book report on the original Hardy Boys adventures.

I may not be a mental giant. But I pride myself on being smarter than the average dude.

Going through college with Cathy – at least for the year that we went through it together – she never once took me for a dumb person. One of the few in our class who respected my intelligence as I recall.

She should have known better.

Despite myself I turned to Cathy with hot eyes, my fists clenched and ready to bite someone's face off. Her eyes widened in surprise and she took a half step back and away from me as I readied some harsh words.

Cathy was frightened.

Of me.

The other disadvantage of being bigger than most? Even people who cared about you were often also scared of you.

Deep breaths, Joe. Deep breaths.

After a moment of silence we ended up talking over each other.

"Joe, I'm sorry. I know you're not stupid."

"I'm sorry. Cathy. I didn't mean to get angry."

Silence.

And then we both laughed.

Not loudly or hysterically. Just genuine, heartfelt laughter.

After a very stressful night, fighting with gang-bangers and then the ordeal at the Police Station both of us were having trouble dealing with the tension. It felt good to laugh. To be alive and able to laugh.

"Okay, I will go on the record right now and admit that this was a bad idea." Cathy conceded, wiping delicately at one eye. Her smile was bright but tired. "God, what was I thinking?"

Her arms were crossed with fingers gripping at her biceps. Despite the heatwave during the day, Winnipeg could still be chilly at night. Without a word I shucked out of my battered leather coat and draped it over her shoulders. It brought me within unusually close proximity to her as my jacket swallowed up her tiny form, the hem reaching down past her hips.

Cathy's eyes were very wide as she looked up at me.

Is that a ruler in your pocket, Joe?

I cleared my throat quietly and took a half step back, my small smile firmly in place as I hoped the shadows were hiding the colour in my cheeks. The hopeful, dreamer part of my brain thought Cathy looked slightly regretful as I stepped back. But that part of my brain's been batting zero-for-a-thousand since I was a kid, so I brutally locked any of those thoughts away and tried to stay on topic.

"The record shall show that on this day, Cathy Greenburg admitted to fallacy in the first degree."

She smiled in return. "Thank you, Your Honour. If possible I'd like to plead for leniency prior to sentencing."

I nodded with good grace and peered into the minimal traffic on Main Street hoping to flag down a cab. "Granted, Miss Greenburg. Bail shall be set at the price of lunch later this week or possibly next."

"Done." She then sighed quietly and huddled deeper into my coat. "I feel like an idiot."

"There are worse feelings."

"Joe, I got arrested. I got you arrested. This'll be on our records going forward."

I shrugged. "They didn't press charges. Technically we got detained. That isn't too bad if you think about it."

Cathy mulled that over.

"Have you been arrested before?"

I paused in my flagging down attempts to peer at her. "Hmm?"

"I mean... Well, you've worked a lot of clubs."

"Working as a bouncer equates to getting arrested?"

It was her turn to shrug. "You get in a lot of fights, don't you?"

"In theory I stop a lot of fights." My head shook slightly and I raised my hand at an oncoming *Duffy's Taxi* which threw on a signal and began to change lanes towards us. "But for the record; never arrested."

"Really?"

"Nope."

"Damn." Cathy's lips quirked into a smirk. "I am definitely a bad influence on you."

My small smile quivered. "The worst. My mother is ashamed to tell her friends that we hang out."

"How is your Mom?"

"Sleeping peacefully I hope. Will make sneaking into the house in an hour a lot easier." The cab came to a stop in front of me I opened the back door for Cathy. "You've got your wallet and stuff, right?"

She blinked up at me. "Of course. Wait, why another hour? Aren't you getting a ride too?"

I shook my head. "Your condo's ten minutes away. It makes sense for you to head straight there and put this night behind you."

"What about you?"

I motioned with my head in the other direction. "I gotta pick up the van. She's only a few blocks away and after what happened I could use the walk to clear my head."

Cathy's expression was worried. "Are you sure?"

"Definitely. Go home. Spend time with Captain Max and your cats."

"We don't have cats." She winced. "God. What am I going to tell Max? He's going to freak out."

"Start with the truth. Saves time."

She bit on her lower lip, clearly concerned.

I put my hand on her shoulder reassuringly. "Go. He's crazy about you. He'll understand."

Cathy nodded and started to shuck out of my coat.

I tucked it higher on her shoulders. "Keep it. I'll be good. The walk'll keep me warm. Just hand me my wallet and keys."

We exchanged my essentials and without more words I helped her into the cab. Within moments she was riding down the road towards the most famous intersection in Canada, Portage and Main.

Right past the vacant, bulldozed lot that used to be the hottest night club in town.

Until it burned to the ground around me.

I took off my hat and ran my calloused palm down over my tired, stubbled face.

Am I ever going to get past that night?

No one answered. I wasn't surprised. Expecting a higher power to answer my questions wasn't something I went for anymore.

So I resettled my hat, pocketed my wallet and keys and took off at a steady jog towards my van.

Not too long ago this was something you'd never see me do. With a bad knee and near three hundred pounds of flabby mass, Joe Donovan was not built for jogging. Oh, I tried a lot. Every couple of weeks I'd have a "fuck it" moment and go nuts on a treadmill or around the block at home. Inevitably I would suffer the same fate within a matter of minutes: breathlessness, aches in all my joints and a certain sense that I was going to have a heart attack.

Since getting shot? I loved jogging.

The freedom of it. Feeling light and energetic. Being able to sustain a pace for ages at a time. The track record I set with Tamara was almost two hours at a continuous, steady jog. Just seeing the world pass by me as I held a good clip felt... Well, like I said: free.

It was an amazing feeling. And despite my headache and the horrible trouble at the end of the night, it felt good to let it all wash over me as I jogged away.

Until it stopped feeling good.

It didn't happen right away, but when the tingle at the back of my neck that fed the energy my body used began to turn into a painful cramping I knew something was wrong.

My headache progressed quickly from "manageable" to "ice pick behind left eye" and I began to falter and stumble. Streetlights along Higgins Avenue flickered heavily as I staggered by, trying to keep my balance.

Finally my right knee seized up and I lost my footing, charging headlong into the chain link fence in front of an auto body shop.

Ow.

I lay there on my back for several long minutes staring up at the bright sky and wheezing great gulps of air into my lungs. My limbs were shaking with what I could only assume was fatigue while my stomach cramped and protested in time with the ache in my skull.

Tears escaped my eyes, blurring my view of the constellations as I tried to regain some sense of composure.

Now what the fuck is going on?

Using the links on the fence I managed to pull myself up to my feet and flex my knee. It was tight and a little bit swollen. Worse then it had been in months but nowhere near the worst it had ever been. It held my weight so it would do. There was a stitch in my side that wasn't helping the cramping in my guts and I had a nice new set of scrapes on my arms that were bleeding slightly.

"Come on, Joe." I grunted under my breath. "Get your ass in gear before a passing squad car mistakes you for a drunk and throws you back in jail."

My van was only another block away.

It was a slow limp getting there, but I made it.

Didn't expect to see all those *Native Posse* members surrounding it when I got there though.

Chapter 10

Deep in the shadows under the Disraeli Bridge was my beat up and ugly van. Parked right in front of it was a brand new, black, four door sedan complete with shiny rims and a brightly polished front bumper. Four men were lounging around, dressed in denims and sleeveless tees. Their bandanas and neck tattoos would have been enough to identify them as members of Winnipeg's most notorious street gang. But the man walking towards me with a dark scowl on his face confirmed it.

The last time I had seen Shawn he had been on his knees in an abandoned flop house, holding onto a broken hand and crying in pain. I had assumed that by leaving him in such a state with members of his gang as eyewitnesses that his days in the gang were numbered.

Apparently gangs believed in second chances.

How progressive.

Gulp.

The smirk that blossomed on Shawn's face as he approached was unmistakeable. His buzzed scalp glistened as stray moonlight hit it between the shadows. Dressed in a loose white tee and fitted jeans Shawn continued his easy stride until he and I were just out of arms' reach of each other. A wise precaution considering what I'd done to him the last time we were able to reach out and touch.

He'd muscled up some, just something the back of my mind took in while my inner child screamed in a terrified fashion. I examined the positions of the other three *Posse* members as they crept away from the vehicles in a vague semi circle around the two of us. Clearly Shawn had decided after our last encounter to hit the gym and literally increase his power base in the gang. He didn't suddenly look like an Olympia contender or anything but he'd easily added another ten pounds to his shoulders and back.

Never mind the five pounds of iron he probably had tucked into the back of his jeans.

My chest scars itched, adding another uncomfortable feeling to my head and belly. Oh yeah, and the road rash on my forearms.

Big damn hero. That's me.

"Look at what we have here, boys." That was Shawn doing his best Vin Diesel impression. Deep, gravelly talk with very little in the way of enunciation. His eyes never left mine as he motioned with his head. "Looks like the bouncer's decided to clean up after himself and grab his piece of shit ride." General chuckling commenced. Shawn had a real peanut gallery on hand to laugh at his jokes and back up his words.

Must be nice.

A grunt forced its way past my lips. "Careful, you're gonna hurt her feelings."

"What's that?"

I motioned vaguely with my chin towards the van. "No one likes name calling."

Shawn's smirk widened and my stomach sank further than before. I was in real trouble. The way I was feeling a troop of Girl Guides could've whupped my ass never mind these four. On my best day it would be a near thing, four on one is still four on one. Anyone could get a shot off or jab a knife into me while I'm busy with someone else.

The only hope I had was in living off past glories.

Time for some bluffing.

"You've got explaining to do, big man." Shawn turned his body slightly, putting his left foot forward and angling his hand back and away from me. Intentional? Maybe. Could've been reflexive too, unconsciously hiding the hand I'd broken.

I stared a hole at Shawn for half a second and then consciously dismissed him to take in each of the other three *Posse* members.

One of them was barely out of his teens and clearly scared shitless. The other two were a bit older and seasoned, but even they could barely seem to keep their feet still.

Shit like this ain't like you see in movies people. Where everyone assumes a dramatic pose and spouts one-liners at each other until the fight choreography begins. No one here was going to start some wild kick boxing routine in super slow-motion under the Michael Bay orange sepia tone.

Real violence is scary. Really. Scary. Your adrenaline is both your best friend and your worst enemy in these situations. And the only way to get it under control is sadly to get into more and more of these kinds of terrifying situations until – no matter how crazy it gets – the surge of pure testosterone ends up working in your favour instead of against it.

The youngest *Posse* member off to my left was twitching and trembling. The fear and excitement was visibly getting to him. And while his two companions were more seasoned, the sheer nervousness of Young Boy was starting to affect them too.

"I don't like answering questions. The police already asked me a bunch tonight." Never hurts to mention the cops to a bunch of scared gang-bangers Might make them second guess their actions and stuff. "Why should I answer yours?"

Shawn shrugged slightly. "It's only one question."

I returned my gaze squarely to Shawn.

"Just one?"

He nodded.

I pretended to think about it for a moment while taking a mental inventory of how I was feeling.

In short, I felt lousy.

Back to bluffing.

"Okay. Shoot."

Dude. Poor choice of words.

If anything Shawn's smirk deepened. Casually he reached behind his back and withdrew the pistol I'd correctly assumed was there and thumbed the safety off. The barrel was pointed at the ground but its sheer presence heightened the fear I was barely containing to the point where I had to clench my fists to keep my fingers from trembling.

"Who else were your bosses working with?"

Okay, not the question I was expecting.

"What?"

"You heard me," Shawn growled, unconsciously taking a half step towards me while the gun barrel weaved vaguely in my direction. The other *Posse* members picked up on their spokesman's mood shift and shuffled some more. Young Boy made a sound like he was going to throw up. "Who else were your bosses at the club working with?"

My mind whirled.

Everyone knew this story by now, didn't they?

I said so.

"It was all over the news. Aaron and Parise - the cop - were dealing with some Korean douchebags. Working on a pipeline for women to be sent to Asia for some even bigger douchebags." I stared Shawn down, fists still clenched as I kept my eyes on his and tried to ignore everything else. "Cops and RCMP are involved. They're convinced that's as far as it went through the club."

"That's fucking bullshit, big man. There's more to it than that."

I shook my head carefully. "I don't have another answer for you. I didn't even know what was going on until I ran into you the first time at Keimac's old house." Shawn's eyes twitched, remembering how that meeting ended I'm sure. "Police have followed the money trail. The media has followed other trails. Bottom line, what happened at the club is considered done. Case closed."

Shawn's eyes twitched again, his gun hand wavering slightly.

"That's the answer you're gonna die for? Those fuckers can't pay you off now that they're dead."

Despite everything I felt rage build up inside me.

"Nobody's paid me off over those girls and nobody ever will." My voice was hot and ragged. The guilt and anger I felt over being present at *Cowboy Shotz* while women were being coerced, duped and ultimately shipped off to foreign countries to be abused and worse by power hungry sociopaths made my blood boil. The fact that I'd taken money from the club made me feel indirectly involved even though I knew different.

Didn't make me feel better though.

No wonder I couldn't let the events of that night go. I can't get past feeling responsible.

Shawn measured my response thoughtfully, his gun still moving vaguely in time with his breathing.

"Tell me about Selkirk."

I blinked.

"What?"

"Selkirk. Tell me about it."

"What am I, a fucking travel guide? Go read a book or something."

Emotion flashed across Shawn's eyes and his gun hand twitched.

"You saying you know nothing?"

"About Selkirk?" Images flashed in my aching brain, trying to make a connection between my experiences working at the club with the City of Selkirk.

I drew a blank.

"What's to know?"

Shawn's gaze focused sharply on my face for a long, quiet moment. Then to my surprise he sighed, thumbed the safety back on his pistol and tucked it away in his jeans.

The relief that flooded through me nearly buckled my knees. As it is I took a small shuffling step to hold my balance.

"Wait, that's it?" This came from the *Posse* member I was mentally calling Baggy Pants. His face was tight and he stepped over to Shawn, grabbing his arm. "We're just done? That's it?"

Shawn stared his man down. "Fool doesn't know anything."

"So we believe him? We let him walk?" Baggy Pants got in Shawn's personal space, his sparse goatee thrust out belligerently. "White boy and his TV bitch show up and get into *Posse* business and they walk? That ain't right."

"Yeah. They walk." Shawn's voice dropped half an octave and added even more gravel. His eyes never left the man challenging him. "Media girl keeps the story of our missing girls on TV. Keeps the police honest. Keeps our crew honest.

What happened tonight doesn't change that."

Baggy Pants' face sneered, showing a gap in his teeth from previous violence and no dental plan.

"You're full of shit." He looked back at the rest of the *Posse* crew. Young Boy might actually have thrown up when I wasn't paying attention, he looked that scared. Baggy Pants motioned the barely hairy chin my way. "This' the white boy who fucked you up before. Everyone knows that. What he done to you has made you a pussy. Never thought you'd turn pussy on your *Posse*."

Shawn's expression never changed. Neither did his posture.

Then a smack of flesh cracked loudly into the night air and Baggy Pants was down, crying out in pain and clutching one side of his face from Shawn's lightning quick, opened handed slap.

"Not a pussy," Shawn growled deep in his chest, accompanying his sentences with a stiff kick to whatever body parts were available. "White boy is TV girl's friend." Kick. "Something bad happens to him for no reason, her story changes." Stomp. "Suddenly the *Posse* is back in the spotlight and people stop caring about our missing family members."

Baggy Pants flopped on his back unconscious after Shawn's last kick, which would've done wonders converting an extra point. Young Boy and the last crew member were appropriately cowed and hanging back, not willing to meet

Shawn's menacing gaze.

A long moment of silence followed, broken only by one man's unconscious whimpering.

Shawn turned his head minutely, speaking to me over one shoulder.

"Tell TV Girl no more bullshit. The free passes are done." Shawn's eyes smouldered with venom as he glanced at me. "You show up in our business again you're dead."

I nodded imperceptibly and fished for my keys with trembling fingers. I took half a step towards my beat up old baby but couldn't stop myself from asking one question.

Chapter 11

"Why Selkirk?" Cathy asked.

I shrugged unconsciously before realizing that she couldn't see me over the phone. Which was a good thing given my dishevelled state of morning attire. Trust me, no one likes my morning look, all frazzled hair and rumpled boxers. I stifled a yawn with one hand as I rolled out of my old, twin bed and touched feet to the linoleum floor, holding the receiver to my ear as I heaved my tired and achy ass to a standing position.

"Shawn says the last three of their girls who disappeared were visiting family in Selkirk in the week or so beforehand."

"Which ones?"

"Didn't say."

"When?"

I scratched at my unruly mane of hair. "Recently, he said."

"How recently?"

"I didn't exactly get a timeline, Cathy."

"It's not much to go on."

"It's better than what we had before."

"We?" I could hear the smirk in Cathy's voice.

I ignored it.

"Not related. The girls, I mean. He said that much. But definitely visiting family. He was clear on that one."

"Not sisters?" Cathy muttered. I could hear fingers typing madly in the background, Googling like a champ.

"Not related. But visiting family. Those were his words." It was getting tough to stifle my yawns any further and my morning rituals needed handling. "I'll call you back in a few and see if you found anything. I gotta call my work."

"Okay. Thanks for this." Cathy's voice was excited as her typing continued. I could picture her peering intently at her computer screen. Her lips all pursed in thought heedless of her hair or how the top button on her blouse was barely containing her...

I shook my head and hung up before I let my nocturnal fantasies get out of hand.

No jokes, perverts.

I stifled another yawn and quickly dialled the *Canada-Pharm* front desk to beg forgiveness for the late sick call. My friend Lisa at reception picked up. Lisa had been working reception at the internet pharmacy since it's inception in the early two-thousands and was one of the few people there I got along with. I'd been working there fairly steady for a couple of years, primarily for the huge discount on Mom's medications. Canadian Healthcare couldn't cover everything, so working a crap job for a crap wage was the price I paid to keep her going. More than worth it.

That said prior to this day the only times I'd ever missed a shift at the call centre had been while recovering from a triple-GSW. Since then, the office had been more than cool about anything I'd needed as far as time off. Mostly because they did their very best to gain whatever positive exposure they could in the press and medical journals and with other staff members by employing a stalwart and upstanding citizen like myself. Coming down on me for missing my first shift ever due to... Let's call it illness... Well, let's just say it wouldn't do wonders for morale with the rest of the staff.

"Yeah, you definitely sound feverish, Joe." That was Lisa, buying my fib hook, line and sinker. Her voice was conciliatory and encouraging. "Don't worry about your shift today, just try to call in before it starts next time. I'll square things with Troy for you."

"Thanks, Lisa. I owe you one.

"I like flowers."

I blinked.

"Huh?"

"Or Chinese food." Her voice had gotten strange. Flirtatious? "You know, in case you're hungry when you feel better. I know a place where you can pay back the favour."

"Uh..." I racked my brain for a response while my belly rumbled at the mere mention of food. Lisa was a nice lady but I'd never really considered the mother of two working at reception as dateable material. Though to be honest I didn't spend a lot of my time considering anyone as dateable material. Starting with myself.

"Joe? You still there?"

"Yeah. Uh... Yeah. Just..." I cleared my throat uncomfortably, still trying to think past the throbbing in my skull for something to say. "I'm just not feeling good is all. Might take tomorrow off too. Next time I see you maybe we can talk about... Yeah. Talk."

"Sounds great, Joe. Get a doctor's note if you're taking the weekend. Always goes better for the paperwork."

No chance of that. I avoid my doctor like he had the plague.

"Do my best. Later, Lisa. Thanks again."

I hung up before the conversation got any weirder and jammed both heels of my hands into my eye sockets, rubbing tiredly and trying to sort myself out.

The events of the previous night-slash-early morning were

weighing heavily on my mind and starting to concern me. I couldn't remember the last time I'd felt so exhausted and depleted. The headache and perpetual hunger weren't anything new, I'd been dealing with that off and on for months since getting shot. Tamara's ideas about my metabolism or whatever suggested a reason behind them, but that didn't stop me from worrying. I'd gotten used to the idea of being somewhat more of a physical presence than I had been before, and the thought of not being able to perform – I repeat, settle down perverts – at the same level of intensity was more than a bit frightening.

I opened my eyes, blinked at the sharp glare from the basement lamps and staggered off to my bathroom.

Must be getting old. Never had to call in to work before. Even when bouncing at clubs every night.

Clubs.

Shit.

I made a mental note to call Shelby after I got out of the shower, see if she needed an extra body for the weekend. Just because I was blowing off my day job didn't mean I could afford to go without working some hours. Bills got to be paid and all that.

After a quick but scalding shower I wrapped a towel around my waist and wiped at the mirror, hoping to give my stubble a quick trim before getting back to Cathy.

"What the fuck..." I muttered, nearly dropping my blue Bic into the sink.

I looked terrible.

And thin.

Not skinny. Given my muscle mass and skeletal structure I wasn't genetically built to truly be skinny. But thin skinned. My cheeks were sunken in and I could visibly see the outlines of my ribcage against the flesh on my torso. Every sinew was visible on my arms and the flesh around my collar bone was tight. So stunned was I by my appearance that even the revelation of the six-pack and no more belly fat that I'd always dreamed of wasn't a reason to celebrate.

It was one to panic.

The phone rang.

Cathy.

I forgot all about shaving and towelled off rapidly. Mom's weak voice called down the stairs at me, confirming my suspicions. The thought of Mom seeing her son like this added a higher level of panic to my actions and I stumbled back to my bedroom, calling out "I'm coming, don't worry. I'm coming" in reply.

"Wow, you're out of breath." Cathy's voice laughed into my ear before turning wicked. "Did I catch you with your pants down?"

"Is there something in the drinking water with you ladies today?" I grumbled while trying to awkwardly step into a fresh-ish pair of jeans.

"Oh, so more of a private moment?"

I sighed heavily.

"Did you call with an update or to tease your poor and lonely friend?"

"I... Well an update of course." Cathy's paused, her voice dropping to a conspiratorial level. "Joe, I didn't know... You've never said you were lonely before. Like, *ever* before. I have friends if you want to... "

My free hand wiped over my face in frustration.

"I'm fine. I promise." *Aside from the whole wasting away to nothing part, just fine. Thank you for asking.* "Selkirk. Talk to me."

"You sure?"

"Cathy!"

"Okay, fine." Her verbal backing off was clear as day. Odds were good I'd even offended her slightly. I'd make it up to her later. Maybe she also liked Chinese food. "Okay, three of the missing women, all with known ties to the *Native Posse* went missing at different times over the last six weeks. This was the first time the police had anything resembling a pattern to work with and followed the trail as far as they could. But *Posse* affiliates being what they are, only so many of them would even talk to the police, never mind give much in the way of details."

I scavenged around for my belt and cinched it in two notches tighter than I had to yesterday to keep my pants up. "Similarities in disappearances?"

"Not really. Two of them just didn't return home from work one day. The other was heading out grocery shopping and didn't come back."

Near the back of my closet I found an old, long sleeved oversized grey tee shirt and slipped it on. What used to be snug on me now fit like a tent. Perfect for hiding the lack of body mass from my mom.

"Not much to go on."

"That's been this whole story. No connections."

"So what did you find?"

"A connection."

"Details?"

Cathy cleared her throat primly. "The three missing women in question were not related but they were fostered by the same family when they were kids. Mrs. Sonya Kubrakovich and her husband took a lot of foster children into their Selkirk home back in the nineties. Lots of part timers mostly, some of them were in and out of there a few times given the failures of the system."

"Huh." I scratched at the itchy stubble under my chin and considered going back for a quick shave. "So they went to this lady's home? Like a visit?"

"The foster home's been closed since Mr. Kubrakovich died, so I don't think so. But I'm certain they went to visit her."

"New place?"

"Yup. Selkirk Mental Health Centre. Diagnosed with moderate level schizophrenia in two thousand and five. Been under the systems' care ever since."

I grunted again. Genuinely stumped. "Well, she's not gonna have much to say."

"Probably not."

"Still," I scratched at my wet mop of hair absently. "Probably worth the drive for you to check it out. I mean, the cops didn't go. Maybe you'll shake something loose."

Some women smile in a way that you don't have to see it to

know they're doing it. Cathy's was like that, dimples and all.

"I couldn't agree more."

"Cool. Well, Good luck with that. When are you going?"

"I'm not. You are."

Chapter 12

"And you agreed? Just like that?" Tamara asked teasingly from the passenger seat.

I scowled faintly without taking my eyes off the road. Early weekend cottage-goers were littering the highway ahead of me and driving like a bunch of morons.

"No. Not just like that." I took a huge bite of double teen burger with extra bacon and tried to settle the beast that was my growling belly for a time. "But she's right. Someone should go and check the hospital out."

Tamara smiled lopsidedly from behind those librarian frames, tilting her head slightly to peer at me. "I get why she can't go. What with the police telling her to back off the case and not wanting to lose her job. Makes sense." She took a sip from her bottled water and looked out to the road ahead. "Doesn't explain why it had to be you."

I growled quietly and jammed another bite into my craw.

Bacon. Not quite the cure for all that ails you. But it's close.

She wasn't wrong though. It had taken Cathy almost ten minutes to work her way through all of my obvious and pointed objections for keeping my big nose out of this whole issue. But since I hadn't told her Lieutenant Connell's unvoiced suspicions about my previous vigilante activity at *Cowboy Shotz* I didn't even have that as a hole card to use.

I don't know why I didn't tell Cathy if you're wondering. When it comes to all things weird in my life it's like I have a mental block with my old friend. One that forces me to keep her at a safe and discreet distance.

"Seriously, Joe. With this Connell guy having his suspicions about you I really don't think making this trip is a smart move."

Telling Tamara however was a no-brainer. And no, I don't know why if you're still wondering.

While I've only known my miniscule massage therapist-kinesiologist-in-training friend for a couple of years, most of that only professionally via the downtown YMCA where she worked while I lifted heavy things and put them down there's always been an easy understanding between us.

You know how some people in your life are friends that you're social with but can't really trust? And how others you trust to a point but about nothing really important?

Yeah, Tamara's neither of those.

Somehow we just crossed a line into pure trust.

Which to be perfectly frank has been essential for me. I don't know what the fuck I would've done without being able to talk to Tamara about the weird things I was dealing with. Hell, she says it's been good for her too. Apparently her work with my training advancements and testing has done wonders for her

Health Sciences grades at the University.

Yay, friendship.

If she wasn't dating my buddy Mark she'd be perfect.

Yay. Friendship.

"What's he gonna know?" I replied after getting some gristle out of my teeth. My signal flicked on – at least it did inside the van, the outer blinker may or may not have been on the fritz – and I gently pulled into the passing lane to get ahead of a small family hauling an ancient pop-up camper. "Worst case scenario if anyone asks I had the hugest urge for a classic Skinner's Wet'n'Wild Water Park hot dog and I went for a drive to satisfy my craving." My stomach gurgled angrily at the mention of a Skinner's dog. Wordlessly Tamara reached into our shared A&W lunch bag and handed me my second burger. "No harm no foul."

"I suppose," Tamara agreed absently, staring at the road ahead of us. Her feet were up on the dashboard which would've been an annoyance were anyone else to do so while riding in my baby. But since she was wearing a very short pair of cut offs and tank top combo I decided the view was worth the infraction. "I mean, it's not like the police or the RCMP have you under surveillance or anything. Right?"

My shoulders shrugged and grease dribbled into the scruff on my chin. "Who knows? RCMP might have different rules about that sort of thing. The feds just passed a bill about spying, maybe I'm on their list now." My sleeve took care of most of the grease though I knew I probably looked like a messy infant.

Fuck it. It's my van dammit, I'll look like a mess if I want to. Until I can get out and clean up of course. I'm not a complete savage after all.

"Though I doubt it. Odds are he and the WPS have enough on their plates tracking down the few leads they've got getting a handle on this missing women case without throwing budgets and stuff away on a guy like me."

" 'A guy like you?' What does that mean?"

I shrugged again, this time a bit self consciously. "I don't know."

"Yeah, I think you do."

My face started to heat up.

"Come on, spill."

I jammed the rest of my burger into my mouth to buy some time. But that only worked for a moment. Because Teen Burgers are amazing and I couldn't chew anymore slowly when my belly demanded beef that strongly.

"Well?"

"Look, Tamara. Let's face facts." A road sign on the right indicated only another seventeen kilometres to Selkirk. Half an hour give or take from the Mental Hospital.

"What facts?"

"Factual facts. I'm a thirty-three year old undereducated bouncer who lives with his sick mother while working two jobs. I have no other family and no criminal record to speak of – prior to last night, obviously. Hell, if it wasn't for last night I doubt Mr. RCMP would've ever had a name to put to the smoky picture of me that he's holding on to." I let my eyes drift off the road for a moment to give Tamara a pointed stare. "Those facts alone tell me that no matter what he might suspect the odds of him being able to legally do anything are small at best."

Tamara nodded thoughtfully. "Makes sense. So why did he give you his card? Why even bother voicing his suspicions in the first place?"

"Maybe he thinks I have an honest face?"

"You do have an honest face, when it's not scowling or going purple from too many deadlifts that is." I chuckled softly. Tamara smiled and adjusted in her seat, much to the admiration of my libido. Stupid libido. "I just hope he doesn't know anything else about you."

"Frankly, I don't think he knows *anything* about me. Aside from you no one really knows anything." My fingers tightened on the steering wheel as the now familiar tingling faintly returned to the back of my neck. I managed to keep from sighing in relief. "Besides, who'd believe me?"

"I believed you."

"I gave you empirical evidence."

"Lots of big guys are strong."

"Can they make neon signs blow out on command too?"

She stuck her tongue out at me.

My small smile returned and I took a deep breath, settling in for the rest of our short drive.

Silence stretched for a few moments. The van's radio lost anything resembling a signal ten minutes outside of Winnipeg and Tamara wasn't a fan of my choice in cassette tapes so no road tunes.

Fine by me.

Save for how it started to feel awkward.

Putting my peripheries to work I spied my tiny friend carefully. Her smile was intact but her eyes were off in space, staring away.

Sadly?

I cleared my throat softly.

"You never did tell me what was bugging you."

She blinked and looked towards me and then away again quickly. "No, I didn't."

"Any particular reason for that?"

Tamara paused carefully before answering.

Silence equals yes.

"No. No reason. It's just something I need to work through."

"Huh." I passed another minivan with way less mileage than my baby absently. "Afraid of what I might say?"

She shook her head too quickly. "No, not at all."

"Huh." I rubbed at my still greasy chin with one hand before staring at it in disgust. Tamara handed me a napkin without being asked. "Well, if you need anything at all..."

"You're my guy, Joe. I know." Her fingers rested on upper arm for a moment and gave a quick squeeze. "With all you've confided in me, I know I can trust you. But for now I need you to let me work this out for myself."

And that was that.

Or at least it would've been if I had been able to keep myself from taking one more indirect stab at it.

Attack B-Four.

"Well, it was nice of Mark to be cool with you spending your day off with me. Between your schedules I know it's been tough for you guys to get together."

Tamara's face betrayed nothing as she responded. "Well I had that early doctor's appointment this morning. And it turned out there was a shift he could pick up, which since he's still rebuilding his credit after being off work for a few months..." Her voice trailed off as her gaze turned purposefully away, effectively ending the conversation.

Direct hit. I had sunk her battleship.

My mind immediately began to race, assuming all kinds of horrible things. It's an extension of the Neanderthal in my guts, always going into a hyper-protective mode whenever the people in my life are having trouble. With a small effort I was able to shut those thoughts down and keep things in perspective. Tamara wanted to keep me out of this, and if it involved relationship issues between herself and my buddy then she was absolutely right. It was absolutely none of my business.

"How is Mark doing, anyways?" I asked casually, unable to

stop myself from fishing. "I know he's recovered from his injuries back in the spring and is working again. But since we don't toss drunks out of clubs together anymore, seems like I barely ever see him."

"He's good." Still not looking at me as she spoke. Definitely a sign. "His new warehouse job keeps him busy. Always lots of overtime available."

"Makes sense. Sun's shining. Make the hay. Et cetera."

Silence again.

Awkward for sure now.

Dumbass.

Couldn't leave well enough alone.

Highway sign. Selkirk in eleven more kilometres.

The tingle at the back of my neck made it's presence known ever so slightly as my heart rate went up. I had no idea what to expect or what I would find once we got to the hospital. But even this tiny level of excitement at doing something that felt like it was worth doing was enough to get the juices flowing.

Of course, the extra tingling started to awaken the ache in my skull that had been quiet for a few hours. Which reminded me of how wasted and thin I had looked in the mirror. Which made me wish I'd grabbed a third burger. Which sent my stomach rumbling loudly into the silence.

"Oh!" Tamara started in her seat and turned back to me. "That reminds me. I think I've figured out how to keep you from getting headaches."

Chapter 13

Cold.

Delicious.

Refreshing.

At the worst of times, there are few things better on a hot summer day in Southern Manitoba than a Slurpee from your neighbourhood Seven-Eleven.

But when you've been avoiding these delicious, calorie laden treats like the plague for over a year in a desperate attempt to shed excess body fat and because – frankly – as a thirty year old man I felt a bit silly enjoying a kiddie drink... Bloody ambrosia.

Given that Winnipeg was the reigning "Slurpee Capital of the World" and had been for a decade and counting it was increasingly difficult to avoid the temptation as summer rolled around. It seemed like everyone was gleefully consuming one right in front of me as an added taunt and torture.

Those fuckers.

But so worth the wait.

The head rush that hit me was so intense it nearly I stopped in my tracks, my stumbling self nearly bumping into Tamara who laughed at my Slurpee-drunken stagger good-naturedly as we approached the doors to the Selkirk Mental Health Centre.

"Easy there, champ." Tamara laughed at me, her eight ounce cup looking huge in her tiny hands. "We're here to talk to a patient not become one."

I mock glowered down at her, using the brim of my hat to add stern emphasis to my pseudo displeasure. My diabetes inducing thirty-two ounce cup was over half empty as I took another huge pull of frozen sugary soda deliciousness and felt the rush hit my belly, sending pure energy racing through my system.

"Quiet woman." My growl was much too cheerful to really be called a growl, but that's what I was going for so that's what I'm calling it. "What have you done for me lately?"

Her pert eyebrow cocked high over the brim of those damned teasing librarian rims at me. "Aside from show you a way to keep from starving yourself into endless headaches and cramping?"

"Yeah. Besides that."

"Asshole."

"You love it."

"Don't push your luck. You're not that cute."

I chuckled and purposefully did not make any sort of flirtatious follow up comment.

The tingling at the back of my neck was constant but muted. It was an amazing transition from feeling so depleted and wasted. The literal sugar rush was intense. I knew I wasn't back to normal (check that, back to my *new* normal) but there was no doubt that I was on the right track.

"What made you think of Slurpees of all things?"

Tamara's smile faltered slightly. "Honestly it was from a new patient one of the nutritionists at the University was speaking with. I was in the other room working on a paper last night and could hear them through the door of the consultation room."

"Big guy?"

"Huge. Clearly a food addict." Tamara paused, taking a small sip. "Poor guy just had all of the worst kind of habits. Too many sugars, starches and no concept of exercise."

Flashbacks to my more slovenly three-hundred-plus pound days of sitting on the basement couch eating nachos and feeling sorry for myself rolled on the internal film projector.

I shuddered. "Been there."

"Not like this." Tamara's smile faded slightly, lost in her own thoughts. "Doctor's were warning this guy about his blood pressure, the risk of heart disease. All the usual things you expect in a heavier set person later in life. This guy is twenty-three."

That killed my good mood as well. "So, buddy's seeing the nutritionist?"

"Yeah. And it was just so obvious listening to the basics of proper nutrition being explained to this poor man. The concept of good calories over bad. Intake versus output. Proper water consumption." She shook her head slightly as if having trouble understanding herself. "Remember what we talked about yesterday? About how elite athletes need to balance their intake to match their output of energy just in order to keep their body functioning? To avoid muscle atrophy and headaches and so on?"

The mental image of my epic face plant into the chain link fence surrounding the car shop on Higgins the night before made me wince and rub at my forearm where the road rash was itching beneath my sweater sleeve.

"I remember."

"Well this poor man was immediately put on a calorie deficit diet, and so he should be. Until he's at a level of health where exercise of any sort won't be dangerously strenuous the only thing he can do is manage his addiction and cut down to the sheer basics. Proteins, vegetables and light, fibrous carbohydrates."

"Well duh." I snorted. "I've been doing that off and on for years trying to lose weight. One of those easier said than done things but also a no brainer if this guy's health is that bad. But what does that have to do with these delicious beverages?"

"I was just getting to that. The good news for this man comes from learning that his main vice was... ta-dah! Slurpees!" Tamara took a loud sip to make her point. "The nutritionist immediately explained to him just how many hundreds if not thousands of calories were in one of these jumbo sized beasts. Just by cutting them out of this guy's diet..."

"He might drop into a calorie deficit right away." I nodded thoughtfully. "Makes sense. I was doing much the same thing in a desperate attempt to shed the love handles."

"But now you have the opposite problem, Joe. You're like one of those elite athletes." My face may or may not have gotten a touch smug at that point. Words I never thought I'd hear anyone say without trying to make fun of me. "The way I see it you may not be able to keep up with the energy output your metabolism is burning through these days."

My turn for the eyebrow to quirk, first at Tamara and then at the Super Big Gulp in my hand.

"That seems way too easy. I mean... Well let's face it. I'm not like a normal guy anymore, am I? Sure, some people can move the weights I can in the gym, but not at the... Well... When I'm really letting this power loose it's not the same thing at all."

Tamara blinked at me as if I was an idiot. "Joe. Energy is energy. Newton's Third Law proves that for every action there is an equal and opposite reaction." My eyes started to glaze over the second I started hearing science being thrown about. *Focus dimwit!* "So for every kilojoule of energy you expend, whether it's walking to your car or bench pressing four hundred pounds fifteen times the energy you're using will leave your system and leave *you* in a state of withdrawal. Hence muscle fatigue, headaches and stomach cramping for not replenishing fast enough."

"I told you I got a D in high school Physics right?"

"We're talking chemistry and biology. Now pay attention, here's where I think this applies directly to you." Tamara stopped us short of the hospital entranceway by grabbing my arm. Her tiny fingers were Slupree-cool even through my sweater.

Her eyes were very serious.

"Joe. According to the Law of the Conservation of Energy the total energy of an isolated system cannot change. It can neither be created nor destroyed. However it can change form – like from a chemical energy," she raised her Slurpee cup and gave it a little shake. "To the kinetic energy you've been using like crazy the last few months." Her eyes travelled up and down my body briefly, making me feel a touch self conscious. "In addition, this energy can also be conserved or stored in a vessel until it can be used at a future time. And since I can see your cheekbones and every muscle fibre in fine detail I think that you might be out of stored up energy."

The memory of a wasted, thin skinned me in my bathroom mirror made me shudder.

"Huh." I chewed at my bottom lip. "I can't decide if I have the best problem ever or the worst."

Tamara tilted her head as she peered up at me. "Some people would be very happy to know that their metabolism burns faster than they can keep up with."

"I used to be fucking jealous of those guys. But this... This is crazy. Am I supposed to have a jumbo Slurpee every day? That can't be good for me either."

She shrugged."It's loaded with fast burning sugars and water which carry electrolytes through your system. I'm sure your dentist will disapprove but until you can find a better way to keep your body level this might be a decent short-term solution."

My head was shaking.

"This is crazy."

"We also might want to start cutting back on your training sessions, Joe." I blinked at her in surprise. Her expression told me that she didn't like the thought either. "As much as I want to keep tracking your progress, the sheer amount of effort you're putting forth has only been depleting your reserves."

"You mean my fat ass."

"I mean your reserves!" Tamara's eyes narrowed, fingers squeezing tighter on my arm. "Professional body builders risk their lives every time they drop below five percent body fat for a competition, Joe. It is very dangerous to not have any fat on your body. Again, it's where electrolytes are stored to keep the rest of the system nourished. Deplete it too far..."

"Headaches. Cramping. Injuries. Muscle atrophy." I sighed heavily. "Got it."

Her smile slowly returned. "I don't want to stop outright, Joe. But maybe take a week off. Eat properly. Get the house sorted for your Mom's realtors. Get some rest. Let your system recharge."

She was right. My whole life the very thought of taking a break from anything – work, the house, Mom, the gym and more work – was impossible to consider. I was a sixty-hour-plus work week kinda guy, not used to taking a break until sleep kicked my ass.

But taking a week off from the gym... Man.

"Okay." My head was nodding thoughtfully and my small smile was returning. "Okay. Maybe you're right. We'll check in here for Cathy, ask a few questions. I may have to work the club this weekend, but that's pretty slack." I saluted her with the brim of my cup. "And you're officially off Joe-duty for a week. I promise."

Her infectious smile was back.

We entered the hospital and approached the front desk. Two ladies were working the front counter, both making apologetic motions to us as they were tied up on phone calls while a man in hospital scrubs was turned away, working at the filing cabinet behind them.

"Who are we meeting again?"

I rummaged around in my pocket for the paper I'd scribbled on this morning. Eventually it came free and I began unfolding it.

Which was when the man turned from the cabinets and started in surprise.

My eyes were drawn to the motion and I met his face.

And I froze.

The Slurpee cup slipped from my suddenly numb fingers, splashing icy syrup all over my sneakers and the white linoleum floor.

My heart started racing and the tingle at the back of my neck exploded.

"Holy shit," I whispered.

Chapter 14

Memories.

For months I had been finding myself having bursts of memory that were nearly as clear as the day they happened. I was remembering things in full Technicolor during brief, intermittent flashes.

Old TV shows.

The smell of Dad's pipe.

Donald's face after I walked in on him making out with his girlfriend.

The exact essay I'd written, verbatim for English class in grade nine.

Crazy accurate and detailed stuff.

All coming to me in brief, storming lightning bolts behind my eyes.

They'd last for a couple of seconds tops.

Would feel way longer.

I was having one now.

Simon Pritchard.

Wearing hospital scrubs and standing right behind the reception desk where he stared back at me.

I hadn't seen him since...

Lightning flashed behind my eyes.

Cue the highlight reel.

Cub Scout Camp. I must've been eleven years old. Cub Scouts was the level above Beavers but not experienced enough yet to become a Venture – don't look so confused, these are just the Canadian designations for being a Boy Scout.

Yes, they're named after wolf cubs and beavers.

Canadian.

Let's move on.

So yeah. Cub Camp. A whole weeks worth of sticky, uncomfortable hell in the Whiteshell region of northwestern Ontario.

Hot. Wet. Insect riddled. Eight kids to a tent. Canoeing. Fishing. Archery. Woodworking and trailblazing.

Tons of kids loved it.

Not me.

I'd stopped being the tallest kid in my class the year previous. I kept on growing of course, but it was growing to fat as opposed to height. Quickly my peers began to look down on me and take advantage of it. Lots of schoolyard bullying, face in dirt and name calling crap.

Tough to deal with at school for a few hours a day. Harder for a whole week with minimal supervision and no Mom to cry to or Dad to lift my spirits with stories and dirty tricks to use in my defence

So yeah.

It sucked.

Simon made it worse.

Mostly because everyone thought they could trust him.

You see, Simon was a Venture. A Scout Leader

Older than the rest of us by a couple of years and earning more badges for leadership with every Cub Camp he helped out at. Over the course of one summer he helped out at all of them, six or seven in total I think. A real outdoorsy type was how the other leaders and chaperones referred to him. "Terrific with the kids" was a common phrase overheard at meal times.

And it appeared to be true. Simon was usually surrounded by groups of us Cubs. Whether it was in the lake, during mountaineering classes or any of the sporting events there was always a good crowd of kids that stuck with him.

He was free with advice. Always offering to help with crafts or adventures. More than often he had a shoulder to cry on and an ear to listen for the kids who were upset or homesick. He would often be seen leading one of the younger boys who was having a rough time off to one side to chat, offer some advice. A friendly hug.

Turns out, Simon was giving more than just friendly hugs.

It took years for the truth to come out. This is the sort of crime that is deeply personal and incredibly difficult to talk about, especially with your family.

But once the first young man came forward to the police, accusing Simon of molesting him over the course of time it opened the floodgates for more.

In total there were over a dozen young men and women (Girl Guides graduated to Ventures as well) who took the stand and told horrific stories of abuse, manipulation and deceit. Most of it was too graphic to print in the news. All of it completely damning and likely not even the tip of the iceberg when it came to the true number of victims.

And since I know you're thinking it; No, I wasn't one of them.

Simon had always creeped me out for some reason. The things he would say and the way he would act around others... I always found it incredibly fake and unconvincing. Like someone who knew the right words to say but didn't know how to say them. Like the acting on regional commercials, all stilted and wooden.

But I guess people, more importantly young people, are just happy to hear what they want to be told. Especially when they're emotional and confused and looking for direction.

During raids of his apartment police found evidence of child pornography and worse buried in the hard drive of his computer. E-mail correspondence with some of the victims and others that he was working his way towards making victims.

The Pritchard family attempted to stand beside him during the trial. But once the evidence began to pile up and the people's outrage rose to dangerous levels, Simon's widowed father famously said in an interview with CTV; "If my wife had lived to know the horrors her son has committed it would surely have killed her. It may kill me yet."

Simon was convicted on multiple counts and sentenced to prison. He was placed in general population at Headingly Penitentiary which was nearly the same as a death sentence given how the rougher inmates usually treated rapists and child molesters. It wasn't long before stories circulated of multiple suicide attempts and therapists started coming to his aid, trying to "learn more about the mind of such a sick man."

Eventually one therapist was able to convince the Crown that Simon Pritchard was "less a criminal in search of hurting others" and more of a "damaged human being in need of care, examination and potential rehabilitation."

I remember clearly reading the story in the Free Press when it broke a few years ago, detailing the public outcry and the victim lobbying to keep Simon behind bars. The story had been buried deep below the fold in as small a space as possible to try and minimize the public outcry. Somehow, despite all of the negative community sentiment and his criminal convictions Simon was granted permission to relocate to the Selkirk Mental Health Centre to be kept under constant surveillance and segregated from the rest of the populace.

Three square meals a day. Time in the exercise yards under minimal supervision. No bars. No cell. Nurses and therapists to check on him during the day.

You know, the kind of care that his victims had to pay through the nose for in order to cope with their shattered lives while this creep got it at the expense of the taxpayers.

Justice. It isn't blind. It's damn near non-existent in today's world.

Chapter 15

"Can we help you?"

That was one of the front desk attendants. I think. My mind was still whirling and the hairs on the back of my neck were dancing from the tingle racing up into my skull, shooting energy through every fibre. My toes twitched and my fingers clenched spasmodically. I was filled with a million thoughts and a million urges.

Simon stood there behind the desk eyeing me carefully. He looked different than I remembered, not surprising over the course of time. But no mistaking him.

Shy of six feet but not by much. Back in the day he had been lean and fit, all that time on Scouting adventures keeps a person in shape. These days he'd changed to just plain skinny. Wrinkles had developed on his forehead and crows' feet were blossoming. His dark hair was cropped short to hide his receding hairline and prominent streaks of gray ran throughout. He was unshaven and dressed in typical hospital scrubs, looking more like a nurse's assistant than a patient.

His eyes though. Brown. Calculating. Speculative.

And given his expression, he recognized me as well.

My knuckles cracked softly as hands became fists.

Tamara's hand on my arm broke the spell.

I shook my head, forcing myself to take in everything that was going on and started taking steady breaths until my tunnel vision collapsed.

The overhead halogen lights stopped flickering so heavily while the ladies working reception tried to keep helpful but distant expressions on their faces. Simon hadn't moved from behind them, still holding some manila file folders in his arms and staring back at me.

I found my small smile and plastered it hurriedly on my face. Stepping forward towards the desk made a squishy wet sound.

Right. Dropped Slurpee.

Idiot.

Thankfully Tamara took over at that point. Turning on the smile and bubbly personality I'd seen hundreds of times at the YMCA. Apologizing for my behaviour by making up some plausible fiction about hospital phobias and asking for assistance with the mess.

"Of course," said the blonde receptionist before turning back to Simon. "Would you be a doll and grab a mop?"

Simon blinked, coming out of his own stupor. A false smile – well, it looked false to me – flashed onto his face and his eyes warmed up considerably, putting down the folders and turning to leave. "Of course. I'll be right back, Shannon."

My eyes tracked Simon all the way down the hall on my left until he was out of sight. Tamara continued her stream of pleasant banter with the ladies, explaining the reason for our visit. Or at least the reason I had concocted to get us into see Cathy's target for investigation.

The greying blonde receptionist looked over her computer screen, tracking down what I presumed was a list of names and rooms. Given how my mood and emotions were up I kept a few feet back from the desk, not wanting to let my freak show aura cause any further problems.

"Kubrakovich?" she asked absently, her finger now tracking along the screen.

Tamara eyed me over one shoulder. I nodded tensely, trying to keep my breath steady. Her eyes behind her librarian frames tightened fractionally, though her voice remained pleasant in reply. "Yes, please. We're friends of the family. Just popping by since we were in the area."

Okay. It wasn't a great story. But what would you have tried?

Squeaking rubber wheels announced Simon's return, pushing a bright yellow mop bucket ahead of him. The false smile was still wide on his lips while his dark eyes took in the whole lobby, not missing anything.

The belligerent Neanderthal in my belly growled as he approached.

I stubbornly stayed stock still, my feet in the middle of the mess my cup had made.

Simon stopped just out of my reach.

Intentional? Possibly.

His false smile froze.

"Can I get you to move, please?"

His voice.

More memories flashed. Campfire songs. His lessons on wood crafting and trailblazing. Annoying jokes other kids laughed at that I never found remotely funny.

That smile never wavered. His eyes got darker if that was possible.

Suddenly there was an itch at the back of my head in that moment. I can't describe it any better than that. An irritating new sensation that mingled with the more familiar energy surge. Like a sudden urge to scratch at a mosquito bite right at the base of my skull.

Very annoying.

I didn't move.

Simon's eyes blinked while his false smile seemed to tighten slightly.

"Joe?" Tamara's voice once again bringing the rest of the world back into focus. Both receptionists were back to eyeing me warily. A pair of security guards were now within eyesight at the end of the hallway to my right, keeping a close watch on the lobby.

Keeping a close watch on me. The potential threat in the lobby.

Chill out, man.

I took another deep breath. Raised one hand in what might have been a non verbal apology, might have been a dismissive wave and stepped out of the puddle and onto the doormat where I attempted to wipe off my sneakers.

Everyone seemed to relax. Simon's expression didn't change as he began to mop up my mess. The security guards dispersed out of site and the ladies at reception went back to work.

I could hear Tamara apologizing for me quietly, referencing recent trauma and hardships at home causing temper flares and other issues. The ladies at reception nodded understandingly, which I suppose shouldn't be a surprise given the type of difficulties they likely saw and dealt with on a daily basis here in the hospital.

Simon's mop made wet slopping noises as it soaked the

laminate flooring. That damned smile never wavered even as he eyed me cautiously.

I forced myself to look away. My guts were twisted with impotent rage and that damned itch at the back of my skull was getting stronger, turning into an annoying pressure.

"Right. Sonya Kubrakovich." The greying receptionist said at last. "Sorry for the delay, she's recently been transferred between wards."

"That's all right, I'm sure it's a common practice." Good ole' Tamara, making everyone around her more comfortable. "Is it all right if we go see her? To pay family respects?"

The other receptionist peered down at the screen briefly and blinked. "Well you can see her. However, I warn you now that she won't be very responsive."

That caught my attention. I cleared my throat carefully and tried to keep my voice calm and concerned. "Has her condition worsened?"

The first receptionist replied. "Her condition changed dramatically in the last two weeks. Apparently she reacted badly to her treatments and is now in the critical care ward."

"What does that mean? Is she dying?" Tamara asked.

"Her vitals are stable however she is unresponsive. Her doctors have her listed as being in a coma."

Chapter 16

Ever seen someone on TV or in the movies who's supposed to be in a coma? How they're just laying there, barely breathing and completely unresponsive?

Turns out that's one of the few things that Hollywood got right.

Mrs. Sonya Kubrakovich was a slight, painfully thin woman. Wispy hair and very pale skin that was beginning to go grey and pallid. Her current state of health made her appear even older than the mid-fifties her chart said she was. There was an I.V. and catheter tube in place to regulate her intake and output while the heart rate monitor strapped to her chest beeped away fitfully from the monitor over her head. There were sticky diodes attached to her temples, apparently to read and record brainwave activity. The screen those were attached to showed a number of wavy lines that her chart explained showed signs of dreams and mental acuity.

Hence; coma instead of brain dead.

"Well." I grumbled under my breath. "This is disappointing."

I was keeping a safe distance from all of the electronic equipment. Given the shock - rimshot, please – of seeing Simon in the lobby I was still feeling off and over emotional. The tingles were still shooting from the back of my neck and making extremities itch with pent up energy. Usually I was able to keep a firm grip on the side affects to my weirdness, but I didn't trust myself here.

Tamara skimmed over the chart some more, chewing on her lower lip pensively.

"When did those missing girls come to visit again?"

Numbers and dates flashed behind my eyes.

"Six weeks ago. July seventeenth. Disappearances occurred separately but all before August first."

Tamara blinked and adjusted her glasses to look at me.

"That's pretty exact."

I shrugged.

"No one likes faulty data. Not even Brent Spiner."

Tamara blinked some more, her expression blank.

I sighed, feely suddenly very nerdy.

"Seriously? Brent Spiner? Data?"

"I don't... Is that supposed to mean something?"

Kids these days.

"Forget it. When does it say Mrs. Kubrakovich fell into her coma?"

Tamara went back to the chart. "August nineteenth. Apparently in the week prior she began having strange reactions to her medications and treatment. Lashing out in ways she'd never shown before, having screaming fits and refusing to eat, making wild accusations to staff members and volunteers. Eventually she started refusing her medication which never ends well in this environment. Then one day she just didn't wake up in the morning and here we are. No change since then, but there are strong readings on her brainwave activity. The doctors have made positive notes on those readings." She glanced up from the chart to gaze sadly at the immobile woman. "They're hopeful of a recovery."

I leaned against the doorframe and sighed, rubbing fingers against my temple. The weird itch had been replaced by the faint stirrings of my more familiar headache which was never a good sign.

"I shoulda stayed home. Helped Mom get the house ready. Keep sorting through the shit we've had piling up forever."

"This was worth the trip, Joe. At least now we know this is a dead end." Tamara shamefully gasped, pressing fingertips to her lips. "Oh my, God. Poor choice of words there."

I managed not to laugh at her.

"S'okay. I won't tell."

Tamara glanced over at Mrs. Kubrakovich apologetically all the same.

I moved my fingers from my temple and ran a palm over my face heavily before pushing away from the doorframe, energy racing down my spine from the sudden movement and pulsing in time with the ache in my skull.

"Okay. Let's bolt. Her doctors won't talk to us. She can't talk to us. Security won't have anything to tell us about our missing girls due to privacy laws and neither will the receptionists. Let's get out of here so I can grab another Slurpee for the road home. Maybe I can get some house stuff done for Mom before I head to work at the club tonight."

Tamara fell in step beside me as I turned purposefully away from the resting woman's room. Fatigue and frustration warred equally within me as I stalked out.

"I thought you were taking the day off?"

"I took the day off. The night is different. Still got bills to pay."

"You hate working weekends now though. Too many bad memories or something?"

I shrugged, slightly embarrassed. "It's not so bad at the new club. I just prefer working mid week when it's quieter. Same pay, less bullshit."

"Plus, more weekends off."

A mirthless laugh escaped my lips. "Yup. More time to workout, stress about money, take my mother to church and wonder what the next fucked up thing that's going to happen to me that I'll have to figure out how to control will be."

I could feel Tamara eyeing me archly. "You could always go out. Have fun."

"Do I look like a social butterfly to you?"

"Grabbing a drink or a movie with friends hardly qualifies you for butterfly status, Joe."

"I see movies. I drink beer."

Tamara shook her head, raising her palms up in mock surrender. "Fine. Don't listen to me. I'm only your friend after all. It just might be nice to see you outside of your workouts or whenever you decide to put on your cowboy hat for extra curricular junior detective adventures."

That pulled me up short, stopping abruptly in the middle of a hallway. Frustration over a wasted trip and running into... Anyways, frustration made my voice sharper than I preferred. "Is that what you think I'm doing?"

She crossed her arms beneath her breasts and met my stare defiantly. "What would you call it?"

"I'm helping a friend. That's it."

"Joe, helping a friend involves things like carrying a couch. Or watching their cats."

"Cathy doesn't have a cat."

"That's not the point."

"You have a point?"

"Yes."

"Then let's hear it!"

Tamara took a deep and steadying breath, clearly calming her nerves and collecting her thoughts. Realizing that my voice had grown in volume as well I did much the same, embarrassed colour rising in my unshaven cheeks.

"Tamara, I'm sorry. I'm just thrown because..."

"We'll get to what's thrown you. Believe me. But you asked me a question, and I have an answer I think you need to hear."

Her eyes were deadly serious. Sexy as hell behind her librarian frames, but deadly serious.

She reached out and gripped at my upper arm, tiny fingers barely making it halfway around. I could feel warmth and hesitancy in her touch. Hesitant for my reaction? For her words?

"Joe." Her voice fluttered nervously, forcing her to stop and clear her throat before continuing. "You are one of the most stubborn men I have ever met."

She paused.

I blinked.

"Not exactly what I was expecting."

"Shut up, I'm not done."

"Right. Sorry."

"Stubborn. Self-deprecating. Earnest. But you're like a dog with a bone when a problem is bugging you. A big, German Sheppard sized dog."

"You saying I need a haircut?"

"Shut it. I'm saying that you're not here in Selkirk because Cathy needed a favour. You're here because both she and this Lieutenant Connell are right about you." Tamara's eyes didn't waver from mine. The look got very intense. "You want to help. You're compelled to help. Not for Cathy. But for you."

My feet shuffled uncomfortably but I was unable to break eye contact.

Her fingers tightened on my bicep.

"Something about these missing women bothers you deeply. It angers you. Maybe it's..." her voice dropped to a whisper unnecessarily as no one else was in the hallway with us, but I appreciated the gesture. "Maybe it's because of the stuff at *Cowboy Shotz* and how you couldn't help those women. Maybe it's something else."

"Tamara..."

The fingers of her free hand poked me hard in the sternum, cutting me off.

"What I know for certain is that this is something you need to do. Because you know that you can. And the sooner you admit this to yourself - that this is just who you are – the happier you'll be."

I blinked, slightly overwhelmed and just a little bit confused.

"I'm happy."

"You're miserable."

"What?"

"Not just right now. You're generally miserable. And grumpy.

And pissed off at the world. Yet despite all of that you're a good man at heart." Her hand squeezed my arm once more before letting go. "Now stop beating yourself up for a wasted trip. Let's make another run to Seven-Eleven and hit the road."

A new emotion threatened to take over me for a moment. A mixture of the embarrassment from before and something I wasn't altogether familiar with. I couldn't even put a name to the feeling. So let's just call it warmth, because that's how it felt in my chest to hear those honest words from a dear friend.

We were in motion heading back towards the front entrance. I was fishing my keys out from my jeans pocket when Tamara spoke again.

"Before I forget, what got into you with that patient when we first walked in?"

I was about to answer when we rounded a corner and saw Simon ahead of us, mopping at the floor to the hallway en route to the main lobby.

Warmth vanished. Replaced with sudden cold.

"Let's have him explain it to you."

Chapter 17

It was very hard not to stalk down the hallway since I wanted to keep my approach as calm as possible.

As far as my emotions went what I wanted to do was way out of order for civilized society. Plus, Tamara was right there and had just said all kinds of nice things about me. Smashing this predators' teeth out of his fool head might have totally destroyed her impression of me.

Still. It was a close thing.

Simon was resting his chin and folded hands on top of the mop handle as we approached. His patently false smile was in full force while his eyes calculated. My headache pulsed in time with the extra tingle at the back of my neck. The itch at the base of my skull returned in that moment as well, but I pushed that irritant out of my mind as I focused on remaining calm.

"Joseph Donovan," Simon drawled. His voice was higher pitched, an upper edge tenor in the campfire choirs in my youth as I recall. His eyes remained focused on mine, the dark shadows in them more than just my imagination I'm sure of it. "How long has it been?"

I stopped a few feet from him with Tamara just to one side. Her posture felt surprised to me, though given my reaction since we stepped into this building she shouldn't have been.

"Not long enough." I was keeping my voice as low as I could manage. What I wanted to do was bellow and rage to force a reaction. Something to justify any sort of bullshit self-defence claim. But I knew better. Simon wasn't going to make things easy on anyone.

His smile twitched. "Well, that's not a very nice thing to say."

"I'm not a nice person."

"I remember you being such a good boy in camp."

"I know what you did to other good boys at camp."

Tamara's shocked gasp broke the tension as she understood. "Oh, God. You're him. The *Scout Stalker* from the newspapers."

His expression finally became something genuine. Disgust and distaste twisted his lips, like he had tasted something foul.

"Please. Can you call me Simon?"

"No, I don't think I can."

I stepped slightly ahead of Tamara, partially shielding her from Simon's leering eyes.

"You should be in prison," I growled.

He blinked up at me while his smile returned. The itch at the base of my skull intensified.

"According to Federal medical and psychiatric staff I am a sick man. Someone not criminally responsible for my actions." His patently false sigh of sadness made my clenched teeth ache as Simon put on a sorrowful expression. "Of course I regret my activities. But now that I am here, under the watchful eye of these excellent physicians I am doing much better."

The Neanderthal in my belly raged, urging my hands to lunge forward and shake this piece of garbage until his head popped off. I even took a half step forward before I caught myself.

Deep breaths, Joe. Stay calm.

"Too bad your victims don't have the same access to care." My voice was barely above a whisper. I didn't trust myself to even speak at a normal volume for fear of not being able to remain in control. "Those people have to live the rest of their lives dealing with what you did to them. Your abuse of their trust. Their bodies."

Simon nodded in sad agreement. "I wish there was something more to be done for them. But at the time my relationships with those people..."

"Children." I spat. My pulse rising in time with the energy flowing in my veins. The halogen lights along the hallway began to flicker in time with my thoughts. "Not people.

Children. Little boys. Girls. Teenagers. People implies consent."

"I never lied to any of them. No matter how sick I may have been prior to treatment, I do know that at the time my lovers were enjoying themselves."

I nearly threw up at those words. A low growl began deep in my throat.

"You say that," Tamara broke in. "You say that as if it justifies your actions."

Simon shrugged sadly. "At the time I didn't think I was wrong to have those feelings. Those urges. They seemed perfectly natural. In my mind I was only following my heart. Giving in to the natural desires I was feeling." He met Tamara's gaze steadily, locking eyes. "Isn't it wrong to deny how you feel to another person? To want to demonstrate affection?"

Tamara looked like she wanted to answer but her voice was caught somewhere in her throat.

"You knew you were wrong." My words were sharp. Heated. Simon's eyes snapped back to me, the itch at the base of my skull intensifying. I brushed it aside mentally as I focused on the man in front of me. "You *knew*. When you were confronted by your victims and the police you denied everything. You tried to destroy your hard drives. Just like you destroyed the lives of those..."

"Of course I did. I was scared." Simon shook his head as if regretful but with a perplexed look in his eyes. "As I got older and understood what societies' opinions and beliefs about sexual behaviours were I knew that I had to keep my feelings to myself." He looked me in the eyes again, setting that itch aflame. "Do you have any idea how that feels? To have to hide your feelings to everyone you know? Everyone you love?"

My hand lashed out of its own accord. The mop went scattering down the hallway with a loud clatter, spraying water in a wide arc. Simon stepped back and away from me in a flash, pressing his back against the wall, his face showing its second genuine emotion of the day.

Fear.

I was right in his face without intending to be. Toe to toe and staring down at the slightly older man. In his eyes was genuine terror. His whole body pressed back against the wall, trying to dissolve into it as a means of escape.

"Joe, don't do this." Tamara's hands were on my arm again, this time trying to pull me away. "You can't do this. Not here."

Off in my peripheries I could see security guards stepping out of their office. One of them bringing a radio mouthpiece up and speaking into it as he and his partner slowly advanced on our little scene.

Tamara's grip on my arm got more frantic. "Please Joe. He's not worth it."

"Listen to her, Joseph." Simon blurted, the itch at the back of my skull getting frantic while energy raced down my spine. "I am a patient here. A guest of the Crown. Legally sentenced here to pay for my crimes."

"Mopping floors? Sorting files? What kind of punishment is that?"

"I'm making progress. All of my doctors say so."

"Horseshit. You're manipulating them somehow. The same way you manipulated your victims."

"They were willing. I didn't coerce anyone. I am a sick man."

"Joe, please!"

"Repeat, requesting immediate assistance in hallway number one. There's a guest getting threatening a patient. Needing backup and possible police presence to..."

I tore my eyes away from Simon's terrified gaze and glared at the approaching security guards. My rage needed a release. This fifty year old man saving up for a pension didn't deserve my wrath but I was too incensed to care.

Energy pulsed from the back of my neck, washing away the itch and headache as I expanded the sensation throughout my whole body. Hair rose across my entire flesh as I built up the charge and released it haphazardly down the hallway.

Sparks burst from the battery pack charging the guards' walkie-talkie as it overloaded, forcing the man to toss the useless handset aside as if it were on fire. Come to think of it, it probably was on fire.

All the fluorescent lights along the hallway suddenly burnt out in a wave away from me, passing over the guard and extending down to the main lobby where I could hear one of the secretaries curse as her desktop computer suddenly went dead.

Silence in the sudden darkness.

And embarrassment.

Mine.

God, what's the matter with me?

Tamara's pressure on my arm continued. I gave into it, allowing her to pull me away from the terrified man. The energy released suddenly left me as fatigued as if I'd finished an hour of sprinting around the track. My stomach rumbled and my headache returned with a fury. Down the hall the guards' silhouettes remained frozen in place, clearly freaked out and wondering what was going on.

I turned my eyes back to Simon. He was still pressed back against the wall. In the sudden darkness he was harder to make out save for the gleam in his eyes and the reflection off his too white, government of Manitoba paid for dental plan teeth. His eyes were speculative and calculating once again. A smile had begun to force its way back on his face.

"Good to see you again, Joseph." His gaze flickered to Tamara and leered at her. "You feel free to visit anytime. I don't get many guests."

The Neanderthal wanted to rage again but I was too spent. Tamara's comments on pushing myself too hard and depleting my reserves rang true in my ears as my stomach rumbled.

So I settled on spiteful words.

"Go fuck yourself. Hope that you never see me again."

I turned on my heel and let Tamara lead me down the hallway, past the stunned guards and out to the main lobby.

Simon's words echoed after us.

"You never know. I'm gonna be here a long time."

Chapter 18

"She's in a coma?"

"Yeah."

"Since when?

I repeated the question to Tamara. "Few weeks ago," she replied.

"Few weeks ago," I parroted wearily into the payphone.

"Well, *that's* convenient." Cathy sounded tired and irritated. I couldn't blame her. I felt much the same. "Were you able to get anything from her doctors?"

I glowered at the receiver before answering. "On what premise? We're not family. Hell, we're lucky we were able to check her out in person."

"Did you see her chart?"

"We did see her chart, Joe."

My glower shifted to Tamara unfairly. "Do you want to do this?"

"What?"

"Joe?" Cathy's voice was in my ear again. "Her chart?"

I sighed and went over the little bit we had been able to glean from the clipboard at the end of Mrs. Kubrakovich's bed.

"Well that seems odd. If she was responding well to treatments what would cause her to suddenly have a reaction and slip into a coma?"

"I know. We thought the same thing."

"Did the doctors change her meds?"

I posed the question to Tamara who shook her head. "Nope."

"Dosage?"

Same process. "Still nope."

Cathy swore under her breath. I could picture her twiddling a pen frantically in her spare hand, an old habit from whenever things got complicated in college.

"Got any other ideas?" My stomach rumbled as my brain pulsed with gradually increasing pain. "I'm fresh out and should get back to town to help Mom with the house."

"Let me work a few things on my end. Maybe we can get you back in there with some credentials. Get you to have a look at her files more closely. Her visitor log as well."

"Me?"

"Joe, we discussed this. I'm on notice after the deal with the police last night. My boss didn't make a public statement but told me in no uncertain terms to leave this case alone until I had something resembling evidence."

My palm was rubbing over my forehead, feeling at the sweat damp curls threatening to drop down beneath the band on my black brimmed hat.

"Joe? You still there?"

"Yeah. You'll have to find someone else to come back here, Cathy."

"What? Why?"

Tamara motioned with her head to the convenience store entrance we were standing in front of, her expression questioning. I nodded, grabbing some change out of my pocket and handing it to her. "Anything with protein, please."

She smiled tiredly and turned away. My eyes would have had to have belonged to a better man than I to not have stared at her ass as she walked away.

"Joe?"

"Sorry. What?"

"Why can't you go back to the hospital for me?"

"Oh yeah. I got kicked out."

"*What*?"

Even over the staticky payphone her muted shout hurt my ear. I flinched back and made soothing gestures she couldn't possibly see with my free hand. "It's okay, Cathy."

"How is it okay? How could you get kicked out checking on a comatose patient?"

"It wasn't her that got me kicked out."

"Well I should hope not."

"I know, right?"

"So who kicked you out?"

I sighed heavily.

"Can we just let this go? You'll have to find another person to..."

Something thumped mutedly on the other end of the line. Fist on table? Coffee mug? Foot on desk?

I got nothing.

"Joe!"

"Fine." My face heated up as I looked around carefully, hoping no one was close enough to overhear me. "I nearly beat up a janitor."

Pause.

"Are you kidding me?"

"Technically he's a patient. Doing menial tasks as part of his rehab."

There was a long silence on the other end of the line. I rolled up the sleeves of my long, grey sweater and regretted the decision to wear it as the heat of the day began to peak. The road rash on my forearms was healing nicely, but more slowly than I was used to. Still red and angry, possibly infected in a couple of the deeper gashes. Didn't hurt though, so that was something.

"Okay, Joe." Cathy's voice was resigned and weary. The lack of sleep she had gotten the night before was starting to catch up with her voice. "I'll play along. Why did you nearly beat up a patient who was working as a janitor?"

So I told her what happened. Simon. Our history in the Scouting program. How he started a conversation with me. I got angry. Security guards. All of it. Okay, not all of it. Lights burning out and computers dying as a result of my anxiety fuelled energy wave didn't make the list. But everything other than that. You know, the important stuff.

When I finished there was more silence on the end of the line.

It started to make me nervous.

"Cathy?"

"Hang on." Frantic typing on the other end. Lots of it. Some more muted cursing and muttered thoughts out loud.

Tamara was back, handing me a brand-nameless Coke Slurpee and a bag of beef jerky. My tummy growled eagerly and my face must've shown my pleasure as her lips quirked in a smile.

"Let me get this right," Cathy's voice returned, sounding all businesslike and in full bore investigative journalist mode. "A convicted sexual predator of boys and girls under his supervision while operating as a Scout Leader – convicted I repeat – is not only no longer serving his sentence under constant watch in a federal prison, he's now wandering free in a minimum security mental health centre mopping floors and filing documents for the staff?"

"Yup."

"*What kind of society do we live in?*" Cathy's shout over the phone made Tamara blink behind her glasses and choke on bottled water. In the background I could hear other people admonishing the emotional anchor for her outburst. When she came back on the line her volume was much more moderate though no less heated. "I swear to God there are people in power in this country that have their heads so far up their sponsors' asses that they couldn't do the right thing if someone spelled it out for them in crayon."

She couldn't see it but my small smile agreed with her.

Cathy made a disgusted noise over the line. "For God's sake. I'm looking at reports right now for some of Pritchard's victims. You can't imagine the hours of therapy and medical assistance these poor people have needed. The difficulty they've had reintegrating in normal society. Learning to trust new people in the workplace, or any place where people just interact." More typing. Another disgusted noise. "One of the victims has needed to see a therapist twice a week for two years just to help cope with her paranoia." More typing. "Medication. Fees. Her family had to take a second mortgage to help pay for all of this while the man who abused her, the man who took her sense of innocence and trust away is mopping a floor and enjoying walks around the damned hospital garden!"

My hand tightened around the payphone receiver, making it creak in my ear. "Now you know why I got kicked out."

"I might've gotten kicked out as well."

I snorted a laugh. "Bullshit."

"What?"

"You're the most professional person I know. Oh, you'd have been furious to see Simon wandering around with that shit eating grin on his face. But you'd have kept your cool, asked your questions and then put together a piece exposing the whole story for the six o'clock news."

Silence.

My smile got a bit less small.

"That's what you're going to do now, aren't you?"

Cathy's voice was positively vicious in its determination. "The missing women story has hit a stall. We'll come back to it later. Simon Pritchard's perversion of justice has gone long enough without being in the spotlight. Time to make a bunch of politicians squirm uncomfortably during question period. I'm seeing a three-part story on this piece of garbage."

"Don't sensationalize him."

"Not a chance, you have my word." Her sudden sigh seemed to wash fatigue from her voice in exchange for a newfound purpose. "Okay, I have a special piece that needs pitching. You go help your Mom."

"Will do. I'm at the club tonight and likely the weekend as well. So, please no more early morning-late night adventures? I have to sleep sometime."

Her laugh was rueful. "No worries. Max and I are flying to

Calgary for a charity golf tournament this weekend. Sleep is a priority until then."

"Right. Talk to you later."

"Say hi to your mom for me."

"You say hi to her. She watches you every night as six."

Finally, a genuine laugh. We hung up. I took a huge swig from my no-name Coke Slurpee and led Tamara back to my now very hot van for the trip back to Winnipeg.

Chapter 19

"Simon Pritchard," my mother exclaimed breathlessly at the dinner table. She looked harried and gaunt, even more so than usual. "My God, his poor family."

I managed not to snort derisively in her face.

Mom crossed herself with a trembling hand and leaned back in her chair. "How many years were you two in Scouts together for?"

My shoulders shrugged as I shovelled another huge mouthful of pasta into my piehole. " 'Couple." I mumbled out between noodles.

Mom sighed heavily, her eyes still staring into the middle distance. "What a terrible shame. I remember speaking with his parents many times over the years at your events. His mother in particular was so proud of Simon and his efforts with the Scouting program."

My teeth began to grind through the starchy goodness. I swallowed heavily and began to choke like a nitwit. Thank goodness for water.

Mom stared at me from under an arched eyebrow. Mom Stare in full force.

"How many times have I told you not to stuff your face like a farm animal?"

More coughing and water sipping.

"Seriously, Joseph. You're not a little boy anymore."

The redness in my cheeks slowly became embarrassment instead of asphyxiation.

She shook her head in resignation.

"Are you ever going to grow up?"

Tears of pain in my eyes were dashed away and my throat clear allowed a witty retort to bubble clear.

"Fuck no."

Mom Stare.

More embarrassment.

"I mean... Heck no."

She sighed again.

"So how did things go with the realtor?" Anything to change the subject.

"Good, thankfully. Mr. Fairlane took a long tour of the house and made a lot of notes while taking pictures. He mentioned many good things about the house structure and the work we've done to maintain it." Mom Stare returned briefly. "Obviously I didn't let him into your disaster of a room but he said it wouldn't be an issue so long as you managed to tidy it up prior to putting the house on the market."

"I'll do it tomorrow."

"You have said that for two weeks' worth of tomorrows."

"For real this time."

"Regardless, given the state of the housing market in Winnipeg these days and the area Mr. Fairlane anticipates a quick sale. A bidding war might be too much to hope for but getting the asking price shouldn't be a problem."

You ever felt relief and dread at the same time? It's an unusual sensation to describe but it was exactly what I felt rush through my gut in that moment.

Relief at the thought of having the mortgage paid down. Having Mom in her medical care facility where she would receive the best of care without needing my help so often anymore.

Dread at the understanding that this was suddenly real. We were really going to sell the house. Our house. The only house I've ever known. My safe haven. The literal centre of my whole world.

Change is scary. Sometimes good. Sometimes bad. But

inevitable. Ever since Dad and Donald were killed in that car wreck I've been unchanged. Working the same types of jobs. Doing the same routines. Living the same life.

But now...

"Have you figured out where you're going to live yet, Joe?"

I blinked, reverie broken. "Hmm? Oh, sort of. I've looked at a couple of apartments. Some of the guys at *Canada-Pharm* have made some recommendations." I shrugged again. "I'll find something soon. Don't worry about me."

"I'll always worry about you, Joe. That's just how it goes. I'm your mother."

"Well don't worry. I've got options." Just nothing confirmed and nothing solid. No point in getting her stress up any higher than it already was.

Besides, worst case scenario there was always my van.

"Have you talked to Mark?"

I blinked.

"You said Tamara and he weren't living together. Perhaps he would like a roommate."

Relief and dread left my guts and were replaced with faint

concern.

Must've showed on my face. "Has something happened? Aren't she and Mark still..."

I put my fork down and leaned back from my overloaded spaghetti plate. "I don't know what's happened, but it's clear something did." I scratched at the still shower damp curls at the back of my neck with a grimace. "Tamara made a few remarks and has been a bit off the last couple of days. She says it's nothing serious and is asking me to stay out of it."

"But it involves Mark?"

My grimace deepened. "She has said as much in every way possible without actually saying as much."

"So it definitely involves him."

"That's what I figure," Mom gets me. Any ounce of intuitiveness I may have or proclaim to have comes from her. "But she doesn't want to talk about it. So..."

"So you stay out of it. Fair enough." A cough escaped her lips. Not the most painful sounding one I've heard from her but always a concern. I was half out of my chair before she waved me off, wiping at her mouth with a serviette.

"Mom, can I..."

"Stay." More coughing behind the napkin. A bit wetter than before. She calmed, taking a sip of water herself. Colour returned to her face and she settled back into her chair. I followed suit. "Sorry. A bit of dinner caught in my throat I suppose."

I knew a lie when I heard it. But it's always bad form to call bullshit on your mother.

"What've I told you about stuffing your mouth like a farm animal?"

Her brow arched again but ironically now.

My small smile appeared and I dug back into my pasta.

It felt so good to eat with reckless abandon. After a decade of self flagellation for being overweight and frankly ashamed of my appearance it was just so refreshing to not have to worry about the calories piling into my mouth. And it felt like I could do this forever. Just shovel pound after pound into my craw and feel it hit my ravenous belly like a rush of cool air on a hot day.

Clearly there would be a limit to what I could ingest. But if Tamara was right – and all the empirical evidence suggested she was – my body was in desperate need to build my energy reserves back up. So for the first time in a long time I enjoyed every mouthful. Truly enjoyed it.

It was so damned good to eat.

"It is so good to see you eating, Joseph." Mom was smiling softly at me. "You've been wasting away lately."

No shit.

"Well, I've been making some breakthroughs at the gym." That was my standard line. Seemed easier than talking about being able to feel electric currents in the air and that it somehow helps me to run forever and lift like a superman. "Diet's a big part of that."

"Your clothes have been practically falling off of you. How many new holes have you punched in that belt?"

"Maybe a couple."

Her head was shaking softly again. "You've gone too far. I'm glad you're coming back the other way."

"Heh. Me too," I mumbled.

"Now we just need to get you some new clothes."

"Come on, Mom. I'm thirty-three years old."

"And you need new clothes."

My face buried into my palm. "I'll go shopping when I have time. I'm working tonight."

"You're always working. And I thought you didn't work the club on weekends anymore?"

"First, it's only Thursday. Not exactly the weekend yet." Mom made a face so I hurried on. "Second, I had to take today off to help Cathy. Money still needs to come in and Shelby's always trying to give me hours. I work this weekend and can make it all up, plus extra."

Mom's face deepened to disapproval. "You know how I feel about you working there."

"You know how I feel about not paying the bills." The last of the pasta hit my gullet with a thump and I sighed contentedly before collecting the dishes. "Trust me, Mom. I am safer at Shelby's club then at any place I've ever bounced before."

Disapproval turned into the Mom Stare.

I started cleaning the table. I had to be at work in an hour.

Chapter 20

Contrary to popular belief, watching attractive women take their clothes off gets old after a while.

Peeler's Burlesque Palace was a bit off the beaten path for Winnipeg's nightlife. Stuck between downtown, the south end of the city and kitty corned next to the St. Boniface industrial park; this den of sin and chicanery had been an institution in town since before I was born. Connected to a hot sheet motel at a major intersection where thousands of cars pass by every day, the location alone has kept the establishment in business through seven provincial regimes. No matter who was in power – conservative or liberal – *Peeler's* has stood the test of time and provided smiles, fantasies and empty wallets for over thirty years.

The very first time I went to *Peeler's* is a fairly common story. Sixteen years old with some buddies from high school during a spare period between art and math class. We had planned for this day all week and were doing our very best "grown up" look, complete with fuzzy attempts at moustaches and puffed up self importance. We'd heard stories about the lunch time shows and wanted to see what the fuss was all about.

Needless to say one look at the lady performing in her shiny skivvies on the phallic shaped stage sent a couple of the guys into full on "astonished face" and got us busted before we'd even cleared the cover charge desk. I'm not ashamed to admit today that I had been one of those with his jaw near the floor. The image of that lady reaching for the clasp on her bra just as we were being ushered out the door has been burned in my mind ever since.

It was a short visit. But memorable.

For many years after that *Peeler's* took a lot of flak for being a shabby dive run by biker gangs through money laundering front men. During that period I rarely entered the establishment but read a lot about the activities that went on there. Several drug busts. Lots of brawls on the patio and in the club itself. More than a few allegations of ladies being busted for soliciting sexual favours to big spenders and vice versa.

So basically, the sort of stuff you'd expect from a strip club.

Reputations can take a long time to change. But in the nightclub industry sometimes all you need is a new coat of paint, a bit of redecoration and a change in ownership.

When Shelby called me out of the blue to offer me the head of security position I had been surprised to say the least. After years of working in top end clubs - and after the fall out from *Cowboy Shotz* - the thought of lacing up my steel toes and getting back into bouncing wasn't high on my list of priorities. But Shelby had always had my back when we'd worked together before. She was very big on taking care of the guards who were taking care of her while she served the high rolling patrons. After leaving *Cowboy Shotz* Shelby had managed to secure enough financial backing to lease out the old, dilapidated strip club and was looking for good people to help her make it a fun and safe place to spend seven dollars on drinks while ladies took their clothes off five nights a week.

I was skeptical. But Shelby was a compelling speaker and let's face it, ridiculously hot. Getting into operating a strip club was the sort of entrepreneurial decision you'd expect from a woman who paid for her Business Administration degree by being an exotic dancer in college. So meeting with her to talk over a few Coronas didn't seem like a terrible idea.

It turned into a good fit for both of us. She agreed to keep me off the books and let me choose the nights I wanted to work in exchange for being the guy who hired and fired guards as necessary. Essentially being a layer of professional insulation between security and ownership. Which made a lot of sense given the type of morons who typically want to get into the bouncing game.

The first month of operation was crazy busy with me working every night from Tuesday to Saturday all while maintaining my daytime hours at *Canada-Pharm* as we set up the club for its new direction. Shelby went out of her way to hire responsible and experienced servers who knew the game and how to control their patrons while I worked one on one with a variety of muscle bound, testosterone filled dudes who were chafing at the bit to get paid while watching women get naked.

Seriously. Stereotypes exist for a reason. Especially in the nightclub scene.

By the time June rolled around Shelby and I had managed to

get things running fairly smoothly. So with confidence she managed to launch an official "Grand Opening Party" without much of a hassle. Hundreds of men and women came through the front door that night, some of them returning to a place where they once hung out in shame and with dangerous dudes. Others for the first time just wanting to check out the new digs.

It was a hell of a weekend. There were a few fights but nothing serious. My crew of guys was solid and knew how to end issues before they started. Shelby's servers were fantastic at keeping the people happy without over serving them and the dancers were top notch talents who toured on the Canadian circuit.

Since then Shelby had been exceedingly cool with my request to only work Tuesday and Wednesday nights. They were slower business nights and were easy enough for me to handle by myself, allowing her to keep the rest of my crew working the weekend party nights. Occasionally I would come in to help during big promotional times or just to pop in to check on my crew. Maybe spend an hour supervising and making sure everyone was working efficiently before grabbing a beer and heading home to sleep.

Without question, working at *Peeler's* was the best, safest and most profitable bouncing gig I've ever had.

So when I came in that Thursday the last thing I expected was to get punched in the face.

Like I said, watching attractive women take their clothes off gets old after a while. Not just for me but for drunken fools who'd been cut off by the servers.

My Thursday night crew consisted of two university students named Dave and Jordan. Both of them were battling to keep their spots on the school's football squad academically in order to keep up their scholarships. Both of them were big, polite and hard working dudes who were more than happy to earn some cash to back fill the education expenses not covered by their deals.

The only trouble with these guys was their lack of experience. Plus Dave had the face of a fifteen year old, killing the level of intimidation often required to stop things before they got physical.

Thankfully it was only a glancing blow that I managed to take off my forehead. The drunken lawyer in the thousand dollar suit threw like a sidearm pitcher giving me plenty of advance notice to tuck my chin and take his knuckles off the hardest part of my skull. The cry of pain he let out could barely be heard over the heavy bass groove blasting from the speakers strewn about the club.

Lawyer's group of buddies were on their feet in a flash and ready to make things into something more than what it was. But as the lawyer held his likely broken hand tight to his chest I grabbed a firm hold of his ear and twisted, bringing him arching up onto the tippy toes of his expensive leather shoes.

The rest of his crew stopped dead in their tracks.

So did Dave and Jordan, their eyes wide and suddenly terrified.

Everyone paused in that breathless moment.

My stomach rumbled and my head pulsed in time with the bass groove.

With the scent of lavender preceding her by half a step Shelby strode past me and faced the suddenly rowdy patrons.

On the worst of days, Shelby McMasters made a stunning entrance. Tall. Bottle blonde. Exquisite make up without appearing garish. Tanned to a golden brown with a cosmetic white smile to light up a room. Eyes that radiated intelligence to anyone who made it up past her plastic surgeons' masterpiece of a rack. Dressed in professional looking dark slacks, a purple-ish chemise and stilettos Shelby would've turned heads in any crowd.

And when she needed to, she could command attention from a group of drunks.

"Gentlemen," her voice shouted to be heard above the din from the deejay booth. "Is there going to be a problem here?"

Lawyer squirmed against my grip, opening his mouth to make some retort. All that escaped his lips was a gasp of pain after I pressed my thumb deep into his ear canal.

Shelby's well maintained left eyebrow quirked inquisitively at me, her lips pursed to keep a smile from ruining her severe posture.

I shrugged.

"He hit me."

"I saw that."

One of lawyer's buddies began to bluster, stepping forward. "This is outrageous," he sputtered, the scent of low-grade whisky hitting me in the face. The man began to sloppily rearrange his loosened tie in an attempt to regain some measure of bar passing professionalism. "Your head thumper here is way over the line. Given the amount of patronage we have given this establishment tonight there is no need for this level of animosity."

Big words.

Show off.

"Dick," I growled, motioning with the Lawyer's head which caused another cry of pain. "Buddy here keeps pawing at our servers. They've had enough. So have I."

"Listen, I'm sure there's been some kind of a misunderstanding. The last thing we need is a legal investigation to bring unfavourable attention on this admittedly immoral establishment."

All trace of humour left Shelby's face in a blink of her eyes. She rounded on the speaker with intent, towering over his undersized frame.

"If you even consider making a legal scene out of this there will be footage of members of the Court of Queen's Bench popping up all over the newspapers and the evening news complete with eyewitness accounts and bar receipts." She motioned with a slight tilt of her head over to the lawyer writhing in my grip. "What do you think your friends' chances will be to take over as Premier of Manitoba after that type of footage gets out?"

The diminutive man's face got hesitant as reality set in on him. The rest of his group began to look in other directions, not wanting to be seen to be watching the dressing down of their superiors.

"Imagine the field day the blogosphere would have if word got out about members of the New Democrats drinking at Winnipeg's hottest strip club while using the party's corporate credit card."

Logic trumps drunken ego nine times out of ten.

Lawyer looked at the man in my grasp and the rest of his crew. "Maybe we should go."

Shelby smiled and motioned to me.

I gave the soon-to-be failed politician one last twist before shoving him towards his suited compatriots. They gathered their belongings and I motioned for Dave and Jordan to escort them out.

Shelby sidled up next to me as we watched the legal beagles take a brisk walk of shame past the half full bar. Her lavender perfume – body wash, whatever – hit my nose in a pleasant way. The proximity of her body to mine hit other parts of my anatomy in a different way.

"You okay?"

I nodded, wiping my waxy thumb on my blue jeans subtly and kept my gaze on the lawyers until they'd completely left the room.

"Need any ice?"

I glanced down at Shelby managing to maintain eye contact in the process. "Nah. All good."

"You sure? You've been wincing all night and look even more tired than normal."

My shoulders shrugged as the ache behind my eyes continued merrily. Dinner had been a number of hours ago and I wasn't interested in having any more soda or sugary drinks. The refreshing rush from the Seven-Eleven Slurpees had done wonders for my energy levels but absolutely nothing for the sticky taste of syrup in my damned mouth.

"Was out late yesterday after booking off here. Busy day today. Lots of running around, prepping Mom's house for showings."

"Jordan did fine filling in for you last night. Figured you needed a night off to sleep. Turns out you went out partying at a different club?" she teased.

"You know me. Party animal."

"Have you eaten?"

My stomach rumbled heavily against my ribcage.

"How're the hot wings?"

She smiled.

"One pound or two?"

My small smile graced Shelby with its presence as I held up two fingers. She winked and motioned over to my usual spot at the back of the club away from the deejay booth and the video lottery terminals. "I'll bring it over in a few minutes."

With a nod to her I made a brief circuit of the club, making sure all the remaining patrons were behaving appropriately and to maintain my presence as the alpha male to anyone else who wanted to misbehave. After that I assumed my usual perch at the one spot in the club where I could see everything and everyone in the building without being in a position to muck with any electrical equipment.

Feeling the cool wall against my back as I sat my tired butt down on my regular stool I leaned my forearms on the tall bar table before me and tried to stop thinking about the whirlwind that had been the last twenty four hours.

Part of my mind couldn't stop fretting over Mom and the house. All the last minute work I still needed to do to get it ready for sale. Her needs and items that needed to be packed or donated before she moved into her assisted living home and just plain worrying about her in general. Her health seemed to have stabilized according to her recent doctors' visits but she was never going to be really healthy or active. Plus the guilt I felt at the prospect of having more time to be me without having to be Mom's sole caregiver.

Then there was the faint lead about Selkirk and the mental hospital. Should I be calling Connell? Letting him know about the connection? He seemed to imply he knew about my involvement before at *Cowboy Shotz*. He practically said that I should keep an eye on things and get information back to him. But this info wasn't anything at all. Some gang-bangers' girls went missing and they all happened to go to Selkirk. No real connection there.

My eyes felt like they were full of sandpaper as my knuckles rubbed at them.

"Why is nothing ever easy?" I muttered.

"Easy's for suckers, man. You know that."

I snapped my gaze up and focused.

Mark.

My bouncing buddy and sometimes gym partner.

And Tamara's boyfriend.

Whom Tamara all but said without saying that she was having issues with earlier today.

Shit.

Chapter 21

"Mind if I join you?"

I motioned to a nearby stool with my chin while trying to keep my poker face from looking like a poker face.

He pulled it over while I eyed him surreptitiously. It's a strange thing not seeing a buddy all the time anymore. When we worked every weekend and had each other's back it formed a solid bond. One that felt stronger than mere friendship. I liken it to how hockey teammates or soldiers would feel as they went into battle. A thing where no matter how different you are from each other once you're both on the same side of an issue, you're on the same side. Period.

It carried over outside of the club too. Late night coffee chats. Gym time. Bullshit sessions about girls and the like.

I don't actually have a lot of friends in case you hadn't noticed. Maybe because I'm such a pitiful navel gazer every time I start to get to know someone.

Sigh.

I managed to shove my concerns over Tamara off to one corner of my mind to be re-evaluated as this conversation wore on by taking a moment to scan the room. A new dancer was taking her turn on the main stage while two of the earlier acts were mincing around in lingerie and high heels, attempting to score private shows from the half full crowd.

Slim pickings tonight now that the high rolling lawyer crew was ejected, but nothing ventured nothing gained.

Dave and his teenage-boy face was back at his regular post at the cover charge desk, looming over the tiny woman stationed there and looking like the most unlikely giant to ever be working at a nightclub. Jordan was on patrol checking every corner, heading to the restrooms and eventually the patio. The more he moved around the less likely there was to be problems. The constant but subtle reminder of authority that made more of an impression than you might think.

Mark settled next to me heavily and mirrored my posture on the elevated bar table, leaning his weight heavily over crossed arms with a weary sigh. I noticed absently how he flexed and straightened the knee on his bad leg – the one broken by our old bosses after he asked too many questions.

I didn't make a mention of it.

What was there to say?

"Tired?" I asked

"You're one to talk."

"I'm always tired."

"Who's fault is that?"

"Can I blame you?"

"Might as well, everyone else seems to."

Strike one for the blind fisherman.

Mark's expression turned sour, his gaze focused intently on the table top.

My suspicions over Tamara's problems regarding Mark started trying to make some noise from the corner of my mind where I'd shoved them. It was clear that something was bothering him. Which, oddly enough, made me feel better about the situation. At least it was a mutual issue and not a one-sided situation.

Though I would be a liar if I didn't admit that the selfish part of me was quietly rooting for Team Breakup.

Focus. He's your friend. Took an ass-kicking because of you. Respect that.

So I nudged his arm with my elbow. "Dude. Talk."

Mark glanced up at me and then around the club, a grimace on his lips. "Is there somewhere else we can go?"

"Why? Are the girls making you nervous?"

Finally a chuckle. "Yeah, 'cause I've never seen half naked

women before."

"You shoulda seen Dave's face the first night he worked here."

"Kid working the door?"

"Yup."

"He looks like someone stuck Harry Potter's head on Refrigerator Perry's body."

"I've been using a Peter Parker and Juggernaut comparison myself, but you're not wrong."

Mark chuckled again, leaning back from the table. "For real, can we talk somewhere else?"

The scent of fried chicken and Frank's Red Hot hit my nose just before the scent of lavender wafted along behind it. I motioned with my head towards the equally enticing odours.

"You'll have to ask my boss."

Shelby's approach was even more impressive than normal since she managed the trip carrying a massive plate in one hand and two ice cold bottles of Mexican Magic in the other. I swear nothing is hotter than an incredibly sexy woman bringing me beer and wings. Does that make me sexist or just a regular patron at Hooters?

My stomach rumbled gratefully as she slid the plate directly in front of me. Shelby's smile lit up the room first for me and extended to the man on my left whom she greeted with a quick hug.

"My God, Mark. It's been months. How are you feeling? I haven't seen you since... well..."

Mark's grimace returned briefly. "Yeah, since before Parise's boys tossed me down a flight of stairs."

"I'm sorry, I didn't mean to..."

"It's good. No serious damage. I'm barely limping anymore."

"Well good. That's good." Shelby shook her head faintly taking the both of us in. "I still can't believe Aaron and those cops would do that to you guys. You're the best bouncers I've ever worked with."

"Well, given everything else that was going on in that club..." Mark glanced over at me as he spoke. "It's not like being good at our job was gonna matter once the truth came out."

Shelby crossed her hands and rubbed at her arms as if suddenly chilled. The emphasis this put upon her magnificent breasts wasn't lost on either of us, though I'm pretty sure I kept myself from being too obvious.

"God. Those poor women." She rubbed her arms some more. I didn't notice some more. "To think we were there supporting that whole fiasco. Those pricks all got what was coming to them, that's for sure."

I cleared my throat quietly to gain her attention and not in anyway to change the subject. "Can you spare me for a few? Mark wants to chat."

Shelby blinked in surprise. "Of course. You know you don't have to ask."

"You're the boss, Shelby. I always gotta ask. Sets a bad precedence for the boys if I don't."

"Oh please. You're practically my partner at this point."

Not according to my bank account.

"Not according to the others working here," I replied without a trace of bitterness. "Or to the patrons. Never hurts to show the person in charge being in charge."

Shelby rolled her eyes and laughed, waving one hand like a conductor. "Fine. Whatever. Go out to the patio and have your man-talk. I approve."

I gave her my small smile and I stood up, grabbing my hot wings and both Coronas.

The patio was practically empty by that time of night. One of the dancers was sitting with three dudes and trying to talk them into a private show while sharing a smoke. I glanced at the clock over the door. Given that it was creeping up on one in the morning I was surprised to see as many people as there were. Friday morning workers these people were not.

A yawn tried to force it's way out, reminding me about my own Friday morning worker status.

One day I'll get some sleep. Maybe.

Mark limped over to the glass Wal-Mart special patio set furthest from the doorway next to the exterior fence and sat down gratefully. I placed a beer before him and set the wings in the middle of the table between us, generously offering to share my food. We clinked bottles as I sat wearily and drank.

Silence.

Suited me fine. I was hungry.

Before the first wing passed my lips Mark spoke.

"Did Tamara talk to you today?"

Typical.

I eyed Mark in silence and proceeded to expertly clean the wing before answering.

"Yeah. She helped me out with an errand earlier."

"What kind of errand?"

I blinked. Bit suspicious sounding?

Let it go, see where this leads.

"I was helping my friend Cathy out with one of her stories, doing some research for her. She needed to find some info and Tamara offered to tag along. Thought you knew about it. She said you were picking up a shift."

"Huh," Mark grunted, stealing from my vocabulary. He took a swig. "You guys do that a lot. Tag along. Help each other out."

I leaned back in my chair chewing thoughtfully. I tried to keep my voice level despite the Neanderthal in my belly beginning to warm up his war drum in response to Mark's passive aggressive challenge.

"You trying to say something, Mark?"

My voice may have been too level. His eyes snapped to mine, suddenly defensive.

"Shit. Dude, no. Sorry, I don't think you're fucking my girlfriend. Not you."

Is it weird I felt both relieved and insulted by that?

"But you think someone is?" I clarified. Seemed like a better question than "what do you mean 'not me??' "

Mark shrugged slightly, staring down at the bottle in his hand. "Pretty sure, yeah."

My turn to frown. Knowing what little I did about Tamara's own concerns from earlier I had to concede that it was possible for her to be seeing someone else. Knowing the kind of open and honest person she was, those kind of shenanigans would weight heavily on her mind and make her uncomfortable. She just wasn't the type of person to be dishonest like that.

Which is why I liked her so much. Made her a better person than me.

Speaking of which.

"So what's bugging you the most?" I asked directly while reaching for another piece of meaty goodness. "The fact that she might be fucking around or the fact that's she's doing it before you've had the chance to?"

Mark's face darkened, though mostly with shame.

My eyebrow quirked. Strike two for the blind fisherman.

"I know I'm not a saint, Joe. But ever since what went down at... With Parise and the other cops. You know, I've been wanting to change. Be a better person." He sipped beer and went quiet. "Tamara's been really cool. Truly one of the nicest chicks I've ever met. Not a bitch at all. Totally helpful during my rehab and stuff. Committed to her school."

"So what? How does everything you just mentioned make you think she's fucking someone else?"

Mark shook his head with finality.

"No, I know she's fucking someone else."

"How?"

"Because she's pregnant."

Chapter 22

The obvious question needed to be asked.

"Are you a fucking idiot?

Mark blinked, somehow surprised. "What?"

I was mad now. Madder than I would've thought possible given who I was talking to. Or maybe because of that. My beer bottle rapped loudly off the cheap glass table with a crack, nothing broke thankfully though the dudes smoking with April O'Kneel across the patio glanced over. My glower killed their curiosity but did nothing for my mood.

Mark still seemed surprised by my question. "Why do you think I'm being an idiot?"

For real. That was his response.

I forced a deep breath before responding. All of the subtext I'd been reading from Tamara began to line up in my head. Making me even angrier.

"Dude. What the fuck is the matter with you?"

Mark leaned back in his chair, his expression still confused. "I don't... I don't understand."

"What's to understand?"

"Why you're so angry?"

"Do I have to explain how babies are made to you?"

"Fuck off."

"No, fuck you." My teeth ached from the gritting; nicely accompanying the headache I had almost forgotten about. "If Tamara's pregnant why do you automatically assume the baby belongs to someone else?"

Mark shook his head, looking away. Embarrassment? Confusion?

"It can't be mine."

"Bullshit. You gonna tell me you're waiting for marriage?"

Still looking away. "Just... It just can't be mine."

I made a disgusted noise, pushing the wings slightly away as my stomach soured.

"Fuck. You talk about wanting to be a better person but I never figured you for one of those guys."

"One of what guys?"

My knuckles cracked loudly as my left hand formed into a fist. "One of those guys who can't take responsibility for his dick."

"Excuse me?"

"How many of the guys that we bounced with have kids you

figure?"

"What"

"How many?"

Mark looked puzzled. "I guess a couple."

"More than a couple, trust me." I took a swig of beer to try and calm down because alcohol's always been the solution for hot-headed words and actions in the past.

"So what?"

"How many of them you figure take good care of those kids? Took responsibility for them?"

"Joe, what are you..."

"Dude, you have no idea how much it pissed me off to hear those guys talking about their kids like they were a burden. As a mistake. As if somehow it wasn't their fault that they knocked up the mothers." My fingers tightened further, bringing my forearm veins into clear view. Memories flashed in my head of guys making awful statements with disgusted expressions. My stomach soured further, remembering the desire to smash each and every one of them and then being sickened with myself for doing nothing. "I never figured you for one of those guys, man. I thought you were better than that."

"Joe, you don't get it." Mark's voice was quiet; his eyes

glanced around the patio quickly, making sure there were no eavesdroppers I suppose. "It's not like that. If the kid was mine I'd be all over taking care of things."

I grunted, reaching for my beer to try and wash the awful taste out of my mouth. "So what, you got a Pat Test on Maury Povich or something? He said that you are not the father?"

"No man, it ain't…" Mark ran a hand over his face and stared down at his feet. "It can't be mine."

"Why not?"

"My sperm count's too low."

My rapidly warming bottle of Mexican Magic froze at my lips.

Mark face was red and his eyes remained focused on his feet.

"Say again?"

He sighed. And repeated himself.

The hamster wheel in my skull began to turn.

"Huh." I drank some beer and thought. "So like, you've had it tested?"

He nodded.

"When?"

He shrugged. "Couple years ago."

"How come?"

If possible his face got redder. "You know big jacked up Dave from *Cowboy Shotz?*" I nodded, absently realizing I've worked clubs with a lot of Daves. "How he was always trying to get the other guys on the juice with him?"

Ah.

"You didn't…"

His shameful expression deepened. "Went pretty hardcore for a few months man. Got real sick off it too. Docs said my natural numbers were super low and that I needed to dry out."

"Huh." More thoughts rumbled through my head. "I don't remember you getting all jacked."

Mark shrugged. "It ain't a magic pill, man. It's just drugs. If you don't train right and eat good you're just pumping your body full of chemicals."

I shook my head.

"Well that was dumb."

"Tell me about it."

"So now docs say you can't produce? You're firing blanks?"

Mark glowered up at me, his face completely flushed.

"Said maybe one day I might recover. That after enough time passed I might be able to have a normal testosterone level again. "

"One day," I muttered.

"Yeah."

I thought some more.

"So why not today?"

Mark blinked at me.

"You said it yourself man. You did that stuff a couple of years ago. Maybe you've had enough time to recover."

Mark's lips twisted in a grimace.

"You ever go back for more tests?"

He shook his head. "I hate doctors."

"Me too. But this might be a good time to get it checked."

"Do you have any idea how embarrassing that test is?"

"Do you have any idea how little I care?"

"Fuck you."

My glower cooled Mark's rising voice almost immediately. He leaned away from me in his chair, embarrassment fading from his face along with the heated words. For the first time I noticed the super dark bags under his eyes. Looked like he'd sleeping even less than me over the last few days.

"Dude. Get it checked."

"Yeah. Maybe."

"Do it tomorrow. Be sure."

"Yeah."

He sipped beer and mulled thoughts over for a while. My stomach recovered from its sourness and demanded more chicken wings. I obliged my stomach, still lost in my own head. April must've finally convinced the crew of dudes behind us to go for a private dance as she led the three of them inside leaving Mark and I to ourselves.

"So what happened?" I asked between hot wing mouthfuls.

"With what?"

I scowled at him. "With you and Tamara?"

He shrugged again, staring down at his beer bottle. "She called me up on Monday. Said she hadn't been feeling good for a bit. Decided to take one of those pregnancy tests. Came up positive."

"You freaked?"

Tears legitimately started welling up. "Yeah," he muttered brokenly. "Yeah I totally freaked."

I deboned another wing and waited him out.

He scrubbed at his eyes. "I said it couldn't be mine. Told her she was lying. That I wasn't able to have kids." He stared at his feet again. "I said some awful shit."

"I bet."

"Did she say anything to you?"

I shook my head. "But I figured something had happened."

Mark put down his barely touched beer and laid both palms on the table before me, meeting my gaze for the first time in a while.

"You gonna kick my ass?"

I was considering it.

"Jury's still out," I replied, my voice level despite the mixed emotions I was feeling. Conflicted, treacherous emotions. "Depends on what you're gonna do next."

"Do?"

"Yeah. Do."

He nodded and took a deep breath. "I'm gonna talk to her. Get things checked out. Make sure of things."

I nodded. "That's a start."

"Then... I guess then we'll see."

Not exactly the answer I was looking for, but not every guy is responsible enough to just make the leap from "reformed bachelor" to "suddenly parental." God knows I'd freak out if a woman ever surprised me with that kinda news.

Of course I'd probably have to get laid more often than every other leap year first.

Stay on target, Joe.

"You should call her, man. Right now." I stood up from the table, ostensibly to give him some privacy but really to make sure he didn't have any phone trouble. My emotions were likely strong enough to play hell with his reception. I gathered up the last of my wings with the intention to scarf them down once I got back inside. "Get in touch. Say you're sorry. Say whatever you need to say. But start talking with her, man."

"Yeah. Yeah, I will." Mark dragged his phone out of his jeans and stared at it blankly, his face still a wreck. "Hopefully she'll answer this time."

"Can't blame her for avoiding your calls. Though I'm surprised she hasn't tried to talk to you."

Mark started tapping the screen. "She tried calling. Well, texting mostly. I kept ignoring her 'til today." I could hear a faint ringing coming over the line and took a few steps further back.

"Oh?"

The ringing changed to a dial tone and Mark glowered at his phone. "Yeah. We were going to meet up tonight once she got back to town after helping you. But I haven't been able to get a hold of her."

Chapter 23

Mark's words hit me like a punch to the gut.

"What?"

He tucked away his phone. "Yeah. All my calls ring once then cut to dial tone. No voice mail. All my texts bounce back. I can't even get her on Facebook. Nothing."

My heart rate began to pick up. Reflexively I took a steadying breath to keep the tingle at the back of my neck at bay.

"That's been going on all day?"

Mark nodded. "Yeah. We haven't been in touch since she told me you guys were taking a trip."

My stomach sank a bit further.

Be cool. Think. Tamara has good reason to ignore Mark.

"What is it?" Mark's voice had picked up on my concern though his expression was more confused than anything else. "Joe, do you know something?"

I shook my head minutely as my brain went racing down a million worst case scenarios as the tingle at the back of my neck flared, sending shooting shocks along my nervous system. The surge made me twitchy, wanting to jump into action. Fly to the rescue. Up, up and…

I shook my head more vigorously, deep breathing continuing.

"Joe?"

I held up one hand to Mark while pressing firmly at the bridge of my nose with the other, anything to quell the sudden pressure from my energy surge and headache combo.

Think, dammit. Know facts. Assume nothing.

"You got a key to her place?"

"What?"

My eyes must've been something wild since Mark started back at my expression, nearly dropping his smartphone in the process.

"A key. Do you have a key to her place?"

Mark blinked in surprise a few times but his hands fumbled to his front pocket where I heard the jangle of metal. "Yeah. I think... Yeah she cut me a copy a few weeks back. Why?"

Take no chances.

"Go there. Right now. Knock on her door. On her window. If she doesn't answer use the key."

"Dude, I'm trying to apologize for being a dickhead. Won't banging on her apartment at one a.m. and letting myself in piss her off?"

"Not if she's not there."

"Where would she be?"

I closed my eyes for a moment, worried thoughts and an intuition that couldn't be ignored swirling my stomach."

"Just go. Please. Go there now and make sure she's there."

Mark was still lost. "Dude, are you okay?"

I nodded, forcing my small smile back onto my face. *Don't panic him. Don't panic.* "Yeah man. Just... This issue is a big deal for you guys and I think it's really important that you get this worked out as soon as possible."

Mark's expression changed slightly, a light going on behind his eyes as he understood my concern. "Oh shit. Joe, you don't think she's been..."

"Just *go*, dammit!" I snapped, concern overwhelming my good sense as the energy continued to fire up my nervous system and make my fingers tremble from the inactivity. "Go there now and call me either way. If she's there you guys can have a good laugh at my expense before you talk about what's really important."

Mark found his keys, checking to make sure her apartment key was on the ring and nodded.

"Okay. Yeah. I'm off. I guess I'll call the front desk as soon as I can."

"I'll be here."

He limped past me at a quick trot and I held the door open for him as he hobbled through the club to the main lot across the street. I watched him go with my stomach seizing up in knots.

Having an active imagination can be fun. Having an over active imagination can be fucking terrifying as a horrible thoughts flicker through your brain like an old school flip book displaying awful images in rapid succession.

I shook my head savagely and plopped my ass back down at my usual perch, mindlessly plowing through my now chilly hot wings as I tried to calm my nerves. No matter how sour my stomach was I figured getting the calories into my system was going to be essential if I needed to rush out of *Peeler's*.

So I ate. And brooded. And kept eating.

Habits. Emotional eating has always been one of them. Tamara's suggestion that it might be necessary to keep me alive given my messed up metabolism should've justified the action and removed the self loathing normally attached to it. Sadly it didn't.

Roughly half an hour later with the scent of lavender preceding her arrival by a moment Shelby minced up next to me in her ridiculous stilettos to rest one hand one the bar table and the other high on my shoulder.

"Everything okay?" she half shouted to be heard over the din.

I nodded fractionally, trying to find my small smile and failing. I settled instead for wiping my buffalo sauce covered lips with a soiled napkin.

Her eyes were direct and not letting me look away. "Mark took off in a hurry. You guys have a fight?"

I shrugged, trying to avoid spreading my worry. "Not really. He's just gotta check on something."

"Something important I take it?"

"Yeah. Kinda important."

"Okay." Her lips pursed slightly as she scanned her eyes around the bar. "Well, if it's that important you can take off too. We're probably going to shut this down soon unless we get a rush of big spenders."

My chin nodded again as I found a hollow version of my small smile. "Thanks. I might have to take you up on that. Mark's gonna call the front desk in a bit. I'll know more when he does."

Shelby's manicured purple fingernails squeezed my shoulder firmly.

"Okay, sounds good. Your boys can close up without you as usual." Her eyes examined my face for a long moment, trying to read my mind the way a lot women thought they could. Thankfully I still have a poker face that's better than average.

Her gaze started making me uncomfortable.

"What?"

"You know you can trust me, right?"

I blinked.

"What?"

Shelby glanced away, the eye contact having gotten intense for a moment there. Her hand loosened on my shoulder as she started to turn away. "Never mind, it's okay."

Reflexively I reached out and grabbed her hand, turning her back to me. "What's okay? Are you okay?"

She blinked a few times and pursed her lips again, clearly choosing her words carefully.

"It's just..." she cleared her throat and began again. "Ever since we've been working together – since you've been helping me get this place up and running I mean – it seems like you're always keeping me at arms length. Maintaining this stoic wall between us."

My turn to blink as confusion replaced the sense of dread. "Huh?"

"Even earlier tonight. Asking for permission to take a break. Making it clear that I'm the boss." Shelby cocked her head slightly and held my eyes. "You know that we're practically partners at this point, right? I couldn't have gotten this place ready and safe for the crowds and the staff without your help."

I felt a slight flush creeping my cheeks but I kept it at bay by opening my mouth, aiming for a sardonic tone.. "You asked me to do a job. That's what I did."

"Really? Is that all you did?"

Now I was really confused.

"Shelby, I don't know what you're getting at."

"No, you really don't do you?"

"Are we agreeing on my confusion?"

Finally she laughed.

Shelby's hand squeezed mine before sliding out of my grip and reaching up to my scruffy cheek. I blinked again in surprise. "I'm just saying that you've been more than a business associate. You've helped me turn this place into something I can be proud of. Something that's helped me provide for my son without needing to work for anyone else. I trust you completely and have a ton of respect for you." Her lips quirked into a shy smile. "I'm just letting you know that when you're ready to, you can trust me too."

Then she walked off leaving behind a warm sensation on my cheek, the pleasant scent of lavender in my nose and more than a slight sense of discomfort in my jeans as I watched her prim posterior sashay away from me in an exaggerated way.

I remained frozen in place for more than a few moments as my brain tried to process what had just happened. If I didn't know better I would've sworn that my ridiculously hot ex-exotic dancer, ex-high end bartender and now nightclub owner had just made a very strong pass at me.

Me. The thirty-something bouncer without a pot to piss in after his mother moves into the assisted living home and sells the only house he's ever known.

"There just has to be something in the water today," I muttered, shaking my head.

On the plus side, it got my mind off of worrying about Tamara for a few minutes.

Until I saw Jordan waving at me from the other end of the club making the universally accepted hand gesture for "the phone is for you."

After weaving my way between tables and a few liquor-and-naked-lady-distracted patrons I passed by Jordan with a nod and stepped through the staff door near the main stage, escaping the hyperactive bass groove into the relative quiet of the lobby. Ordinarily this scene change would fill me with a sense of relief.

Not this time.

I took the phone receiver from the creepy mid-fifties dude

who always seemed to be working the front desk with a nod.

"Mark?"

"She's not here, Joe."

Shit.

His voice was panicked. I tried to make mine as calm as possible.

"No sign of her? Nothing to say she'd just stepped out?'

"What am I, a detective?" I could practically see Mark in my mind, stumbling around Tamara's disorganized and tiny university area apartment. "There's no one here. Hell, she might not have been here for days for all I know."

The tingle at the back of my neck returned in a blaze sending shivers down my spine and electric jolts to my brain. With a deep breath I managed to keep from crushing the old-school phone handset in my grip while I focused my thoughts.

"Mark, I need you to chill."

"Joe, has she been abducted like those other girls? The ones not taken through the club?"

"Mark, I don't know anything. But you're there and I need you to look for something. Anything that might be able to tell us where she is."

"Oh Christ, Joe. I was such an asshole to her. If anything's happened I don't know what I'm gonna do." There was some rustling in the background; I could hear him shuffling papers and other objects. I could smell lavender again and with a quick glance noted that Shelby had stepped into the lobby. Her expression was concerned as she waited a few feet from me.

"Keep looking man. Is her computer on?"

"I don't know, I'll... Wait. Yeah. It's on I... Shit!"

"What?"

"I found her cell phone. It's been smashed."

"She dropped it?"

"No man, there's a hammer here on the table next to it. Jesus. Why would she smash her phone?"

Worry seeped deeper into my stomach.

"Check her computer. Maybe she sent an email. Maybe there's... I don't know man."

"Hang on." I heard the clicks of a keyboard. "That's weird."

"What's weird?"

"Why would she be looking at bus fares to Selkirk?"

Chapter 24

I ignored the rest of Mark's concerned question and turned on my heel while throwing the handset back into the face of the stunned front desk clerk. My entire nervous system went up in a blaze, gooseflesh tingled all along my body as the back of my neck flared with energy. More images and horrible ideas tried to flash in my brain that I clamped down on viciously as I strode towards the door.

Shelby's voice cut through the mental noise.

"Is there anything I can do?"

Despite the animalistic urge to fly into motion the question brought me up short.

Think fool! Don't be an idiot.

So I took half a second. Forced myself to think.

Huh.

Go figure.

"Yeah." I reached into my back pocket and found the now soft and wrinkled business card still tucked away there. I turned back and handed it to her. "Call this guy for me."

Shelby stepped forward quickly taking the card and blinking at it in obvious surprise. "RCMP? Joe, are you in some kind of trouble."

"I'm about to be," I muttered, my feet practically dancing with the need to move.

Her eyes found mine. "What do I tell him?"

"Tell him I'm going to Selkirk."

"Selkirk? Why? What are you going to do there?"

I grimaced, thinking back to the conversation at the police station.

"Tell him I'm going there to do the right thing."

Shelby's eyes went wide.

"Joe... What are you..."

"I gotta go."

She nodded, clearly still confused but understanding my sense of urgency for what it was. "Be careful."

"Hah," I grunted turning on my heel and settling my battered felt hat more firmly as I trotted out the door. "Careful."

Fighting the urge to give into my reflex reaction to tap into the energy surging through my body wasn't as easy as you'd think. My heart rate was racing in time with my mind as I fumbled keys out of my front pocket while sprinting across the street to where my battered baby was parked.

I fired her up and quickly checked the gas gauge because nothing would be worse than getting halfway to Selkirk and having to jog the last few kilometres there. My knuckles were white as I gripped the steering wheel and shoved all of my panicked thoughts and concerns to the back of my mind, resolving my attention to a steely focus.

Hang on Tamara. I'm coming.

Chapter 25

Getting out of Winnipeg from the St. Boniface Industrial Park is usually a pain in the ass given the often winding state of roads and idiotic traffic. But since it was well into the wee hours most everyone was in for the night and out of my way. Turning what should have taken me nearly half an hour into a fifteen minute trip.

I may also have been somewhat reckless in my attention to things like traffic stops and speed limits.

What? Like you pay attention to these things when you're late for work, never mind terrified for your friend's life.

My battered baby hummed along in protest as I flew by the Pritchard Farms housing development some thirty kilometres over the speed limit, passing the few cars on the road without slowing down. My eyes continually scanned the sides of the road searching for any signs of people, hitchhikers or otherwise. In my head I was toying with some faint hope of seeing Tamara wandering aimlessly along the highway away from Selkirk, possibly having just escaped from her abductors and trying to make her way home. Possibly hurt, likely battered, certainly terrified but with the information I needed to follow her steps back to the people responsible for hurting her and others and...

Horns blared. Headlights flashed brightly in my eyes.

I yanked on the steering wheel, bringing the van back into my own lane and narrowly missing a head- on collision with a semi-trailer driving into the city.

My heart hammered up into my throat as I berated myself.

Focus idiot. You know where she is.

Which of course was pure insanity. I didn't *know* anything. I had no evidence. I had no facts. The best info that I had was a screen on Tamara's computer implying she was checking out bus fares.

"Always trust your gut, Joe."

I blinked in surprise.

Lately the memory flashes I'd been experiencing were getting more vivid. More detailed. But this was the first time one had manifested so strongly to the point where I could hear my father's voice from over twenty years ago.

A haze opened on the memory in the back of my head, acting like a second screen feature on those new fangled TVs that I can't afford. Allowing me to keep focused on the road while reliving that damned day from high school.

Back in Grade Eleven the unthinkable happened. I finally hit my adolescent growth spurt. Over the course of eight weeks I grew damned near a foot and stretched out my dumpy, overweight frame to a much taller but still dumpy frame that looked like the younger version of the man I am today. Just with more acne and an inability to grow proper facial hair.

You know, the good old days.

But because of this sudden change in my stature everyone in school had begun treating me differently. Gone were the days of being body checked into lockers by random groups of hockey hair mulleteers in between classes. I was no longer being picked on as openly by the cooler groups of kids who didn't understand my desire to get higher than a C-Average in all my classes.

Also gone were the days of being completely ignored by the phys-ed teachers.

Two years prior I had opted out of gym class figuring I didn't need to give the other students more ammunition to see me in volleyball shorts or have free reign to hammer me with sporting equipment in the name of "education." As a result my fat ass quickly dropped off the radar for the sneakers and whistles sporting members of the faculty.

But now that I was suddenly half a foot taller than most everyone else in my class Mr. Trubiak wanted to talk my ear off about joining the schools' football team.

"What did he say, son?" that was my dad, reclined comfortably in the same brown leather chair I occupied these days while reloading the pipe Donald and I had gotten for him that Christmas.

"He said I'd make a good addition to the defensive line," my cracking tenor replied, making current me's face wince at the memory. Growth spurts and sudden hormonal changes suck ass, just in case you don't recall. "I tried to explain I don't know football at all but Mr. Trubiak said it didn't matter and that they'd be able to teach me during the summer over training camp."

Dad puffed thoughtfully for a moment considering his next words carefully.

"Sounds like a good opportunity to get into a sport, Joe. I know you've been talking about finding something."

I nodded minutely. I hadn't done anything more athletic than walking to and from school since dropping out of little league baseball.

"Is this something you'd like to do?"

I shrugged again. "I don't know."

"Why not?"

Both current me and memory me grimaced. It was bizarre feeling the same twist in my guts as I drove frantically to Selkirk that I felt while I stood sheepishly in front of my father.

"I don't like anyone on the team," I mumbled. My monstrous feet shuffled on the carpet. "They're dicks."

Dad's lips twisted into his familiar small smile. "Oh?"

"Yeah. They used to... They're just dicks. I don't like them."

From a perspective nearly two decades later it was easy to see that Dad knew exactly what I wasn't saying. "So don't play. If you don't think you'd have any fun..."

"Do you want me to play?" I blurted.

Dad blinked in surprise. "What?"

I shrugged again, embarrassment flushing me from chest to forehead. "I know I'm not like Donald. I don't do sports. But if this is something you think I can do maybe you'd like me to do it?"

Dad stood up, the top of his head barely coming up to my chin. "Joe. Do you think I am ashamed of you?"

I couldn't meet his eyes.

"Joe, why would you think that?"

My already cracking voice trembled slightly. "I've seen the looks you give Mom when I came home with bruises. I've seen you and Donald talk about stuff that I don't get." I shrugged again feebly. "Mr. Trubiak says I'd be able to run over guys on the field 'cause I'm so big now. That I'd be able to fit right in. Get some of those dicks to respect me, maybe get back at some of them in the process. Isn't that something you think I should do?"

Current me grimaced as I drove. Time and experience showed me how horrible things looked to someone whose worldview was limited to his high school circle and couldn't see outside of that bubble. Really made this whole melodramatic moment silly to me now.

But not to my Dad.

"Joseph, if you did decide to join the football team with the intention of running over and getting back at the boys who have tormented you; then I would be ashamed of you." His lips quivered slightly, his small smile threatening to reappear against the attempt to remain all wise and fatherly. "Well, not terribly ashamed."

It was my turn to blink in surprise.

"Let's face it; some of those guys could use a good tackling. Let 'em know what it feels like."

I was so confused.

"So... Should I join then?"

Dad laughed.

"I love you, son. But you're too much like your mother

sometimes." His tobacco stained fingers reached up to grip my shoulder. "You both think too much."

"Huh?"

"If you want to join the team, do it. But do it for you. Don't do it because you think it'll make me or anybody other than you happy." His small smile reappeared. "Trust your gut. The future is always in motion and you can never know what the best course of action is in advance. But deep down you'll know what the right thing to do is, because that's how we raised you." He took away his hand and lighted punched me in the stomach to emphasize his point. "Always trust your gut, Joe. Even when you don't have all the facts at least you'll know your moral compass is pointing you in the right direction."

The second screen hazed over in the back of my mind as I cruised past the "City of Selkirk" welcome sign. Just up ahead I could see the famously ugly catfish statue that was the hamlets' mascot.

The mental hospital was only minutes away.

Chapter 26

At first glance, I thought for sure that my gut had betrayed me.

The parking lot in front of the facility was empty save for a few cars belonging most likely to overnight nurses and security guards. The majority of lights in the building were out and there wasn't a single person in sight after I made a complete scan of the surrounding area.

The frantic energy supplied by the desperation I had suppressed the whole drive up began to subside as a faint sense of doubt began to creep into my thoughts. Again, I had no evidence of anything. I had no motivation. No understanding.

All I had was my gut feeling.

And the thought that Tamara would have absolutely zero reason to come back to Selkirk after our visit earlier in the day without telling me unless something drastic had happened.

If she even came back to Selkirk.

Dad's calm voice whispered in the back of my head again.

I clenched my teeth together.

"Fine," I muttered, firmly setting my battered hat in place. "Let's make sure."

I tried the main entrance for the sake of having a place to start.

Locked.

Not exactly a surprise.

Peering through the windows showed me nothing except deep shadows and not much else. The urge to do something – anything – was becoming impossible to ignore. The tingle at the back of my neck sent shivers down my spine despite the still warm summer night.

To my left the parking lot extended along the front side of the complex until it reached the neighbouring green space where doctors and orderlies supervised the patients permitted to have freedom out of doors. To my right the building extended to a chain link fence that prevented people from sliding down the ravine along the Red River.

No lights on at all to the right and a fenced off river?

Left by default.

Like I've said before, I'm not built for stealth. So I didn't bother trying. My booted footsteps echoed loudly off the hospital walls in the quiet night giving anyone who might be out there ample notice of my approach.

If anyone's out there.

My teeth ground together and my knuckles popped into fists.

I took a glance into each window as I passed by. Between the glare from the streetlights off the glass and drawn curtains I was drawing a complete blank as far anything to go on went. Didn't help my sense of doubt or frustration at all.

Passing into the green space forced me to slow my stride. While the majority of the area was occupied by wide open grass sporadically littered with benches and picnic tables the shadows were much deeper here. The only light aside from the stars and moon came from some ancient lamps that followed along the walking path leading away from the hospital into the denser garden region that I presumed eventually backed onto the river as well.

I stood beneath the faint lamplight for a moment, the luminance flickering heavily overhead while I took another look around.

Back side of the hospital showed nothing. No lights on at any windows or the back doorways. Nothing untoward or even really a place to hide anything along the back wall.

One long walking path leading into a darkened area with some tree coverage and shrubbery surrounding a bunch of fauna.

I stared into the shadows, listening for all I was worth.

Nothing.

"Fuck it," I grumbled, taking off my hat to quickly scrub out my sweaty mess of curls before jamming the wide brim back into place and striding down the path. "Maybe I'll run into the Knights Who Say Ni."

Why do gardens look so damned creepy when the sun's gone down? Take the Leo Mol Sculpture Garden at Assiniboine Park for example. During the day it's one of the most beautiful places in Winnipeg to visit and share with friends and family. After sunset it feels like a cemetery straight out of Gotham City. Great for LARPers and Emo kids I guess but lousy for ambience.

This garden was much the same. With sunflowers, lilies and the like adding a sweet smell to the warm air it would be beautiful and calming under the tree branches during the day. But as I walked along the path all I could see were shadows that moved with every step I took. Both advancing on me and following my every move.

"Gotta stop watching X-Files reruns," I muttered to try and ease my tension while feeling more and more like the victim of the week with every step.

In truth the garden region wasn't very large. Maybe three hundred yards square all told. I walked along the path with my eyes in constant motion and my mental grip on the jittering energy pulsing at the back of my neck firmly in place.

There were no lamps through the garden, likely the trees were too dense and low hanging to make it easy to get any in place.

During the day when this area would be busy there wouldn't be any issues with visibility but at night... Well who goes wandering through this area after dark?

Just me apparently.

And whoever was hanging out in the utility shed at the other end of the garden path.

There was a faint orange glow outlining what could only be a sliding overhead doorway, likely for some heavy duty John Deere sized lawnmowers. The building itself was a decent size, looking more like the utility shed for a golf course than a hospital's garden. Though what I expected a mental hospital's garden shed to look like is not the point.

Roughly twenty yards wide from the front and I guessed ten yards deep. The power lines coming out of the left hand side of the building were easy for me to find despite the darkness as the energy feeding the building raced beneath my feet along buried cables stretching all the way back to the hospital. I hadn't consciously been following this sensation but as I approached my heightened sense of electrical awareness made this sole source of electricity shine like a beacon in my mind. While it wasn't a particularly heavy amount of energy – it was a shed in the middle of the night after all – given the lack of urban interference the cables might as well have been glowing fluorescent pink to me.

This was still a weird thing, being able to sense electricity in the world around me. Most of the time as I wandered around from place to place in the city I seemed to spend the majority of my time consciously ignoring the feeling, mostly because I have enough things stressing me out to let all of that errant energy distract me. It's like being in a crowded elevator with a dozen people all talking at once and clamouring for your attention. Both claustrophobic and somehow exhilarating.

But out here under the stars being able to pick out this single source of energy was a welcome distraction from the anxiety in my belly and acted as a courage booster after all the creepy garden walking.

Warmth seeped back into my limbs replacing the chill and trembling caused by the barely contained tingle at the back of my neck. I stopped momentarily in my approach to the utility shed door and permitted myself a moment to relax. To close my eyes and take a deep breath.

For a brief and wonderful moment – far too short – the perpetual headache and bone deep hunger that had become a regular part of my existence subsided.

Get a move on, Joe. Smell the roses later.

Stupid subconscious.

My eyes blinked open and focused on the faint light coming from out from the sliding door. Very faintly I thought I could hear voices coming from the shed. Nothing specific but definitely voices.

"Well, no point in knocking." I muttered.

Next to the sliding overhead door was a standard, steel reinforced people door. Undoubtedly locked.

The cracking of my vertebrae in the silent night was eerily loud as I rolled my head on its swivel to loosen up and permitted the tingle to send it's torrent of energy and life surging through my body.

Everything became sharper. Full Blu-Ray HD in my vision. All sounds rang like a bell while all the fatigue from another long day operating on precious little sleep completely washed away.

My small smile appeared, supported with an eager and giddy feeling.

It was time to do something.

Finally.

The distance blurred and the heel of my booted foot was driving through the people sized door and smashing it inwards, sudden light blinding me to what was inside.

Chapter 27

When my eyes cleared the sensation of energy and life slowly faded while the more prominent sense of doubt crept back in.

Yup.

No one was there.

In fact, it looked like someone had just left the lights on by accident. And the radio as a monotonous voice droned on about Bigfoot sightings in the Pacific Northwest in the otherwise silent shed.

Shit.

Over on the right was a long work bench laden with different kinds of tools. Shears, rakes, shovels and hoes. A few work knives but nothing that looked menacing for anything other than hedge trimming.

There was a Sears Craftsmaster brand riding lawnmower sitting in the middle of the shed with an old no-name brand wood-chipper standing next to it. I guess the John Deere Company must've lost the contract for being "too American" or something for the federal government people who funded this facility. It happens.

Sets of filthy overalls hung on pegs along the left hand wall accompanied by a bunch of stained smocks and eye goggles. The rancid aroma of too warm fertilizer permeated the shed reminding me of the one brutally long summer I spent working as a groundskeeper at the Windsor Park Golf Course over school break.

I stood in the middle of the shed and tried not to berate the hell out of myself as I turned in a slow circle examining the room.

The sense of anxiety and fear slowly leeched away as doubt and self-recriminations started to take over.

"God dammit," I muttered. "I'm gonna look like an idiot if Shelby got a hold of Connell."

I ran a palm over my face, wiping away the sweat trickling from the brim of my hat.

Make sure. Be sure.

One deep fertilizer filled breath to clear my head and I began a more in depth look.

Despite sharing dark curls with Benedict Cumberbatch it turns out he completely trumps my ass in terms of Sherlocking skills. I minced around the shed as much as a linebacker sized moron in steel toed boots can actually mince anywhere. Still, I took a look in every corner of the building.

The lockers in the back held only more smocks and coveralls. The riding mower looked recently cleaned. Some canvas tarps were stacked neatly off to one side next to a couple of plastic bins, all of them looking in need of a proper washing. The tools were arranged haphazardly along workbenches and hung on pegboards. An old rusted green toolbox was high up on a shelf, likely needing one of the aluminum ladders hanging on pegs across from the tarps in order to reach it.

Everything seemed to be put away neatly but without a plan.

So, yeah.

I had nothing.

Idiot.

As the energy fuelled by the tingle at the back of my neck faded my headache and hunger pangs slowly returned. I shook my head one more time and turned away, glancing at the shattered doorframe to the shed I felt even more foolish as I began to walk out into the darkness once again determined to give the entire compound a complete tour just to be certain. I started to formulate a search plan in my head as I strode away, trying to think of other places in Selkirk to look for signs of Tamara before I tucked my tail in shame and drove home.

I was ten steps into the darkness and trying to blink my eyes into focus from the lighting change when I realized the one thing I hadn't seen in that shed.

Fertilizer bags.

The smell was damned near overpowering and unmistakeable. When I'd worked at the golf course we'd had plenty of bags stacked up in piles to keep things fresh and green. We'd had a dedicated location covered in canvas to keep the bags dry and in one place. Hell, we went through several bags in a day sometimes, especially during the summer heat waves just to keep things lush.

There was a heat wave on right now.

The garden seemed lush even in the moonlight.

I could smell fertilizer.

But there wasn't any fertilizer.

I glanced back over my shoulder at the shed, confusion rattling my brain as conclusions and more began to jump from thought to thought in my fatigued brain.

"No way."

I turned on my heel and quickly jogged around the shed again, making sure that I hadn't missed anything. No bags piled up outside. The garbage bins piled up out back held grass clippings and various foliage trimmings.

No fertilizer bags.

The tingle began again very faintly as the hunger pangs turned to sour please-don't-throw-up twisting in my guts. I jogged back into the shed for another look.

Garbage bins first. Miscellaneous crap. Old tool packaging. Some empty flower pots from Home Depot.

Nothing.

But that smell.

My eyes locked on the canvas tarps.

Guts twisted even further.

I clenched my teeth together and strode forward.

They were heavy and huge. The kind of twenty foot plus tarps you would get to cover your truck in the winter time to protect it from the elements. Good for protecting from the elements as water would roll off it without bleeding through to the items underneath.

I unfolded the tarp hastily, my mind whirling as the smell got stronger.

The canvas was wet.

And stained.

I turned over my hands, dropping the canvas to the floor.

They were covered in a rusty coloured paste that smelled like fertilizer.

And iron.

My stomach nearly betrayed me right there but I clenched my jaw tighter than even before as I stared at my hands.

"No way," I breathed, my fingers starting to tremble. "There's no way."

My eyes needed to look away. I tore them away from blood stained fingers and looked up, trying to focus on anything else.

They locked onto the plastic bins. Also stained the same colour as the tarp.

And the filthy wood-chipper

The staining along the downspout and the intake blades didn't look like dirt and rust.

Not anymore.

My vision blurred and my stomach finally rebelled. I lurched away from the canvas on the floor and stumbled back blindly, bouncing off the riding mower and colliding into the workbench. The sound of metal tools and objects hitting the floor were distant noises as the evenings' supply of hot wings and Corona came back to haunt me and made a mess in the corner of the utility shed.

Tears poured down my face from disgust and anguish while

every scrap of food remaining in my belly hit the dusty floor.

I couldn't remember the last time I'd cried.

After this night I'd never forget.

I permitted myself enough time to finishing puking before forcing my body upright and scrubbing at my eyes and mouth with the back of my hand. Light-headedness nearly buckled my knees and I barely avoided collapsing to the floor.

When my vision cleared my filthy hands were curled into fists, knuckles driving into the wooden workbench to keep me vertical and give me a pain focus from the grit against my skin. It took a few more deep breaths of the putrid air to get me to turn around.

Something clanked metallically against my steel toes as I turned.

It was the metal toolbox, fallen from its perch over head after I'd collided with the bench moments before. The lid had popped open with its contents strewn about the now filthy floor. A few rags. Some work gloves.

And a grey plastic Tupperware container. Roughly a foot long and square-ish. Similar to the kind I used to keep my Magic the Gathering cards stored in.

I picked it up. No markings on it.

It rattled.

I opened it.

At first I didn't know what I was looking at. That's how shaken I was. Something I'd seen hundreds of times. Hell, I had ones of my own in my back pocket at that very moment.

Credit cards.

MasterCard. Amex. VISA. Even a Discover card.

I skimmed through the first couple blindly, unable to determine what I was seeing. Unable to piece what was clear as day through the horror of what I'd found.

Then the names started hitting me.

Women's names.

Familiar ones.

Lightning flashed in my brain. Memories of lists. Names read in the paper. Names under faces during Cathy's six o'clock newscasts. Names on the wall under pictures in the basement in a gang member's flophouse in the North End of Winnipeg.

Names of missing women.

"Holy shit," all breath left my lungs as my filthy hands began to tremble again. "Holy shit. Holy fucking shit."

My mind whirled. I flipped through more cards, flipping through them as quickly as possible. Not all the names were familiar which wasn't a surprise. Not every missing woman was demographic enough to make the news media sometimes. A sad truth but there it is.

I kept skimming, this time searching for a specific name. Hoping beyond hope.

Nothing. Tamara's name wasn't there.

I'm not wrong. My heart pounded with excitement and honest to goodness pride. *Maybe she isn't here yet.*

My fingers flicked along the cards in the box with a delicacy that was really out of character for me. Until they came across a name that made no sense.

"William P. Dinwiddie." I blinked down in surprise, reading it aloud to make sure I had it right.

By no stretch of the imagination was that a woman's name. I mean, I knew a few female Charlies and a Bobbi or two. But William?

Next card: Ronald Smith-Bowman.

The next ten cards were also all men's names.

My stomach lurched again.

"They got it wrong," my mouth kept on muttering as my fingers kept flicking. "Not missing women. Missing people." I got to the end of the half full box, made sure all of the cards were in place and shut the lid firmly. "We're dealing with a goddamned serial killer."

Shadows crossed my line of sight.

Three hospital security guards stepped into the shed. All of them alert. All of them holding their five pound steel Mag-Lite flashlights in the unofficially-official beating a trespasser into submission position.

Chapter 28

Okay there was no getting around it.

At first glance I was in a compromising position.

Middle of the night. Door kicked off its' hinges. Everything in complete disarray. A bloody canvas tarp in the middle of the room. Same bloody substance on my hands. The same hands holding evidence of members of the public who had gone missing over the course of months.

Yup.

I was fucked.

Well, when in doubt start with a classic.

"Guys, this isn't what it looks like."

All three guards stayed stock still and barely moving. No change in the expression on their faces.

I held up the box for them to see, nice and visible. "You have to believe me. I'm here about the women who've been abducted. The missing women in the news... This is proof that they've been near here." I motioned towards the bloody tarp, bins and wood chipper. "You have to believe me. Call the police. Ask for Sergeant Connell with the RCMP. He'll help explain."

Their expressions still didn't change.

Not in a stone faced rent-a-cop way. I would've recognized that one.

As in no expression whatsoever.

Blank slates.

I blinked. Peering at each of the guards.

"Uh... Hello? Anyone home?"

Nothing.

What the fuck?

I lowered the plastic box of evidence slowly as the tingle at the back of my neck started up again, sending shivers along my nervous system.

"Guys. Are you listening to me?" I started creeping away from the workbench and angling cautiously towards the shed door. Finally a reaction as two guards stepped out to the sides to cut me off, setting up in a semi circle between me and the exit.

I kept trying to talk my way past.

"Have you guys called the cops? I'd be more than happy to talk with them." I motioned with the plastic box once again.

"If you guys want you can show me where a phone is. We can call them together?"

"You haven't called them yet?" The middle guards' voice surprised me with both its reply and by how deadened the tone was. Hollow, like he was speaking to me from the far end of a long hallway.

I blinked again, staring at the mid-fifties guard cautiously while his younger co-workers continued to flank me. I kept moving my feet slowly, not letting the other two get out of my peripheries. The tingle along my spine continued to send pulses of energy shooting along my limbs, making my feet itch and fingers tingle. The urge to fly into motion was beginning again and only the slow realization that I was about to indulge those urges was allowing me to hold it back.

"I don't have a cell. Totally stuck in the nineties, what can I say?"

"No one knows you're here then?" Still hollow sounding. And the timber was all wrong. Like he wasn't speaking with his own voice.

I know. It made no sense to me either.

My mind raced trying to understand the situation while my mouth kept trying to stall for time.

"No one." All three guards hefted their heavy Mag-Lites quickly prompting me to continue. "Well, almost no one. A few people."

"Who?"

"No one really. Just friends."

"Who?"

"Friends."

"Not police?"

It was at this point I had a memory flash that was beyond familiar. One that I've experienced many times over the years whenever sticky situations looked ready to get violent.

Me at the dining room table holding a facecloth filled with ice against my bloody nose. Tears streaming down my cheeks as Dad gave me the most important advice of my life.

"Sometimes you can't talk your way out of a fight, son. So don't try."

It was suddenly clear that this was one of those times.

The tingle at the back of my neck surged like an independent entity setting my entire nervous system alight with life and energy. Gooseflesh pimpled along my flesh sending every spare hair on end.

"Fine," I growled. "Let's do this."

I stopped mincing with my feet and took two long strides towards the shed door. The overhead lights flickered like an orange strobe machine while all three Mag-Lites flared incandescent until the bulbs burned out.

The middle aged guardsman had enough time to bring his heavy duty flashlight into a defensive position before I got close enough to grab the front of his uniform tight, directly beneath his sternum. With one more stride I turned my mass and momentum into a forward push - enhanced by the electric thrill racing through my body of course – and heaved the two-hundred plus pound guard away from me.

The poor man sailed ten feet through the air and slammed back first into the overhead sliding door reserved for the riding mowers. The impact echoed like a cannon within the confined space and his body left a significant dent in the metal before collapsing to the cement floor in a heap.

A quick internal conflict erupted in the back of my mind as my conscience berated the Neanderthal raging away in my belly for being so rough on this man who was just trying to do his job. The Neanderthal isn't much of a debater, but the acknowledgement of trying to do as little damage as possible was conceded by both parties before I turned to face the remaining guards who had started to advance on me.

With the energy filling me full of life and power the remaining guards looking like they were coming at me in slow motion.

As they both approached I could make out features, see the wrinkles around the eyes of the one on my left. Hell I could read their name tags.

The dark haired guard to my right ("John" apparently) looked roughly mid-twenties with the build of a hockey player who never made it out of community club leagues. Fit enough but with age and beer drinking catching up to his slight paunch. His Mag-Lite was held high in an attack position as he charged forward.

"Liam" on my left was a bit older than me. Looked like a career guard. Receding hairline had begun creeping into a widow's peak but with the broader shoulders and stature of a fully grown man. He was holding his weapon in both hands and low to his waist.

Neither of them could've weighed more than a hundred and eighty pounds.

My conscience fluttered admonishingly while my caveman instincts roared to battle.

John was half a step ahead of Liam and swinging for the fences. I dodged aside, pivoting back and away and felt the heavy flashlight brush past me in a rush of air as John's momentum threw him off balance and stumbling to the dirty floor.

I finished my pivot in time to see Liam bringing his Mag Lite up across his chest to begin a swing at my head.

He didn't see the plastic box of cards until it hit him right between the eyes.

The box bounced harmlessly to the ground as Liam staggered back, holding his face. With one hand on his chest and a foot behind his knee it took little effort to drive the smaller man hard to the ground with a whoosh of air.

By the time John had regained his footing I had retrieved the plastic box and Liam's now dead flashlight in my free hand.

There was a weird shift in John's eyes, the first real expression I'd seen since the three guards had walked into the shed..

"Don't do it," I growled, hefting the Mag-Lite until I had it gripped at the very end of the hilt. Like a short sword. Or a gladius I suppose. What? I watched Spartacus. The one with Kirk Douglas and the TV show where Xena kept taking her clothes off.

The guards' expression was speculative. Almost curious.

Then John charged, brandishing his flashlight ahead of him in a two-handed grip.

I met his charge head on, swinging the Mag-Lite with the electricity racing through my body.

The heavy trouble thumpers collided with a metallic screech not unlike a car wreck. Both of them shattering at the bulb end, sending pieces scattering all across the shed.

John cried out in pain as he stumbled aside, careening into the riding mower. I did much the same as I dropped the useless hilt while shaking out my hand. Several small abrasions were leaking blood from my knuckles back up to near my elbow.

Nothing deadly, just hurt like a sonofabitch.

"Idiot," I muttered while trying to wipe my now doubly bloody hand awkwardly against my tee shirt and get an assessment of the three guards.

Both Liam and the middle aged man were out of things, hopefully just unconscious. Preferably nothing broken.

John on the other hand had cuts similar to mine on both of his hands as well one larger one just above his right eyebrow that was pouring blood down his face.

Shit.

I looked quickly around the shed for anything to staunch the flow. Scalp wounds are big bleeders but usually not dangerous. Unless you hit an artery. Which I was afraid I might have done given the pulsing flow.

Nothing clean. Nothing useful.

"At least it's a warm night," I grumbled while peeling out of my black *Peeler's* tee shirt, awkwardly holding both the plastic box of cards and my felt hat in one hand so I could wad up the cheap cotton and press it firmly to John's head.

He flinched at the contact, his bloodied hands coming up and instinctively applying pressure through the shirt along with me.

"What's... What's going..." He blinked rapidly, coming out of a daze. His eyes seeming to focus on me for the first time. He blinked some more. "Who are you?"

"Just some guy in the wrong place at the right time. Sorry about the head."

John's eyes flicked around the room, widening at the sight of his fallen co-workers. He started to struggle against me but I had all the leverage necessary to keep him pinned down.

"What... Did you do this to us?"

I shrugged.

"Why are we in the gardening shed?"

"I must've hit you harder than I thought." I mumbled wearily.

"What?"

I sighed. "Concussions. They suck." My left hand held up the plastic box. I rattled it in his face. "I'm going to take these to the police. They will likely have questions for you about them and tonight."

"The cops? Questions?" John's voice got weaker as his gaze got more frantic. "Oh God, am I gonna lose my job?"

"Seriously?"

Tears formed in his eyes to my never ending surprise. "Oh God. I was passing around a joint with friends before work tonight. If they make me take the piss test..."

"Hey. Focus." John's rambling halted, his wild and terrified eyes meeting mine again. His entire body trying to creep away

Confident I had his attention I continued.

"Short girl. Librarian glasses and a pixie style haircut. You see her tonight?"

"What?"

"Did you see her? Might've been wearing a pair of cut off..."

"Daisy Duke style jean shorts?" His voice got more animated, immediately making me re-estimate his age to be something closer to barely twenty years old. His impending unemployment seemed forgotten as he continued. "Yeah. She showed up around six, right at the end of visiting hours. Said she just needed a moment to visit a relative."

Not wrong!

My heart rate picked up speed again. "Did you see where she went after?"

"After what?"

Sigh.

"After she visited her friend. Where did she go?"

John's eyes began to go blank again. For a moment I thought he was about to pass out on me. Then his pupils sharpened once and his voice lowered. He began to ramble, as if reminding himself. "I don't ... I didn't see her leave. I was going to watch her out on the cameras. Same as when I watched her in. I mean her ass was too good to miss. She was heading down the hall, entered the rec area and..."

He trailed off, his eyes spacing out again.

"What John? Who did she meet?"

John's face twisted and the tears began to fall as his chest shuddered. "Why can't I remember anything after that? What's happening to me?"

"John!"

"Why did you kick our asses? I wasn't doing anything to..."

"Who did she meet?" My voice thundered, echoing loudly in

the confined space.

The young man blinked some more. Tears still falling. When he spoke his voice was barely audible.

"Pritchard. She was visiting with the Scout Stalker."

Chapter 29

I was out in the night air and running at top speed before my mind had registered what my body was doing. Life and energy mixed with anxiety and blind panic fuelled the tingling sensation at the back of my neck, propelling my body in a headlong ground eating sprint that found me rocketing through the garden towards the hospital.

There was no plan. No thought process. Just instinct and fear pushing me to my very limits as the rear entrance to the institution zoomed closer.

To my brain's credit, it did try to warm me that my next course of action was foolish at best. It sternly advised me of the ice pick headache that I was ignoring and the cramp in my belly that was beginning to reassert itself. Not to mention the sheer spectacle I was going to make of myself in the process. All sense of keeping a low profile were out the window as wind whistled past my ears and the hospital rushed towards me.

My instincts and idiocy were piloting the ship now, brooking no interference from the noisy yet logical complaints from that foolish grey matter area between my ears.

The rear doors to the hospital were similar to the front ones. Floor to ceiling double paned glass framed in steel.

So the picnic table I hurled through them made a spectacular mess and noise.

Fire alarms rang madly as I stepped through the gaping hole into what appeared to be a common dining area. My stomach cramped at the mere thought of food, fingers now trembling with fatigue as the prolonged exertion of energy began to take its' toll on my system. The surging at the back of my neck had reduced in intensity to a more familiar tingle, warning me that I was nearing the limits of my strength.

Nothing to be done. Find Tamara. Get out.

I stalked through the empty hall, stepping around the wreckage of doorframe and picnic table as glass and debris crunched under the heels of my work boots. Sweat poured from the brim of my hat and down the back of my neck as my eyes scanned every corner of the room. The arctic level air conditioning blasting to combat the August heat wave made the decision to leave my shirt with security guard John's bleeding head seem foolish as the drop in temperature added to my discomfort.

And the alarms were really loud. Not helping the headache.

My teeth ground together as I left the dining area and entered one of the main hallways, finding a directory on one wall. I wasn't sure what area "convicted sexual deviants and mass murderer" was listed under but I felt safe in excluding some areas to search as I skimmed along.

Turns out I didn't get much time to map out the complex.

A slight shifting in the shadows to my left was my only

warning before a heavy mass of humanity slammed into me, driving us both into the wall before the cold linoleum floor rushed up to meet us. A hairy forearm was being ground into my cheekbone by a beefy orderly dressed in red scrubs while he attempted to trap my left arm in a modified hammerlock.

With the breath knocked out of me it was hard to gain purchase with the floor or really anything to gain a sense of traction. The orderly's grip was firm and well practiced, clearly used to dealing with unruly patients or drunks at the local Selkirk bar. He was using his weight effectively, leaning high on my shoulder while sinking in an arm lock. His forearm slid along my face until the point of his elbow sank into the hollow of my cheekbone and leaned heavily forward.

Ow.

Stars began to creep in the edges of my vision. Partly fatigue but mostly pain. My arm and shoulder began to protest from the angle it was being twisted in. And the extra two hundred pounds of pressure leaning directly on top of me wasn't a picnic either..

The thing I remember the most clearly?

The orderly never made a sound.

I've been in a bunch of scrapes. Some more serious than others. But never in my entire life have I ever gotten to grips with another guy where not a grunt escaped his lips, never mind a curse growled in effort.

Nothing.

If the fire alarm hadn't continued to blare overhead I would've thought I'd gone deaf.

The stars began to get more prominent in my vision. I tried to push against the orderly's pressure but despite the tingling still feeding life to my limbs I was in exactly the wrong position to brute force my way out without breaking my own arm in the process.

Shadows moved down the hall looming large in the emergency lighting.

Three more people in scrubs. One more orderly in red with broad shoulders and tattoos running from his wrists up into his short sleeves. Two female nurses in blue.

All of them with the same vacant, emotionless expression on their faces.

One of the nurses carried a syringe.

Time to panic.

With the beefy behemoth on top of me my options for squirming away were limited. No place to post off from or gain leverage.

So I stopped fighting against the pressure.

First rule of grappling according to my sensei from the local community centre where I took three whole judo classes when I was nine? When in doubt go with the flow.

My shoulder and neck protested but the orderly on top wasn't able to prevent me from rolling forward with the pressure and using his leverage to my advantage. It wasn't graceful but it got my arm straightened out and me almost to my knees.

The orderly kept a hold of my arm and reached out with his free arm to try and trap my head.

Energy pulsed. Life flared behind my eyes.

The beefy orderly collided heavily with his tattooed workmate in a rush of air. No one cried out. The only sound I heard came from the impact of flesh on flesh. It was fucking eerie. People make noises in fights, dammit.

Both nurses barely broke stride, merely stepping around the collapsed men and continuing forward. Expressions still vacant. Loaded syringe leading the way.

"Did the zombie apocalypse happen without me reading about it?" I barked out in frustration, my voice loud to be heard over the raging fire alarms. No reaction from the nurses.

Without taking my eyes off their approach I reached down to scoop up the plastic evidence box and retrieved my battered hat, settling it firmly over my brow as they continued their approach.

"Ladies," my voice was firm and direct. I really hoped it would be enough. "Don't make me do something I'll regret. I don't need my mother to be ashamed of me for defending myself against you both."

Both stopped in their tracks. Not independently of each other, but in unison. Like they were partaking in some unknown choreographed routine and that then was the moment to stop.

I repeat. Eerie.

It got more Twilight Zone after that. Both ladies' heads tilted fractionally like a dog trying to figure something out.

Or like someone trying to hear a distant noise better.

"What the fuck is going on here?"

"Language, Mr. Donovan," snapped the syringe bearing nurse, her voice hollow. Distant. I blinked in surprise, the only crack in my poker face. I think.

"You know what the punishment is for bad language and you were never a bad boy." That from the other nurse, her voice also hollow but the exact same tone as the first nurse.

This time my poker face cracked. I took an involuntary step back and away, my skin crawling at the freak show before me.

No fucking way.

Keeping my voice from trembling was not easy.

"Simon?"

Both nurses smirked in unison. "Yes, Joseph." Their replies in sync.

My head began to throb as my fingers trembled. Whether from shock or from the strain of pushing my abilities as far as I had for so long I couldn't be sure.

"How... How is this...?" *Focus, dammit. Don't let him see you sweat.* "Where are you?"

The nurse on my left replied. "I thought you weren't planning to visit me again."

"And besides," right nurse continued. "Is that really the question you want answered?"

Trembling fingers clenched back into fists. Headache and fatigue forgotten.

"Where is she?"

"Your friend Tamara is here with me right now in the atrium on the second floor. Why don't you join us?"

Chapter 30

I left both nurses standing stock still and expressionless behind me as I raced for the nearest staircase. Sadly I wasn't able to reach the same ground eating speeds as before but enough energy kept rushing down to my toes to keep me moving with a sureness of foot that I would've killed for when I was a younger man.

Turns out the atrium wasn't difficult to find what with directional signs and the like. Despite my natural sense of direction I tend to get lost inside big buildings fairly easily. So, yay signage.

The atrium itself was about what you'd expect. A large room with floor to ceiling windows. Natural indoor trees in planters surrounded by couches and coffee tables for patients to visit with family. A kiosk off to one side looked to be stocked with a mini kitchenette for parties including a bar fridge, sink and locked cupboard. Next to that were the washrooms and two well used vending machines, the kind that still took actual change instead of bills and debit cards.

Silhouetted against the light coming in through the windows from the parking lot was a surprisingly large group of people. Roughly a dozen in total. As I neared them I identified a few of them as overnight staff members and the rest of them patients. All dressed in hospital gear, scrubs and all-whites. Staff members had badges to distinguish them.

"Hello Joseph."

That voice.

Flashes of lightning in my brain. Thoughts and memories from cub camps and scout gatherings past tried to interrupt my focus. I ground my teeth together and forced them aside, not wanting any distractions. An added itching pressure returned to the back of my skull, pushing against the tingling pulse that remained in an uncomfortable manner. It made me want to scratch frantically at the back of my head.

I clenched my jaw in a firm grimace and strode forward, focusing on the energy still pulsing weakly down my spine.

Simon stood in the middle of the group. His shit eating grin feigning benevolence like every used car salesman and televangelist you've ever seen. Hands held out at his sides as if greeting a long lost friend while his eyes remained focused on me. It was his eyes that were the giveaway. Some people can lie to your face because they've convinced themselves that what they're saying is the truth. Tone, inflection and proper use of words are deceivers. Simon's lies were just that and he knew it, the look in his eyes betrayed his contempt for other people's intelligence among other things.

Which is why I never understood how other people fell for his bullshit.

But I was starting to understand it now.

As I got closer I began to make out individual faces and expressions on the people surrounding Simon. All of them held that same dead eyed and expressionless gaze I'd seen downstairs with he orderlies and the security guards in the shed.

"It truly is good to see you again." Simon's voice grated against my ears, though with that fire alarm still blaring I confess my eardrums were all kinds of grated against as it was. "I get so few visitors."

I stopped a few feet away from the group and took them all in.

"Where's Tamara?"

Simon sucked air in past his teeth in a way that turned my stomach. "My my you have filled out nicely, Joseph. You were always such a Butterball as a boy." The pressure at the base of my skull increased. "Why don't you come a little closer and let me have a look?"

I shook my head again to clear it.

"Someone from the cops or the fire departments' going to be here any minute." I shook the plastic box of credit cards up where he could see them. "Once they see this your chances of keeping this cushy non-prison gig are shot."

Simon's dark eyes tightened. Frustration? But his snake oil smile widened. "Joseph, I have no idea what that is. Though I am certain if you found it out in the utility shed that the men who accosted you there would know more about such things than I. Why don't you come over here with us, let me take that box from you and we can discuss this further?"

Throbbing in my brain. The tingling being pushed hard by the new pressure. My knees actually trembled from the effort to stay focused.

I scrubbed at the side of my face trying to wipe the pressure inside my skull away. Ignoring the sudden urge to step towards Simon's group and hand him the box.

Stay on target.

"Where's Tamara?"

"Why are you so concerned?"

"If you've hurt her..."

Simon laughed, looking about him expansively. "I am a ward of the Crown, incarcerated for my illness. I am under watch at all times. How could I possibly hurt anyone?"

"You said she was here, dammit. I know she came back here. Whatever issue you have with these people," I shook the box again. "It doesn't involve her. Now tell me where she is or I'll..."

"Is the baby yours, Joseph?"

I froze.

"What?"

"I know she didn't tell you but I suspect you already know. Why else would you be so concerned?"

I had to scrub at my face again. Sweat was pouring down my brow as the raging pressure in my skull continued.

"It's not... It doesn't matter who..." Pain was making me gasp, my knees were getting weaker by the moment. I had the strongest urge to kneel down.

Simon's smile got wider, his eyes more intense. I could almost see a light shining behind his pupils as he leered at me from his pack of drones.

"She has strong feelings for you too, Joseph. Very strong." He paused dramatically, glancing back at his followers. "A shame she doesn't know how he feels. It would explain her dalliance with his friend."

Like the traditional Greek Chorus from an ancient tragedy every member of Simon's group laughed in unison. Not individually as a group, but in unison. Same cadence, tone and syllables. All without smiles or inflection.

"I wonder," Simon continued after his trained troupe cut off simultaneously with a flick of his hand. "I wonder if Joseph even knows how he feels about her?"

Pressure had turned to pain. I couldn't grab a steady breath anymore and finally gave into the urge, collapsing to one knee and bowing my head to the ground. My free hand pressing to the cold linoleum to support my weight.

"How... How are you... ?"

"Tell me, Joseph." Simon took a step away from the pack, his voice changing tone. Sounding triumphant as he approached. "Tell me why you are really here."

Pain. Pressure. Not enough air.

Simon's hospital slippered feet stepped into my blurred vision.

"Are you really here to find your friend?" Small fingers removed my hat and began to stroke gently through my sweat soaked curls. "Or are you really here for me?"

It was his touch that pushed me over the edge.

With my insides crawling at this despicable man from my childhood's touch I found my self exploding up from the floor in a fury, releasing the last of my shortened breath in a rush. My free hand found Simon's tiny neck and lifted him upwards to the ceiling.

Simon's choke of surprise as his feet left the floor emboldened me. The pressure on my head suddenly ceased and the tingling surge of life returned, flooding my limbs with a torrent of rage-fuelled energy and strength.

I held the tiny, twisted man at arm's length for a long moment. Loving the renewed rush of life and control over myself and my body. Sure, I was still weakened. My senses were straining from the extended use of my gifts. But I was damned sure not about to let this sick, child molesting monster have even one more moment of control over myself or anyone.

In the background I could see Simon's group shuddering slightly. Swaying on their feet.

I met Simon's terrified gaze and allowed myself the fiercest version of my small smile.

Then I hurled him across the room.

Simon crashed back first into the Coke machine, shattering the plastic signage and sending sparks flying from the burst halogen lights within. He cried out in pain from the impact, and then cried out some more as aluminum cans fell from their storage shelves to drop onto his writhing form before rolling across the floor.

My knees buckled, sending me back to one knee. The tingle and life drained from my body in a wave that left black spots in my vision. That final burst of effort had finally tapped my reserves and I could feel my stomach cramping in hunger and the pounding in my skull returning as the need to rest and recharge took over.

But I wasn't done yet.

Regular Joe would have to do.

I stood up – which wasn't as easy as it sounds – and stalked towards Simon's prone and writhing body. In the background I could finally hear a new set of mechanical wailing adding to the blaring overhead fire alarm that had been bleating at me for the last few minutes. Selkirk's emergency response time wasn't exactly speedy, but at least they were coming.

"Last chance," I growled, my eyes not leaving Simon's frightened gaze. "Where is..."

Stars exploded in my eyes as a metallic impact rocked my head from behind. Momentum lurched my body forward, stumbling against the remains of the destroyed soda machine until I found myself holding the back of my head in agony while laying next to Simon.

Tamara stood above me in my darkened vision holding a dented fire extinguisher. Her expression dead and vacant behind her librarian shaped lenses.

Chapter 31

Memory gets vague for a bit here. The noise was immense and the pain was impossible. It's safe to assume I blacked out for a time. It's more than likely that I was dealing with a massive concussion if not a fractured skull.

The next thing I do remember was being completely surrounded by Simon's crew as they pulled and yanked at my limbs, trying to get me vertical. I was still in front of the damaged vending machine as it sparked and hissed behind me while two dead eyed patients and three nurses were hauling me up.

Simon stood off to one side, rubbing at his bruised and welted neck with fury in his eyes. Tamara stood right next to him, still expressionless and not noticing that her body was pressed right up to her puppet master in an oppressive, sexual manner.

Sirens were louder but not drowning out the alarm yet. But closer for sure.

The zombified-crew was having a hard time with my dead weight. Not one of these people were exactly large themselves or used to carrying such loads. As it was I was barely up to a seated position.

I blinked my gummy eyes as best I could, trying to get clarity. Everything was a blur. And painful. Everything was also painful.

One of the nurses in Simon's crew bent and reached down out of sight. When she stood up I could see the plastic box with the victim's credit cards in her hands. Simon took the box absently, his eyes staring death at me while he stretched out his chin and neck.

At least he's hurting too.

The crew of people around me were still having no luck getting me to my feet. Frankly I couldn't understand why they were trying.

Until I heard the unmistakable sound of glass shattering.

I blinked my eyes some more. Across the atrium were two larger forms who could only be the orderlies I'd tangled with on my way into the hospital. They were standing in front of a gap in the floor to ceiling windows that had been smashed, presumably by the heavy indoor planter that was missing from a nearby seating area.

The climate controlled air got slightly less arctic as muggy summer heat wafted in through the opening.

My brain began to start working again piecing together what was coming next even before Simon said:

"Throw him out."

The orderlies started making their way across the atrium as every member of Simon's crew turned as one to assist in the task.

There were people pawing and gripping at me every way they could. At my jeans. In my hair. By my belt and bootlaces. Fingernails clawed and scraped at my flesh as they tried everything they could to take a hold of me.

Not that I made it easy for them.

Hey, I don't care how exhausted you are. When people are trying to defenestrate you, you fight back.

In my case, fighting back consisted of little more than writhing and wriggling given how much strength I had left. My head was a mess and my stomach was completely cramped. My mouth was too dry to cry out beyond a few croaks and gasps. Hell, I was so dehydrated that I'd even stopped sweating which is always a dangerous sign. Though admittedly it was low on my worries right then.

By the time the orderlies had gotten back to the group I was already off the ground and starting to be carried away. The only thing holding me back was a white knuckled grip on some sharp plastic and metal pieces which were all that was left of the Coke machine's frame. One of the possessed patients was working on my hand trying to get my grip free, frantically trying to get his fingers under mine.

All the while, Tamara stood dead eyed at Simon's side.

Watching.

The one glimpse of her I had in that moment fuelled me with the tiniest spark of anger. It wasn't much. It was barely anything at all.

But it was enough for me to writhe and wriggle my way enough to free my other hand and take a second grip on the smashed soda machine's frame, turning my view away from the open window and the sight of Tamara with that bastard.

My new view into the bowels of the smashed soda machine made my dry eyes widen in shock, though more at my own sensory deadened stupidity then any real surprise.

Running up the inside of the frame were the electrical cables that powered the machines' cash taking and soda delivery mechanisms as well as the now busted internal lighting system.

Electrical cables that still had power going through them going by the faint pulsing sensation that was mirrored by the pounding inside my skull.

For months I had been able to sense the presence of live wires and electrical signals. I could feel the power resonating and echoing with the tingling at the back of my neck whenever I concentrated on them. Sometimes I could tap into my reserves and find the power sources for machines and fire them up, like I had with a carjackers' truck one time.

Until now this moment it had never occurred to me to try things in reverse and see if an active power source could fire up my machine if I tapped into it.

I redoubled my efforts, kicking and writhing with everything left in my battered body. Ignoring the scratches and scrapes from the fingers pawing at me as I pulled myself back to the machine. Veins popped like roadmaps along my arms from the effort.

For a moment I could feel my fingers slipping.

So I flailed madly with one hand and slapped hard on the exposed wiring, ripping them from their soldering in a small shower of sparks.

And then white light flooded my vision. Pain melted away as the back of my neck exploded, flooding my entire nervous system with vitality. Life and energy surged down my limbs as I was sent into overdrive.

It didn't last long of course. Most household and commercial electrical circuits are designed to prevent massive energy drains beyond certain amperage. It's a perfectly logical safety procedure that keeps appliances from starting fires or fools from electrocuting themselves in the case of an accident. Should appliances or users attempt to draw too much power from for their equipment the circuit breaker steps in to shut off the juice and keep people safe.

Turns out the mental hospital's circuit breaking point was nowhere near the amount of voltage my body could handle.

But it was enough.

My vision cleared.

I was standing in the middle of Simon's crew, all of them were either passed out cold or knocked on their asses and holding their heads in agony. More than a few of the still conscious ones sported confused expressions save for one of the patients who had begun sobbing loudly.

My whole body buzzed with energy. In that moment I knew I was at the very peak of my power.

But I knew instinctively it wouldn't last. I was on borrowed time.

So I wasted none of it.

Simon's eyes were wide and he had both hands pressed to the side of his head. Blood streamed from both nostrils as he backed away from me on shaky legs, the plastic evidence box forgotten at his feet as he stumbled in obvious agony.

Tamara stood in the same spot, her eyes still cloudy and her body beginning to wilt. She was in the process of toppling over now that Simon was no longer pressed obsessively close to her.

The short distance between me and her blurred away. I had her cradled in one arm like an oversized infant, her eyes rolling back in her head as I guided her to the floor.

But she was safe.

For now.

My eyes turned back to Simon.

He was still backing away from me, tripping over his own feet as he stared. Words spilled soundlessly from his mouth as the fire alarm and sirens drowned him out.

I stood up with Tamara held safe in the crook of one arm and began to stalk towards the fleeing man.

Which of course was when the police officers decked in riot gear burst into the atrium with assault rifles at the ready, shouting for everyone to get down and put hands up.

"Officers, you have to help!" Simon screamed as the blood continued to pour out of his nose. He pointed back at me, the shirtless wild man holding what appeared to be a hostage in one arm while surrounded by unconscious and clearly battered patients and hospital staff members. "That man is a lunatic!"

Shit.

Chapter 32

Turns out that interrogation rooms don't get any better the more time you spend in them.

On the plus side, at least I got to nap.

The plain room at the Winnipeg Police Service headquarters was much the same as it had been the night before. Cold. Sterile. Designed to intimidate.

I was sitting in the metallic chair once again slumped over the barren table. My face was pressed awkwardly into crossed arms, trying to keep my eyes closed and get some relief from the various aches, pains and cuts demanding attention from my battered body.

I say awkwardly because the one change from the night previous were the handcuffs binding my wrists. Handcuffs that were also chained to my feet and bolted to the floor.

Now I know that some people are into handcuffs and all that, but I can safely state for the record they do nothing for me.

At least I'd finally stopped shivering. Not that I felt any warmer but someone had provided me with a spare "Winnipeg Police Slo-Pitch League" size large tee-shirt to replace the one I'd left behind in Selkirk. The cheap poly-cotton blend might as well have been spandex for the way it uncomfortably clung to my torso.

Sadly they didn't have a spare size fifteen boot to loan me to replace the one Simon's mindless hoard had ripped away.

Cold feet are the worst.

Right after exhaustion headaches.

And the cramped agony of a completely empty stomach.

And being arrested twice in two days.

I buried my face deeper into my arms and desperately tried to fall back to sleep.

The paddywagon trip back from Selkirk wasn't as unpleasant as you might think. After being cuffed at gunpoint by officers in riot gear and hauled away from the scene things got very blurry. Despite being under armed guard exhaustion quickly took over and let me pass out for the duration of the trip. I barely even woke up while they took my mugshot, though I began to laugh uncontrollably when the electronic fingerprint scanner kept malfunctioning when they put my hand on it. Odds were it had been years since they'd actually needed to use the stamp pads and paper to process a perp. I laughed even more after leaving ink marks on the telephone receiver while making my one call.

After that I had been marched into this familiar room, chained to the floor and left to my own devices.

At which point I no longer was able to sleep.

Worry was making it hard to relax.

Eventually footsteps echoed down the hallway and the door to my room squealed. Something clunked on the table a few inches from my head.

My aching, dry eyes cracked open. Light stabbed at my brain as I lifted my head fractionally.

Tall plastic cup. Filled with ice and water.

Huzzah.

My two handed grip on the cup probably made me look like an oversized toddler as I chugged the water back in one long gulp. Cool relief soothed my throat, eased the throbbing in my head fractionally and massaged the cramping sensation in my belly.

It was a start.

My eyes were slightly less gummy as I blinked them and took in Lieutenant Connell standing across the table from me. He also looked tired. Professionally neat but slightly dishevelled. His collared shirt was wrinkled as were his khakis. Sleeves rolled up with no tie, emphasizing more than disguising his bodybuilder's physique. His piercing eyes had dark circles starting to form beneath them and his five o'clock shadow needed a razor.

I rolled my tongue and tested for moisture before attempting speech.

"So. You got my call?"

Connell grunted before dropping a notepad heavily and pulling out the other chair to sit across from me.

"Could've been less vague," he muttered, scrubbing his fingers over his stubbly head.

"Oh?"

" 'Selkirk' is a bit inspecific as far as directions go."

I shrugged and immediately regretted it. Pain made itself known again from the bruising and abrasions along my skin and muscles.

It took effort not to groan. "Didn't have much else at the time."

Connell checked his notepad.

"Where's Tamara? Is she okay?"

He didn't respond at first. When he did;

"How long have you worked at *Peeler's* for?"

I blinked. Surprised and a bit annoyed.

"Really?"

Connell shrugged.

"Just curious. I haven't been there since I was a kid. Used to be a rough place."

"Not anymore. Not really."

"Good man." Connell flipped through his notepad, his expression sour.

When in doubt, shut your mouth.

I waited.

"What a mess," Connell finally muttered, his head shaking minutely. "I don't even know where to begin.

"Let's make it simple." I met his gaze stoically. "What am I being charged with?"

Connell grimaced. "Even that's not simple. I'm fighting with the WPS brass members who really like you for being behind the missing women case."

Shit.

"Tough to make that stick."

"Not really." Connell began to read from a list. "Breaking and entering a Crown run facility. Assault and battery of patients and employees at said facility. Destruction of private property. Trespassing. Evidence of a potential multiple homicides on your person, likely with your own DNA in a gardening shed where more such evidence is being collected as we speak. A former employee at the nightclub proven to be connected with the missing women case." Connell shook his head again before meeting my eyes. "You can see why they like you for this."

Keeping my poker face up wasn't easy. What I really wanted to do was crawl into a ball in Mom's basement under the covers in my bedroom and hide.

My poker face clearly wasn't that good.

Connell flipped to a clean page in his notepad and produced a pencil from his shirt pocket. "They want you to make a statement."

"Lawyer."

"You'll get one if you need one."

"You should be getting me that lawyer. This was all your idea."

Connell's eyebrow quirked. "How do you figure that?"

Anger wanted to bubble over but I didn't have the strength.

Chewing on ice cubes was taking nearly everything I had left in me.

"Gave me your card. Said you wanted me to look into things."

"I never said anything of the sort."

"Implied. Plausible deniability."

"Tough to make that stick."

Tell me about it.

Connell flipped through his notepad some more, obviously trying to gather his thoughts. Then he abruptly stood up, his metallic chair scraping loudly in the cold room as he turned towards the noisy door. He left me alone briefly. I heard muted voices. When he returned his expression was grim but not for me. Clearly he'd had a discussion with someone that hadn't been pleasant.

"How pissed at me is Officer Swan?" I took a stab in the dark.

Connell chuckled without humour as he retook his seat. "Pretty pissed. But I was talking to someone else. Melissa is working with some of the other people we brought in, taking their statements."

I shook my head. "Good luck to her."

"Oh?"

"I don't think they'll have much to say."

"Why not?"

"Who were you talking to?"

"The officer in charge of recording this conversation."

I laughed ruefully. "Machine's breaking down?"

"Not at all." I blinked in surprise. Connell resettled himself in his chair. "I just wanted to have a private chat."

That took me a moment.

"Private?"

He nodded.

"So, no one's recording?"

He nodded again.

I eyed the two way mirror behind Connell's head suspiciously.

"Isn't that against the rules?"

Another nod.

"Huh." I scratched at my very stubbly chin awkwardly, thanks handcuffs. "Thought that only happened on TV."

Connell's smiled tiredly. "Art imitates life."

"I wouldn't call NCIS art exactly..."

"I asked them to turn off the recording equipment so I could make an attempt to convince you the benefits of making a statement." Connell sat up straight, retrieving his pencil and notepad and made a show of flipping over to a clear page. Literally made a show of it. His eyes never glanced down at the page, they stayed focused on me. "All the evidence and hearsay going on out there is messing with their desire for a cut and dried solution to this mess. Selkirk PD isn't equipped to handle this and since it involves the Missing Women case the WPS and RCMP are taking it over. The WPS is desperate to pin this on someone and for the first time in months they have a suspect that fits enough criteria to make a convincing case."

My head ache pounded heavily. A whole hearted sense of dread and defeat on top of everything else.

"I didn't do it."

"I know that." Connell's eyes got intense. "Now you have to explain to me how Simon Pritchard did."

Chapter 33

For the first time in far too long, hope surged in my chest.

"What?"

"You heard me."

My poor brain tried to rally against the throbbing ache hammering away at it.

Get more information.

"Why do you think Simon's involved?"

Connell nodded his head in a pantomime and began to scribble aimlessly on the pad in front of him, his eyes never leaving mine.

"Come on. During tonight's six and eleven p.m. newscast on CTV your friend Cathy digs up an old story about how convicted sex offended Simon Pritchard is bucking the justice system by serving time in a minimum security mental hospital instead of a proper penitentiary and I'm not supposed to think you like him for this?"

"It wasn't really like that."

"What is it like, then?"

I warred internally with myself, wondering how far I could trust Connell. Overtly he'd given me no reason to suspect him. At the same time, the fact that he'd been so upfront and interested in me and my activities was in itself suspicious.

Logic told me to clam up. Wait for the Crown appointed legal counsel. Ride this mess out.

"Always go with your gut, Joe." I whispered.

"Hmm?"

I bit the bullet.

I brought Connell up to speed about meeting Shawn and the Native Posse crew and the clue about their missing girls visiting Selkirk before disappearing. I told him about confirming this with Cathy and heading up there with Tamara and running into Simon.

"You knew him before?"

I shrugged. "He was one of my scout leaders as a kid."

Connell blinked in surprise.

"Did he... I mean, were you..."

I shook my head firmly.

"Never touched me."

Connell nodded, made a show of writing something down.

"Good."

"Yeah."

"Would hate to think this was a revenge kick, cause then we'd have a different set of problems."

"No revenge. Just concern."

"For your friend Tamara?"

I nodded.

"Why did she go to Selkirk with you?"

I shrugged. "Company I guess. I mentioned I was going, she offered."

"Why didn't she come back with you? Visiting family?"

"No. She came back. I dropped her off at home. I found out later that she'd gone missing."

"How?"

"Her boyfriend."

"Huh."

"What?"

"Nothing." Connell started making some actual notes down at the bottom of his page.

"Now you're writing things?"

"This is for me. Don't worry about it. You found out she was missing?"

"Yeah. Mark – her boyfriend – met me at the club. We chatted. Said he hadn't seen her all day."

"And you figured abduction?" Connell quirked his brow skeptically.

Sigh.

So I explained about how out of character this was for Tamara, leaving out all of the personal details that weren't relevant. After I mentioned receiving Mark's call at the bar from Tamara's apartment Connell chimed back in.

"That's when I got the call from your boss?"

I shrugged again. "I guess. Yeah."

"You trusted her?"

"To call? Sure. I didn't want to wait around."

More writing. "Why not?"

A less tired and achy me would've had a small smile here. "I had a hunch."

Connell's stopped everything to give me a disgusted look.

I made an apologetic gesture with my hands.

"Always wanted to say that," I mumbled.

Connell put down his pen and leaned back, stretching out his neck.

"So how's he doing it? How is Simon abducting these women?"

And that was the twenty-five thousand dollar question.

Truth was, I had an answer.

I sighed again, another cliche loaded and ready to fire.

"You're not going to believe me."

He smiled and fired back with one of his own.

"Try me."

We locked eyes for a long moment.

The silence stretched.

Then;

"You ever watch creepy shows like *The Twilight Zone* or *The Outer Limits?*" Connell's expression didn't change. "No? How about comics? You know who Professor X is?"

Light flickered in the Lieutenant's eyes. "He's played by that *Star Trek* guy right?"

"And James McAvoy in the newer flicks, yeah."

Connell's expression got confused. "You're saying Simon's an actor?"

I put my face in my hands. "No! Well... Yes, kinda. He has got a way with words and convincing people he's harmless."

"So he is an actor."

"I think he's a telepath."

Yeah. I actually said it.

Chapter 34

Connell he leaned forward sharply, his eyes intense.

"A telepath? Are you sure?"

My turn to look confused.

"Uh... Shouldn't you be like... I don't know, calling me deluded or needing mental help or something?"

"Do you really want to go back to a mental hospital tonight?"

Good point.

"Uhm… No thank you?"

"Good. Now are you sure he's a telepath?"

I tried to throw my hands up in frustration but the shackles stopped me short with a clatter. So I settled for a frustrated look.

"How am I supposed to be sure of anything? I mean, how does one confirm if someone has psychic powers for fucks' sake? Jesus Christ, I still get fooled by kids' with fake ID's every now and again!"

"Calm down, Joe." Connell went back to making faux notes on his pad and had settled down in his chair again.

"Calm down?"

"Yes. I need you to remain calm."

I reached out with my hands to show him my bound wrists, rattling the chain. "Get me outta these fucking things and I'll calm right the fuck down."

Connell gave me a level look. Calculating. I kept my hands outstretched.

"What do you think I'm trying to do here, Joe?" His voice was calm but the undercurrent of stress was evident. The corners of his eyes had tightened as had the edges of his mouth. "Do you think I am in the habit of cutting off recording devices for suspects as a general rule? I have pissed off a lot of people to be in this room relatively unsupervised to talk with you right now. WPS brass is going to be breathing down my neck within the hour for making this move."

I snorted. "You ain't doing me any favours."

"I am doing you nothing but favours." Connell leaned back in his chair, stretching out his back again. "You have to trust me."

"I don't trust anybody."

"You're gonna have to make an exception."

"Why should I?"

He paused, lost in thought. Then he put down his pen and leaned forward, keeping his voice low which was odd if the recorders were off.

"Here's what I can tell you right now." Connell's voice was pitched crazy low, beyond a whisper. I could barely hear him at all over the white noise hum from the overhead lighting. "The only person in this police station who will believe you when you say you're not behind the disappearing women case is me. Everyone else will want to chase you for this one and try to score a big win. I am more interested in the real perpetrator."

"Simon."

"If we can prove it's him then everyone will be all over it and you'll be in the clear."

I wanted to tear my hair out in frustration. "How do I prove that he's a telepath manipulating people with his thoughts without sounding like a crazy person?"

"That's not what we need to prove." Gotta give Connell credit, he made sure to emphasize the word "we." "What we need to prove is that he was able to lure people to him. Abduct them from their families and have evidence of that fact."

The faint hope slowly returned in my chest. "The credit cards. You saw the box of cards."

Connell nodded. "We have them. Could be trophies. Could be Simon planned to use them for identity theft purposes as some sort of an exit strategy. He has a few different options there."

"Isn't that enough?"

He shook his head slightly. "Too many conflicting reports. Security guards on site – the ones found in the garden shed – have no memory of the evening. They don't recall the cards at all save for..." Connell flipped back through his notebook.

My memory beat him to it. "John."

"Right. The one holding your *Peeler's* security shirt to his bloody forehead." Connell grimaced at me. "Not exactly the smartest thing, giving a man you assaulted evidence directly linking you to the scene."

My shoulders moved in a slight shrug. "Seemed like the right thing to do."

"Which seems to get you in trouble a lot. Remind me when this is all over to chat with you about *Cowboy Shotz.*"

Guts twisted. Fire. More blood. Sampson's cold eyes behind his dark glasses.

"What about it?"

Connell didn't make a comment on my obvious dodge and

picked up his pen again, flipping back through his notes.

"So here's the dilemma. I know you're involved in this mess but for more altruistic – though, vigilante related – reasons."

"I'm not a vigilante," I spluttered.

Connell's contemptuous expression shut me up.

"You're involved because you were looking for your friend, Tamara," he amended sarcastically. "And not at all because you're disgusted by Pritchard's past crimes and the level to which he's been able to skate justice for them."

Apparently I wasn't too beat up to keep a slight flush from creeping up my cheeks.

"Officially as a member of the RCMP I am obligated to track down every lead in order to make certain the correct perpetrators are incarcerated for their offences. This case has been ongoing for years with little at best in the way of evidence to support any investigation. At least it had been that way, until tonight."

"How am I not screwed again?"

"You're not screwed because I am on your side."

"And why is that? Who am I to you that you're willing to take my side?"

Connell's gaze was direct. His words were more so.

"You're the guy I need to bring this piece of shit to justice."

Chapter 35

"I can't do it," Connell elaborated, his hands back to faux writing on his notepad for the benefit of anyone watching through the two-way mirror. "Not alone. Not with the witness statements from this mess being conflicting at best, impossible to believe at worst. Most of the people questioned can't remember a thing from the evening. The ones who can are unable to give legally binding statements given the kinds of medication and treatment provided to them."

"So my giving a statement explaining how I think that Simon is a freaking Sith Lord that is mind-bending people so he can sexually abuse them and steal their credit cards before running their bodies through a fucking wood-chipper helps you how exactly?"

Connell kept pretending to write. "Your statement is to keep all mention of science fiction locked away for now. All you need to talk about is looking for your friend, finding her being held captive by Simon Pritchard and getting involved in an altercation while trying to assist her."

I mentally flipped through all of the destruction and people who got hurt in the last few hours. It made me wince.

"I may have been a bit over eager in my actions," I mumbled.

"An argument for self-defence can be made."

"Still not sure that'll help you. Or me"

"In the short term it'll do one thing for certain."

"What's that?"

"Allow you to post bail."

I blinked.

"You can't go looking for this guy from behind bars, Joe."

Some wild, vindictive part of my being wanted to holler in excitement at that statement. The beat up, practical and frankly exhausted parts of me had no trouble telling that hero complex fuelled part of me to shut the fuck up.

"I'm not a cop."

Connell almost laughed. "Certainly not."

"It's not my job to go hunting after psychopaths."

"Is it your job to bust heads at a mental hospital?"

"That was different!"

Connell kept writing, not even looking up now.

I rolled my eyes to the ceiling.

"What do you even need me for? I saw your squat team cuff

Simon along with the orderlies and the others. You guys have
him in custody already. Leave him in whatever cell he's
locked away in and throw away the damned key."

Connell didn't stop writing, though his lips twisted with
disgust.

"What?"

"He's not in custody." Connell's voice was quiet but no less
disgusted than his expression.

"What?"

"Are you deaf?"

I felt like throwing up again.

"Just how fast are his Crown appointed attorneys? How could
they get him out of custody so fast?"

Connell's eyes got dark. Angry.

"He never arrived."

I blinked.

"When the head count was taken here in Winnipeg of
everyone apprehended we were one person short." Connell
shook his head minutely, and rubbed a knuckle wearily over

the bridge of his nose. "No one could remember who the last person was or when they disappeared. No name. No description. Nothing."

My spirits dropped even further somehow.

"I don't have any way to explain it. Officially I have to report this as a miscount for the records." Connell put down the pen, giving up on his faux writing to lean back and attempt to relax. "Hell, until you suggested he was a telepath..."

"Might be a telepath."

"Whatever. Might be. Fine. Until then I had no way to explain this at all."

Silence.

"So he's not back at the hospital?"

Connell shook his head. "First place I called. The staff is having a brutal time getting things reorganized. Between damage control and getting the mess cleaned up as best they can they're reporting a bunch of missing patients. Simon's one of them."

I buried my face into my hands with a groan.

"How do a bunch of patients in hospital smocks just disappear?" I looked up to Connell's somewhat shamefaced expression. "Someone must've seen something."

He shrugged with clear exasperation. "No witness reports. No street-cams to speak of in that area of town so we can't pull footage that way. We're planning to get a K-Nine unit out there ASAP to try and pick up a trail but if they somehow managed to snag a ride..."

"He could be half a province away by now."

Connell nodded and made more notes.

Shit.

We sat in silence for a good while. The thought of Simon being on the loose with a bunch of helpless people mindlessly trailing him like some kind of demented Pied Piper was maddening. But not maddening enough to distract me from my real question.

"Where's Tamara?"

Connell blinked, snapping out of his own internal monologue. He flipped through his notepad.

"Women's Hospital. Health Sciences Centre."

I nodded. "How is she?"

"Unconscious and unresponsive so far. Early diagnosis

doesn't think she's in a coma, but there's definitely been some trauma. Doctors are planning an MRI sometime soon apparently."

My teeth ground together painfully. Anger. Frustration. The desire to rage and rampage like a stampede of wild horses riled up the Neanderthal in my belly, but even he was too worn out and sore to do much more than shake a weary fist to the sky in defiance.

Connell spoke quietly. "She's alive, Joe. You were in time."

Small comfort that.

"How many others did he take? How many did he kill?"

"Like you said, not your job."

Unsurprisingly that didn't make me feel any better.

Connell checked his notepad again. "Crime lab will be examining the tarps, buckets and wood-chipper samples from the utility shed in the morning. Hopefully what they discover will give some of the victims' family members closure."

I shook my head. "No closure without a perp."

He nodded in agreement. "Which is why I need your help."

Our eyes met. "Why? Why the hell do you need me? While

we're at it, why doesn't the idea that Simon's got psychic powers weird you out?"

Connell pursed his lips thoughtfully.

Then came a loud rapping on the steel door. It was immediately opened without a pause. Officer Swan stood at the entranceway, her stern face a thundercloud as she brusquely motioned Connell over.

"A word, Lieutenant?" Even her voice was cold, biting on every syllable.

Connell gave me an oblique look as he stood up before turning away, following her out to the hall. While I couldn't make out any specifics, the volume and tone of voice was unmistakeable.

I took the hint and mentally prepared an official statement.

Chapter 36

It was enough to break an already broken man.

The sun was just cresting in the distance, sending shadows and painfully bright glares of light between the downtown city structures. The slight cool of the evening was fading fast as the August heat began to reassert itself while the rest of Winnipeg woke up.

"This is so unfair," I muttered brokenly as I stared at her.

"It's all right, Joe." Cathy replied at my elbow, her voice full of sleepiness and sympathy. "We'll figure something out."

"She didn't deserve this. My God, baby. How could this have happened to you?"

We were standing in the WPS Impound Lot adjacent to the Public Safety Building off King and Logan. Directly in front of us was my ugly ass Ford Windstar with a new feature. An oversized potted plant from the Selkirk Mental Hospital was now residing in the driver's seat, presumably having crash landed there after mind-bent orderlies pitched it through the smashed atrium window.

The roof canopy was wrecked and the windshield was completely destroyed. It looked like the front axel had been snapped clean in half and the new Wal-Mart brand tires I had just put on were complete garbage.

If I hadn't already been so low, I might've cried.

Again.

"It's okay, Joe. We can give you a ride home."

I closed my eyes wearily. Thinking of all the new things I had to add to my mental "To Do List." Top of that list being "rent a truck to help Mom move her stuff out of the house."

"Seriously unfair," I mumbled.

"Man," a precise baritone voice spoke up sympathetically. "I hope your insurance will cover this."

Captain Max Poulin of the *Winnipeg Jets* stood just behind me, peering over my shoulder at my demolished baby. He looked for all the world like getting up before six a.m. was something he did everyday. Dressed in high end jeans and loafers, an NHL brand polo shirt and sporting a watch that would've cost more than my van even prior to it being smashed flat. With a million dollar enamel enhanced white smile and perfect hair Captain Max was the poster boy for the City of Winnipeg. The team's leading scorer, charitable community leader, outspoken education supporter and the fantasy of every interested woman and man who swung that way for over a hundred kilometres.

He was also Cathy's boyfriend.

Yeah. The exclamation point on an already shitty night.

Cathy turned me away from the wreckage with cool fingertips on my elbow. I was too tired to put up anything resembling a fight and let her guide me back into the impound lot's office.

The stern faced clerk behind the desk shoved some papers and a pen across the countertop at me. I signed them mindlessly as his voice droned on about service fees, towing costs and more. Eventually I dug out my credit card and barely even winced as he ran the charges incurred for the tow and eventual removal of my vehicle to the wreckers' yard on it, though he did need to use the old school metal imprint device when the electronic reader couldn't get a signal.

Walking out of the impound lot and mindlessly following Captain Max took more effort than I would care to admit to today. Cathy walked with him holding his hand and occasionally shooting worried looks back over her shoulder at me.

My mind whirled in that weird exhausted state where you knew you needed sleep more than anything else but had so many thoughts running between your ears that even if you were in the most comfortable bed possible that rest would be hard to find.

The events of the last day and a half kept repeating themselves in my head. From Shawn and the Native Posse crew to hurling Simon across the atrium into the Coke machine. Arrested two times. Tamara. Mark. Even Shelby at the club.

My head pounded. I groaned quietly and pressed the heel of

one hand firmly into an eye socket, trying to relieve some pressure.

"Joe, are you okay?" Cathy's cool hand returned, gripping the abused skin on my forearm. "Do you have a concussion? Should we take you to the hospital?"

"No. No concussion," I mumbled, though truthfully I suppose it was possible if not likely considering the walloping Tamara had given me with that fire extinguisher. The lump on the back of my head would've been spectacular if my hair hadn't covered it so well.

"Then what is it? What's wrong?"

I grit my teeth, not wanting to say this in front of Max. But since I'd already fallen my pride would have to goeth right after it.

"Can you call my mom?" I mumbled.

"Your mom? Sure, why?"

I wanted to crawl into a hole and die.

"Because I used my phone call on you. She's probably worried sick about me."

Cathy blinked. "Oh? Oh! Oh God." She started fumbling in her pockets. "Yes, of course. I'll call her right away."

Keys rattled.

Max stepped forward, pressing his car keys into Cathy's hand. "You left your iPhone on the dashboard. Go ahead and make your call. I'll stay with Joe, help him along."

The loving look Cathy shot her boyfriend made me want to dig a hole in the bottom of the hole I already wanted to die in and dive deeper.

"Thank you. I'll meet you guys there."

She trotted away briskly in her sneakers while I limped into step with the hockey star. He matched my pace.

"So do I ask about what happened to your shoes?"

I grunted, ignoring the rocks and grit digging into my calloused feet. "Lost one of them in Selkirk. Made no sense to keep the other one."

He nodded as if that was the most normal thought in the world.

"We've got your jacket in the car." At my confused look, he elaborated with a perfectly straight face. "Your leather jacket. The one you loaned to Cathy last night."

"Ah. Thanks." I hitched self consciously at the too small tee shirt for the thousandth time. "Be good to have it back.'

"Was good of you to loan it to her. Though I wish you hadn't."

It took a moment for my brain to recognize the signals I was getting from Captain Max. In truth I should've seen it right away given how often I give off similar vibes.

I blinked, giving the slightly shorter man a look. "Do we have a problem, Max?"

He met my gaze unflinchingly. Despite his charitable work and male model good looks it was impossible to forget the number of on ice punch ups and heavy hits that Max Poulin had delivered in over ten years of professional hockey. He was a big and fit man used to throwing his weight around when necessary and was heavily respected by his peers.

He was also very good at keeping his teammates in line by getting in their faces when he had something to say.

"Not really. Joe." His voice was level and polite in tone, though he'd dropped any pretence of friendliness. "In fact I wanted to thank you for being with Cathy last night. She is a wonderful woman but impulsive and reckless, especially when it comes to her work. I hate to think about what would've happened if you hadn't been there."

The words conflicted the tone. I could play that game too.

"If it was up to me she wouldn't have been there."

Max stopped in his tracks and faced me head on. "If you had said you wouldn't go do you really think she would have gone by herself?"

I shrugged. "She said she would."

"Do you believe her?"

"I did."

"Bullshit."

Despite everything I nearly laughed. Save for soundless close-ups during hockey broadcasts where you could read his lips you'd never catch the consummate professional Team Captain dropping profanity in public.

"Excuse me?"

"You heard me fine." His expression remained neutral even as his words became more direct. "Cathy asked you for help because she knew you wouldn't deny her. After all, you're the kind of guy who loans his coat to women. How could you refuse such a request."

"So this is about the coat?"

"This is about you. And Cathy. More specifically about your interest in Cathy."

Shit.

"Max." I softened my voice and tried to look as innocent as one could look after being bailed out of jail. "There's nothing going on with Cathy. She's a friend. Someone I've known since college."

His eyebrow twitched ever so slightly. "And someone you've got no interest in whatsoever."

"It's not like that, man. She asked me for a favour and now I've asked one in return."

Max stared me down a few seconds longer, possibly sizing up his odds if he decided to yank the shirt over my head and start wailing away on my battered skull.

"Fine," he said finally with a short nod. "You guys are even then. Hopefully you can keep your nose clean so that Cathy's boss doesn't fire her because you violated your terms of probation and forfeit the bail bond her TV station put up for you."

The not so veiled threat hung in the air for a moment.

"I'll do my best."

"You'd better."

Without deciding to we resumed our pace along the sidewalk.

In the distance I could see Cathy leaning against a top of the line F250 and chatting away on her phone, hopefully making Mom's day in the process.

"You're a good man, Joe."

I blinked.

"What?"

Max's smile was in place again. Like I said. Consummate professional.

"I mean it. You work hard. You take care of your ailing mother and you have your friends' back. Those are good qualities in a man and I want you to know that I respect you for that."

I walked in silence for a moment. Not quite sure what to say.

"Uh... Thanks."

Cathy waved as we got closer. Max' voice softened again even as his grin widened.

"But no matter how much I respect you if you don't keep your distance from my girl you and I will definitely have a problem."

Chapter 37

Mom met us in the driveway as Max pulled up in his dealership sponsored super truck. Mom gushed over Cathy as she always did and made excited small talk with her famous boyfriend who was full of smiles and wishes for her well being. Unsurprisingly he said all of the right things even going so far as to agree to a public appearance at Mom's church in the coming weeks to help draw awareness for a fundraising clothing drive.

By the time he and Cathy left I was ready to pass out right there in the driveway from the pain and exhaustion. I was trying to think of any sort of words I could say to stave off Mom's anxious guilt trip filled concern and justified worry.

But as we entered the house the smell of breakfast hit my nose and moisture returned to my mouth.

Mom smiled tiredly up at me, handing me a fresh mug of coffee from the countertop.

I took it wordlessly, not sure what to say.

"You did a good thing, Joe." Mom's smile was tremulous. Worry hovered just beneath the surface but bolstering that smile was the hint of pride. "You saved your friend. We can talk about the rest after you've eaten. Cathy told me you were starving."

She wasn't wrong.

Half a dozen eggs. Bacon. Toast. Two bowls of no-name Rice Krispies. By the time I'd finished off the coffee pot I finally felt the cramping in my belly loosen as life returned to my weary body. Oh, I was still in pain from plenty of minor injuries and the now mandatory headache, but all of that had become something manageable. Almost normal.

In between bites I answered Mom's questions as truthfully as possible. I left nothing out about why I had gone to Selkirk or what I had found.

Mom shook her head sadly, huddling deeper into her well worn housecoat. "What a sad thing," she said behind the brim of her medicinal tea that I picked up at an herbal shop after the proprietor mentioned how it was for people with breathing issues. "How do you think Simon is controlling those poor people? Some type of drug or hypnosis?"

Okay, I didn't tell her everything. Some things are better left in the land of vague.

"Beats me," I mumbled through a mouthful of crunchy peanut butter and whole grain bread. "Guy always had that Jonestown vibe with me when we were kids. Seemed like he could talk people into anything."

Her eyes got distant behind her mug. "So sad. And to think we knew his family so well."

I swallowed thickly. "Did we? I only remember seeing him at camps and stuff."

"Not so much you kids. But your father and I met his family at church functions and the occasional community centre dinners depending on the season." Mom took a sip and sighed. "His mother was always so proud of him. 'Simon loves working with the Cub Scouts and has such a good rapport with them.' "

I was too tired for the anger to do much more than simmer in my chest.

"That's one way to put it."

Silence, save for my peanut butter chewing.

Mom let the silence stretch. Not wanting to rush me.

Once all the food was gone I stood up from the table with stiffness in my joints and the old familiar pain in my knee. My wince must've been obvious.

"Are you all right, Joe?"

A loaded question. After the previous twenty-four hours there were parts of my brain that knew I would never be all right again.

"I will be." My voice failed to convey the level of optimism I was shooting for. I gathered all the dishes up and tried not to limp into the kitchen. Loading the dishwasher was something I could do to distract my mind from the issues. "Nothing I can't handle, Mom."

She didn't reply. Too polite to call me on my bullshit I suppose.

Mom leaned against the counter behind me while I scrubbed out the frying pan. I could almost hear her thinking behind me.

"I'm sorry, Mom."

"Why are you sorry?"

My shoulders shrugged minutely. "I don't know. Maybe I shouldn't have gone. I shouldn't leave you worrying about me without knowing where I'm at."

Mom didn't reply right away.

"Would you change anything?"

My first gut instinct was to say "absolutely not." Sadly I'd had too much time to think about the events of the evening and couldn't deny the truth.

"Yeah." I swallowed heavily and leaned against the sink's edge, the now scrubbed frying pan forgotten. Guilt was hitting me hard. "I wish I hadn't gone in there at all."

Mom's voice was surprised. "Why not? Tamara needed your help."

"Because I hurt people." *People who couldn't defend*

themselves. People Simon was warping to his will, who didn't know any better. Who didn't know what they were doing. Memories of dropping security guards, lashing out at interns and helpless patients popped up behind my eyes in brief flashes. "People who didn't deserve it."

"Did you know that at the time?"

"Does that make it better?"

"Did you know?"

I scrubbed frantically at my scalp.

"No. I had no idea."

Mom surprised me then. Reaching as far as she could to give me a tiny hug.

"My boy," she whispered into my back, resting her head against my ribcage. "My sweet, gentle boy. You were always so worried about those who can't help themselves."

I tucked my chin to my chest, my large and calloused hands covering her tiny ones.

"I know what it's like to feel helpless."

More memories. Older ones.

Getting bullied and beaten up in school. Trying to keep others from suffering the same fate. The taunting. Exclusion from teams and social groups.

Holding my weeping mother after police officers broke the news to us about Dad and Donald's car wreck.

I closed my eyes, willing the images away. "It sucks."

"It does," her voice mumbled into my back.

Guilt was a powerful emotion. "I should've been more careful."

"According to Cathy you helped a lot of people last night. Not just Tamara."

I grimaced. "That's debatable. Besides, I wasn't thinking. I should've just called the police."

Mom surprised me again by laughing softly, her chuckles vibrating against my back. "Joseph, I have watched you jump headfirst into things your whole life without thinking. You have two modes; full stop and full speed ahead. And when something has pushed you into motion..."

"Are you gonna drop Newton's Law on me too?"

"What?"

"Never mind." I gently broke the hug and turned to face her, leaning wearily against the kitchen counter. "So... Shouldn't you be upset? Angry with me for being reckless? Anything?"

Mom's faint smile never went away though her eyes were a bit sad as she reached for her coffee mug. "Would you prefer if I scolded you? Sent you to bed without supper perhaps?"

My small smile crept into place. "You could tell me to clean my room."

"You do need to clean you room. It's a disaster. And the Realtor is coming by this afternoon to take more pictures for the listing."

I sighed and pushed away from the counter. "I'm on it. After he's gone, if you don't need anything for a bit I'm..."

"Sleep, Joseph. Don't worry about me. I'll be perfectly fine."

Something in her tone rang a tiny warning bell that resonated in my gut. I took a long look at my mother, really looking at her.

She seemed somehow more robust than I had seen her in years. Some colour was in her cheeks. She was standing without a great deal of effort. Even her smile didn't seem forced for my benefit. She truly was in surprisingly good spirits. Don't misunderstand, I didn't expect her to join me in the gym for a weight room session or anything but there was no denying her improved health.

"What?" she asked, uncomfortable at my scrutiny. "Do I have something on my face?"

My turn to chuckle.

"Not at all. It's just..." I didn't know how to phrase it. "You seem more energetic. Not that I'm complaining but I can't remember the last time you've been able to make me breakfast."

Mom smiled slightly and took some more coffee. "I'm not allowed to feed my boy?"

"You know that's not what I mean."

Her shoulders rose in a brief shrug. "I can't explain it myself. Since making the decision to move and to sell the house it's as if there's been a weight lifted from my shoulders. So much stress that I've been carrying around is almost gone and we can move on with our lives." Her eyes got sad as she looked around at our out of date but still functional kitchen. "It's time we moved on."

"Yeah. I guess so."

"And speaking of moving on, if you're up to it..."

"Right. Clean my room. Yes, Mom."

Chapter 38

As I figured, by the time I finally had a moment to think about sleeping my mind was racing too much to let Mr. Sandman dream me a dream.

Though even I hadn't expected it to take as long as it had to clean out my room and pack up the basement in preparation for the upcoming move. By the time I'd finished boxing things up for charity, sorting through clothes and keepsakes I was going to hang onto I wanted to sit on my ass and crash. Sadly I still had to tidy up with a fast sweep and mop before I could think about rest.

Thankfully the realtor had been on time or I might've been photo-bombing his promo pics while passed out on the beat up basement couch. He was a pleasant man. Very considerate to Mom's desires for presenting the house and how she wanted the wording in the listing to read. His concern over her needs was superb and I couldn't have asked for a better guy to help us out.

But when he erected the "for sale" sign on the front lawn there was a small part of me that wanted to punch him in the teeth.

I know. How mature.

After he left and Mom was settled upstairs I finally took a scalding shower to wash away the grime, stress and anxiety of the last thirty-six hours. My hands trembled too badly to even think about shaving and my head screamed at me to lay down.

But first I made sure to call Lisa at *Canada-Pharm* and plead continued illness and book the day off. There was no dating innuendo in the conversation this time around, though even if there had been I was probably far too exhausted to pick up on it.

Eventually I ran out of reasons to delay the inevitable. I wrapped myself up in my well worn and used blankets, flopped down onto the creaky springs of my twenty year old twin mattress and closed my eyes.

Which of course meant I was completely restless.

Typical.

Questions. All I had were questions.

How could Simon just disappear? Sure, Jedi Mind Trick and all but someone must've seen something.

Questions.

Connell. What is his game? Why is he interested in me? Why didn't he seem surprised about Simon having telepathic powers? Shit, how does somebody get telepathic powers?

Questions.

Does Captain Max think I'm trying to get with Cathy? Am I trying to get with Cathy? I mean, yeah... back when we were in college, sure. But now? He's a freaking NHL player making millions. Guys like him got nothing to worry about. 'Specially not from a guy like me.

Questions.

What is happening to me? Headaches and stuff, sure. But this level of agony and steep drop from good-to-go and the shits is out of control. What if Tamara's right and I'm pushing myself too hard? Can I settle down and try to level off? What if my body can't handle much more of this? Maybe I should go to the doctors?

I scrubbed at my sandy eyes, trying to grind away the last question I couldn't escape.

Is Tamara okay?

Sleep was a long time coming.

Chapter 39

I still hate hospitals.

Face it, there's very rarely a good reason to visit one. At least that's always been my experience.

Some people talk about the smell, how the antiseptic odour in the air turns them off. For others it's the oppressing sense of death and doom. Hell, some people just don't like doctors.

Me? Too many bad memories.

"You okay, Joe?" Cathy asked from the waiting room chair next to me, her arms folded primly in her not-ready-for-TV tee shirt. Not that the position of her arms kept every dude who walked by from staring. It was one of those deep v-neck, exclusively for the ladies' tees that were very popular among hockey fans with girlfriends. Or with the girlfriends of the team's captain.

The cold look in Max's eyes flashed into my brain. I blinked several times and scrubbed at my forehead.

At least that mental image banished the memory of being in this same damned room with Mom while surgeons worked frantically to keep our family together all those years ago.

"Joe?"

"I' good," I lied. Small smile forced into place. "Just worried."

Cathy smiled reassuringly. "The doctors expect Tamara to make a full recovery. Whatever psychotics that monster used on her and the others mustn't have had enough chance to do any real harm." Her fingers gripped my upper arm briefly, her smile widening. "You did a good thing."

I grunted non-committally. Psychotic inducing medications was the official story. According to Cathy's hospital sources doctors were at a complete loss how to explain the mass control Simon had over the people apprehended two nights previous. Nothing was showing in the blood tests to give any indication as to what was used or how it could have confused so many people of diverse backgrounds and states of health in one fell swoop. But since doctors and medical facilities never want to appear stumped for fear of causing a justified sense of panic in the community, having a bullshit explanation was always preferable to no explanation.

Correction: "doctors were at a complete loss how to explain the mass control Simon allegedly had over the people apprehended."

Officially no one, other than yours truly naturally, had been actually charged with anything. At present time Simon Pritchard the mother fucking convicted child molesting Scout Stalker was listed only as one of the dozen or so missing people not accounted during the violence and destruction at the Selkirk Mental Health Centre. Words had been bandied about. Cathy had gone on the news and implied her pretty little ass off about his alleged involvement. But in the end, Lieutenant Connell had it right. No one could believe the truth. So a believable truth would be what sufficed.

"What?"

I grunted again, more-committally this time and held up one hand, counting charges off on my fingers.. "I am officially charged with multiple counts of assault. Damage to federal property. Resisting arrest, not true by the way. And currently I am the front runner in the ongoing missing women case according the desperate for a lead Winnipeg Police Service." It was enough to give a guy a headache. Oh wait, that never went away. "A good thing?"

Cathy shrugged and gave me a sad smile. "Well, now that your never been arrested streak has been broken you can officially call yourself a tough guy."

I grunted. It might've been a laugh.

"I blame you."

Cathy's dark eyes blinked in surprise. "What? Why?"

I gave her my best mock glower. "You never talk shutout before the game is over."

It took her a second to understand. When she did a low chuckle escaped her lips.

"You're right. This is my fault."

"Darn right."

"My apologies."

"Accepted. Don't do it again."

Cathy's eyes darkened and she frowned slightly at me. Warring internally with her own conflicting opinions on the topic.

Her fingers gripped at my arm again and stayed there. I gave said fingers a glance as they stayed in position before quirking an eyebrow her way.

"What?"

"I really am sorry, Joe."

My turn to blink in confusion.

"What?"

Her expression turned rueful. "Well... Let's face it, I did ask you to get involved."

True enough. The small petty voice in the back of my head agreed and wanted to lash out at her loudly and with a lot of bad words.

I shrugged instead.

"Never held a gun to my head."

Her eyes searched my face for a moment. "You sure?"

"Yeah." I broke a personal rule and let my fingers cover her tiny ones for the briefest of moments to give a squeeze in return. "It's cool. I'm a big boy. Made my own decisions. All those grown up cliches."

"I still feel bad."

"That's why I called you to bail me out." My expression got very direct and I lowered my voice so that it wouldn't carry past her ears. "Because you kept my involvement with *Cowboy Shotz* out of the news and because you're my friend there was no way I could turn you down. I owed you and you knew that. But we're even now. You hear me?"

Those last words came out harsher than I'd intended when I first planned to say them. Didn't make them any less true to how I felt.

She got the message. Loud and clear. Her fingers slid out from under mine and went back into her lap.

"What would you have done differently?" Cathy's voice was low too, for my ears only.

"What?"

Her expression was sad but also very direct. "If you didn't owe me as you put it and I had asked you to help me with my investigation anyways. All things being equal, what would you have done differently?"

I was silent for a long moment as my conscience warred with the stress of my personal predicament.

"I'd have told you to call the cops and stay home."

Her very faint sneer called me on my bullshit.

I chose to ignore it.

She chose to let me.

Silence.

"How's your mom?"

It felt good to think about something positive.

"Better. She seems a bit more energized. Somehow the thought of moving out of the house has given her a new purpose or something."

Cathy's expression managed to convey sympathy and hope somehow. "Perhaps she's finally ready to move on."

"Huh?"

It was her turn to shrug. "It's been over a decade, right? Living in the same house everyday. Just surrounded by the memory of what was. Maybe the thought of moving out is enough to get her interested in seeing beyond what you've lost and actually try living."

I let that thought simmer for a moment.

"Being in that house isn't what made her sick. It's been our home."

"I know that, Joe. But... Sometimes the only way to make improvements in life is to completely move on. To let go of everything and start fresh."

My guts cramped at that thought. "Man."

"What?"

I shrugged. "That's scary."

"Is it?"

"Kinda, yeah."

"Why?"

I shrugged again. "I just..." My voice trailed off as I ran out of words.

Her tiny fingers twitched like she was going to reach for me again, but instead she chose to nudge me gently with the point of her elbow. "What, Joe?"

My voice was very quiet but for a different reason now. "Maybe all this time I thought I was helping keep her safe I should've been helping her get better." Guilt hammered me just below the gut. It hurt. "God damn, Cathy."

"You did your best, Joe. You've done amazing things for her."

"Yeah. Well, not amazing enough I suppose. Story of my life."

"Joe..."

A door slammed open somewhere down the hallway, echoing loudly. Heads turned that direction in alarm. Patients, staff members and us folks in the waiting room. Footsteps hammered after the echo.

I was on my feet and heading towards the noise before my brain even realized what my body was doing, the tingle at the back of my neck sparking to life painlessly after a full night's sleep and refuelling. In my peripheries I noticed Cathy also on her feet and following right behind me.

Mark came into view around the corner, limping heavily on his bad leg and with a thundercloud expression on his face. As he got closer I could see the redness in his eyes and the tears that had been fresh on his cheeks.

"Hey man, what's going on?" I stepped ahead of him with my hands out to slow his approach, the tingling sensation fading as I did so. No danger here. "Dude, is everything..."

Mark got both hands past mine and shoved me aside without breaking stride. My feet slipped on the linoleum and I quickly found myself dropped painfully on my ass. Shock more than anything else inspired my next heated words.

"Dude, what the fuck?"

He never slowed down, only calling back over his shoulder in an angry and broken voice.

"She'll only talk to you."

Chapter 40

Cathy followed Mark down the hallway as I slowly picked myself up off my bruised ass. "Go see her. I'll try to calm him down," she called back to me over her shoulder, the heels on her insensible shoes clicking away with every step.

I let my gaze follow them until both Mark's limping form and Cathy's quick stepping self disappeared around the far corner. I could feel the eyes of everyone in the waiting room staring, which is always good for making me feel self conscious and nervous.

So I pushed up the rest of the way to my feet and made a show of dusting off my jeans and shirt. It's a hospital floor. They're cleaned practically every hour. Yes, I was just trying to regain composure what of it?

Tamara's room was just down the hall in the opposite direction.

Guts twisted with guilt I turned and walked towards it.

Somehow she had managed to secure a room to herself, though given her police escort into the hospital I suppose I shouldn't have been all that surprised. Likely there's a mandate in place for victims of a crime or special circumstances that prioritizes people into certain categories or something.

Yeah. I got nothing.

The police officer standing guard outside her door checked his clipboard as I approached, confirmed my name and motioned me past him with a nod and a suspicious eye. Only person charged after all.

I found myself stuck at the entranceway to her room unable to proceed and peering in quietly.

Tamara was sitting up in her uncomfortable, convertible bed and staring out the window across from the doorway. She had both arms wrapped around her knees and looked so damned tiny and vulnerable in that ugly hospital smock.

The sun was warm despite the chill coming from the building's AC, its' light filling the whole room with a homey golden glow. The summer heat wave's sunshine managed to make the oppressive and sterile room look less like a polite prison and more like a shitty hotel.

Better than nothing.

Quit stalling. She knows you're here.

"Hi, Joe." Tamara's voice was weak. Bone tired.

See?

I cleared my throat uncomfortably and officially entered the room, taking a moment to slide the privacy curtain shut behind me to block out the hallway. Why? I don't know. Seemed like the thing to do.

The rubber soles on my beat up old sneakers squeaked softly against the linoleum floor as I found myself stopping a few feet from her bed with hands jammed uselessly into my pockets, unsure of what to do. I was unable to dredge up an appropriate action or comment.

So I just stood there.

Awkwardly.

She let the silence continue for a few moments, just staring out the window. Outside the sounds of traffic and construction along William Ave. continued as they did every summer. Horns honked. People chattered in a muted hum. Jackhammers and cement mixers rumbled away.

"I can still feel him inside me." Tamara's gaze never wavered away from the window. One tiny hand crept up from her knees and pressed against her temple with a faint tremor. "In here. He's still in here."

The twisting in my guts ended in a cold rush as my insides seized in sudden disgust and anger. Gooseflesh prickled from my hairline to my toenails as the energy at the back of my neck flared to life, setting my heart racing. My knuckles cracked loudly as fingers curled involuntarily into fists.

Finally she turned to face me. Without her glasses I had an unhindered view of her red rimmed and exhausted eyes. Her tone was humourless despite the words.

"No one likes exploding light bulbs, Joe."

I hadn't noticed the harsh static humming coming from the over head lighting until Tamara mentioned it, the sharp buzzing sound suddenly unmistakable to my ears. It took a moment and a few deep breaths to banish my automatic emotional response. But I did it.

Barely.

Her lips were pursed in the barest fraction of a smile.

"Feel better?"

I shook my head very slightly.

"Why not?"

Guilt. Vile vengeful thoughts. The desire to rage, scream and howl.

I screwed up my courage and met her eyes. It was a near thing.

"I am so sorry." I could barely hear myself through the thickness in my throat. The small, scared part of me wanted to cry once again but my fingernails dug painfully into my palms, keeping the waterworks away while I focused on Tamara.

She blinked. Tears welling up in her own eyes.

"Yeah. You big idiot." Her voice was as raw as her cheeks, scrubbed hard by endless crying and emotion. "You should be sorry."

"I know. I don't..." I was at a loss for words, flagellating myself for getting her into this horrible mess. "I just... I can't go back and fix this."

"Yeah. How dare you violate my mind like that? Getting in my head and making me do and say things against my will? Really, how dare you?"

It took me a moment to hear the truth behind her words. Sue me, it had been a rough couple of days.

The teary eyed stare I was getting demanded an appropriate response.

I cleared my throat again, finding a very faint ironic tone.

"Well if you'd just told me that Mark had knocked you up I wouldn't have needed to get all telepathic on your ass."

You know that place where you're so broken that you can't get any more upset about a situation? The one where tears aren't helping anymore?

That's where Tamara was.

So when she started laughing it damn near broke my heart.

Chapter 41

After a while the humourless laughter subsided. With a small motion of one hand Tamara pointed to the chair I presumed Mark had knocked over and kicked across the room. Dutifully I grabbed the cold metal seat and parked my ass in it right next to her bed.

Her tiny fingers reached out towards me. I gripped them softly in my calloused hand, trying not to shiver at how cold and frail they felt.

We stayed silent like that for a long time.

Then finally...

"So. How've you been?" she asked.

My eyebrow quirked in response.

"Really?"

Her attempt at a smile was a colossal failure but it couldn't be denied.

"You know what I've been up to." She looked around her room with slightly pursed lips. "Don't think you want me to recap this week's episode of The Bachelorette."

"Was it good?"

"Awful."

"I'll bring you some movies if you want."

"Can you bring a DVD player as well?

"Will VHS do?"

Tamara blinked in surprise.

I shrugged.

"For real?"

An embarrassed sigh escaped my lips. "I was playing PS3 a few weeks ago and couldn't get past one level. I was just on the verge of rage quitting and flinging the controller across the room when the stupid machine sparked and caught fire. Now it won't play games or movies."

Tamara's sad smile became slightly wider and a touch more genuine.

"So you dug out a VHS player from somewhere?"

I shook my head. "Mom's had one upstairs on her TV for years and she never uses it. I brought it downstairs. It's been kinda fun re-watching old tapes."

The barest trace of her usual spark flickered behind bloodshot eyes. "What were you playing?"

My arch enemy the embarrassed flush crept up my cheeks once again. "LEGO Star Wars," I mumbled.

She laughed. A real laugh this time, not the broken and devastated one from minutes ago.

I let her laugh uninterrupted. The knots in my belly loosening the longer it lasted.

All good things however.

"Oh God, I needed that." Tamara wiped at her eyes with her free hand, though in truth there didn't seem to be many tears to remove. "Oh Joe, you have no idea."

My fingers squeezed hers gently.

"I can imagine."

She blinked. The smile turning sad again.

"No, I don't think you can."

Her fingers tried to pull away but I held on gently, forcing her to meet my gaze.

"Tell me."

"Tell you what?"

"Whatever it is that you couldn't tell Mark."

Silence.

But I kept holding onto her fingers and meeting her gaze gently. Waiting her out.

It took less time then I thought it would and it wasn't what I expected.

"I'm going to keep the baby," she whispered.

I kept my expression free of surprise and squeezed supportively. "Kinda figured you would."

"I'm so scared, Joe."

"Of what?"

I could feel her fingers tremble in my hand.

"Of everything." She looked away, casting her eyes out the window. "At first I was just worried about Mark, and what he was going to say. How he would react to the news."

"Takes two to tango. He was there after all."

"I know. But after I told him... He was so angry. The things he said..."

Anger began to bubble past the knots in my belly. Keeping it from my voice was tough.

"He told me."

"Did he?"

"More or less. Said he was a complete asshole."

She forced a laugh. "At the very least."

"I was ready to kick his ass all over the patio at *Peeler's* for that."

"Why didn't you?"

I took a deep breath as I thought it through.

"Lots of reasons, but only one that matters." Her eyes prompted me to continue. I let my small smile show itself while I squeezed her fingers again. "When he found out that you had gone missing the panic and concern he showed was unmistakeable." I let my smile widen ever so slightly even as a swirl of complex emotions battled in my head over my next words. "He loves you, Tamara. He might not have said it. After his freak out he definitely didn't show it. But when he knew you were in danger, it was unmistakeable."

Tamara took my words in stoically, seeming to hang on each one.

More silence.

"So what do I do now?" she asked with very quiet voice.

"Honestly, I don't know. But I'd start by talking to Mark. Find some common ground. Give him a chance to make up for being a complete prick about this."

Tamara kept looking away from me, her expression conflicted. "God, I don't know Joe."

"No one ever knows anything. Not really. Not in my experience, anyways."

Her free arm wrapped around her knees once again, hugging herself tight. "How am I supposed to move on, Joe? Never mind Mark and... And the baby." she seemed to shudder. "But how can I move on after what Simon did to me?"

And that was the twenty-five thousand dollar question.

Her eyes bored into me. Hurt. Scared. Angry. Exhausted.

"I... I don't know what you want me to say." More anger bubbled in my guts, this time heating my words. "He got away from the cops. He's able to Jedi Mind-trick any fool he comes in contact with. If he got on a train or scored a ride he could be out of the country by now."

"He's not out of the country."

"He could be..." I trailed off, blinking at the suddenly confident tone in her voice. "Wait, what?"

Her gaze became firmer. So did her voice.

"He's not out of the country, Joe."

Anger continued to bubble, this time mingled with a surge of excitement as the Neanderthal in my belly primed the war drums at the mere prospect of vengeance.

"Are you sure?"

She nodded.

"How sure?"

"Pretty sure."

I glanced back over my shoulder to the closed door and the police officer standing guard out of sight past it.

"Have you told the cops this?"

Tamara gave me an exasperated look. "What am I supposed to say? The telepathic monster that you don't believe in is somewhere nearby and you should go arrest him?"

"Plus they'd be in range for a mind warp and probably wouldn't catch him anyways."

"That too."

Shit.

"Do you know where he is?"

Her exasperated look got introspective. "It's nothing I can... It's not like you think. I don't have an insight to his inner thoughts, thank God. But I get flashes. Impressions."

My mouth suddenly tasted sour.

"Sounds icky."

"You have no idea." Tamara's eyes focused off to something unseen, lost in her own head. "I can't explain what it was like, Joe. At first I felt like I was in control. That I was just following up on our trip to Selkirk on a hunch. Thinking I needed to go back, ask some more questions to the staff and maybe some patients. Then once I got on the bus... the closer I got to... to him." She visibly shuddered again. "There was a pressure in my head. On my sinuses at first and then deeper, near the back of my brain." Her free hand ran over her face, trying to wipe away the obvious discomfort.

My mind flashed back to the other night. To the sensation of pressure at the base of my skull warring with the usual tingle of life and energy I was used to.

"I know that feeling. He did it to me too."

"But he didn't! Not completely." Tamara shifted position on the bed, leaning forward slightly and dropping her voice conspiratorially, protecting the secret I'd entrusted to her even with no one else in the room. "Lots of what happened after the bus is a haze that I can't piece together. But once you came into the atrium everything is very clear. While he had a... a grip on my mind I could sense his frustration and fear. Fear of you."

"Well, I was kinda scary looking at the time..."

"No. He was scared because you were fighting him. Fighting his mind control. Keeping him at bay in a way that I didn't have a chance at."

Memories flashed through my head again. Going over the struggle I felt as Simon's will and words mounted the pressure on me, driving into my brain like the worst headache ever. Forcing me to my knees and immobilizing me.

"He was petrified of you. Simon's been able to control and command people he's made a connection with from miles away. Convincing them to drop everything and come at his command. And yet you defied him." Tamara gripped my fingers this time. "Something about you is different. You can stop him, Joe. I know it."

Hope surged in my belly. The Neanderthal began to wail on the skin of his drum, pounding it in time to the beat of my heart.

"So where is he?" my voice growled.

Tamara's fingers finally slipped from mine to complete the instinctive hug around her knees.

"I don't know," she whispered. "I just know he's not far away."

The Neanderthal howled in frustration, tipping over his war drum as easily as if it was a hospital chair.

Chapter 42

Normally at a time like this a frosty Corona would be the only thing helping me get through the night. But given everything I'd been through I didn't trust myself with anything stronger than ice cold water.

Damned refreshing though.

Saturday nights at *Peelers'* weren't something I was used to anymore. Dave and Jordan had developed into a solid team and didn't need me to babysit them on the regular. So I was mildly surprised to see such a full and well mannered crowd (note: well mannered for a strip club) as I sat in my usual perch sipping on water and brooding.

The events and conversations of the last couple days were starting to overwhelm me. Mom. Tamara. Cathy. Simon. Mark. Even Captain Max. Never mind the legal issues and criminal charges laid against me. Being released on bail wasn't something I'd ever anticipated for myself growing up. Though truthfully I'd never pictured "bouncer" or "electrical freakazoid" on my professional resume either.

Which reminded me, I needed to update my professional resume. After speaking to Lisa at *Canada-Pharm* the word was I had a "performance and attitude meeting" set up for Monday morning after booking off Thursday and Friday without a doctor's note or advance notice. Looks like my newspaper hero status had worn off with the boss-people and I was about to become the example to other staff members.

Probably past time to move on. Hell, with Mom moving into the pseudo-nursing home and the house up for sale I should probably take a look at my finances and...

And what?

I shook my head and sighed.

"Can't even get your own life together, fool. Why do you worry about others?"

"Because that's what good people do," a deep voice half-shouted in front of me.

I blinked, snapping my eyes up from the tiny bar table.

It took me a moment to recognize Lieutenant Connell given his lack of suit and tie. At first glance I thought I was being confronted by an overly muscular Abercrombie and Fitch model given the beige khakis and the stretched to the seams polo shirt. But once I got past the unshaven face and the politely offered beer in his hand I relaxed my posture and leaned back slightly.

"Wasn't aware I'd spoken out loud," I said over the din. Then I blinked, glancing quickly around the club and acknowledging the driving bass and hip hop tracks keeping the ladies on stage in a perpetual state of undress. "Wait, how did you even hear me?"

"I didn't," Connell replied setting his offered beer on the table before me while sliding into the opposite stool.

"Oh?"

He mimed a salute with his own bottle and took a sip before replying.

"Lip reading."

I mulled that over.

"RCMP training covers lip reading?"

He shrugged, causing a slight strain to the fabric over his shoulders.

"Some. Mostly situational awareness and attention to detail. I've worked a lot of stings and stakeouts where the sound equipment hasn't always been great. Gave me lots of practice." He took a long sip and glanced around the bar, scanning the room for threats in the same way I do everywhere I go. Trust me, this action becomes habit after a while to the point where you never turn it off.

I grimaced at Connell while politely sliding his offered beer off to the side next to my empty food plates and took a sip of water.

"What are you doing here?" No point in dicking around with chit chat I figured.

Connell turned back to me about to answer then paused, seeing the empty plates. I sighed, prepared for some chit chat and dicking around.

"Cheat meal?" he asked.

I shook my head and sipped water.

"Huh," he grunted, sipping more beer. His eyes calculating the stripped clean hot wing bones and nacho plates while glancing over at me. "Gonna have to spend time on the treadmill tomorrow to work that off."

I didn't bother responding. My stomach gurgled contentedly and for the first time all day the stress headache I'd been suffering from had faded away.

Connell didn't take my lack of a response personally. He merely shrugged and turned his gaze out into the bar, a man among men enjoying the scenery.

It was a good night. Shelby was near the main bar keeping an eye on the girls slinging liquor and taking cash. When I came in earlier she had voiced a concern over one of the new waitresses and was hoping to catch her in the act of skimming from her till.

Seeing me looking in her direction Shelby smiled encouragingly, silently offering support. Noting I now had company her eyebrow quirked a question. I shook my head minutely in response, trying to dismiss her concern. The way her lips pursed slightly told me I had failed in my attempt.

She's clearly worried about you, moron. Why don't you talk to her? Tell her what's going on?

I shuddered slightly at that thought. The only other person who knew everything I was dealing with was currently laid up in a hospital bed after having her thoughts and of her actions violated by some super powered psychotic. Not exactly the template for bringing in a new confidante.

"Who's that?" Connell asked, motioning towards Shelby.

"Club owner."

"Your boss then?"

I shrugged slightly but nodded. Technically true after all.

"Huh," Connell sipped his beer. "Looks like she should be on the stage."

"Used to be, once upon a time."

"Yeah?"

"So I'm told. I knew her from... We used to work together at another club."

To Connell's credit he didn't push me to admit which one.

"Good looking woman."

"Sure."

"You ever..." Connell left the unspoken question hanging as he peered back at Shelby.

I sighed.

"Don't think I'm her type."

Connell laughed and put down his beer.

I scowled at him. "What's so funny?"

"I've known you less than a week and have seen you in the company of three different stunning women, none of whom you are banging." Connell smirked at me in silent challenge. "Are you playing for the other team, Joe?"

My scowl deepened even as I busted out my raspy Christopher Lambert impersonation. "Why, Connell? You hard up and looking for a piece of ass?"

Connell laughed again. "Nice. I haven't seen the original Highlander in years..."

"What are you doing here?"

No more laughter.

Connell contemplated his beer in silence for a moment as he gathered his thoughts. I drained my water while waiting him out.

"Is it hard to believe that I wanted to check up on you?" he asked.

"Very." Shelby made a motion towards me from the bar, miming taking another drink. I nodded briefly with my small smile. She nodded in return and went behind the bar and out of sight.

Connell's frustration was plain by his expression though it was kept out of his voice. "I went pretty far out on a limb to help you, Joe. You should be in deep trouble today."

"I am in deep trouble." My scowl returned with a vengeance as my fingers clenched tightly into fists. The sudden urge to lash out at anything was intense. "Do I need to list off the charges, Lieutenant?"

"Deeper trouble." He amended, raising a placating hand. Sensing the sudden violence quivering just beneath my normally stoic surface. "Sorry. I didn't mean to upset you."

Two deep breaths, a brief mental admonishment to my internal Neanderthal and a forced unclenching of my fists later...

"It's fine. Little stressed out."

"I bet. You should hit the gym."

I grunted. Tamara's comments from the other day imploring me to take it easy and let my body recover seemed so damned long ago. But after the events at the hospital in Selkirk I couldn't deny that forty-eight hours of proper sleep, food and relaxation had done wonders for my headaches and overall energy levels.

Didn't do much for the anxiety release that pounding iron at the downtown YMCA usually provided though.

Hard to explain that to Connell without explaining everything. And since I had no intention of doing that...

"Yeah, well..." I shrugged my aching shoulders slightly and I tried to find a pleasant expression for the RCMP officer. "Been a rough week. Needed to take a break. The weights'll be there later."

Connell nodded in understanding and raised his beer, offering another salute. "Well I'm sure you'll figure something out. Maybe you'll even get laid."

Shelby's sudden arrival prevented my snippy retort as a million inappropriate comments suddenly needed a repression. Not just from her usual work attire of epic boner producing proportions but from the obvious double entendre she was providing by carrying two oversized water pitchers at breast height. She met my eyes briefly, catching them as they snapped back from their wandering and smirked knowingly.

"Refill?" she asked a touch too innocently.

I didn't trust myself to say anything. So I just nodded and slid my glass over to her.

Connell's mind was clearly going to the same place as mine but his professional cop-face was impeccable. "Love what you've done with the place. Tremendous improvement over the previous owners."

Shelby's smile became much more genuine. She took great pride in her club after all.

"Thank you. It's not much but it's keeping the mortgage paid."

Connell smiled. "I feel like I should be thanking you. If I'm not mistaken I spoke to you on the phone the other night." Shelby blinked in confusion, her smile tightening briefly. "You called on behalf of our friend here," he motioned to me with his beer. "Good thing you did too. He had gotten himself into a whole heap of trouble."

Shelby shot me a sidelong glance with a silent question in her eyes. I shrugged again in answer, giving her free reign to respond as she felt like.

"Well, I don't know much about that aside from what got reported on the news." I made another mental note, this one to thank Cathy again for helping keep details from Selkirk as vague as possible on all the broadcasts. Shelby continued. "However, I know Joe. And I know that any trouble he got himself was only to help someone else. Hopefully the police understand that."

Connell's smile widened at Shelby's admonishing tone though his words were cautious. "Well obviously I don't speak for the entire police force, but I assure you that I understand what kind of a man Joe is." His eyes met mine briefly. "I wouldn't be here now if I didn't believe in him."

Shelby's expression told me she wasn't entirely satisfied with his answer but she was wise enough to keep misgivings to herself. She turned back to me and smiled reassuringly. "More wings?"

My stomach gurgled in response.

What the hell.

"Please. Extra hot if you will. And enough for me and the lieutenant here."

Her eyebrow quirked in faint amusement before turning away, her water pitchers back up at a distracting height. "Two pounds of inferno wings coming up. You boys play nice now."

Both of us would've needed to be playing for the other team to avoid watching her walk away in those heels.

Connell turned back and drained his beer before finally taking the easy joke.

"Nice jugs."

"Fuck off."

"Well, they are pretty damned spectacular."

"What would Officer Swan say if she heard you talk like that?

It was Connell's turn to blink in surprise. Nice to know he could be caught off guard.

"Well, it isn't a crime to look is it?"

"You tell me. You're the cop."

"Besides, things with myself and Melissa are very unofficial at this point. We haven't even..."

"If you don't tell me what you're doing here I won't share my hot wings with you."

Connell went silent for a moment. Then he took up the beer he had originally brought over for me and took a hesitant sip.

I gave him my best poker face stare and waited him out.

Connell went over a few responses internally going by the look in his eyes before finally settling on one.

"I want to help clear your name."

Bitter laughter escaped my lips.

"Right. How do you plan to do that?"

"Easy." Connell's expression got deadly serious. "I want to help you catch Simon."

Chapter 43

"So you're no longer just setting me free to the wild and hoping I'll solve this problem for you?" The sneer in my voice matched by the one I knew was on my lips. "What's changed since yesterday when I made my official statement? Is the Police brass breathing down your neck?"

Connell sighed and sipped more beer. "They're always doing that. But I'm consulting from the RCMP. Technically not in their jurisdiction."

"Well something must've changed. You seemed happy enough to cut me loose."

He shrugged. "That was the best I could do for you until we could process everyone else we'd brought in. Had a chance to compile the statements and see what shook loose."

My heart rate picked. Hope, that oh so powerful yet inexplicable emotion reared it's head once again in my chest.

Play it cool, Joe. You're not a cop. You're in deep enough shit already.Think this through.

"Do you know where he is?" I blurted, disobeying the thoughts of my logical inner monologue.

Connell sighed, his expression souring.

"No. Statements were almost completely useless. Few could remember anything of significance. A couple of them mentioned being sympathetic to Simon's case but nothing to incriminate him as the ringleader. Crime techs are still processing the garden shed samples, though the biggest stumbling block seems to be in separating the human remains and isolating specific victims..."

"Do. You know. Where he is?" I repeated, biting off my words harshly.

Connell sighed again..

"I was kind of hoping you did."

Silence.

"What kind of a cop are you?" I growled at him, frustration spilling out with every syllable.

For some stupid reason Connell seemed taken aback. "What do you mean?"

The temptation to fling the bar table at him was much stronger than I'd normally care to admit to anyone. But since I managed to restrain myself I suppose it's fair to admit it here.

"You have an entire division of cops at your disposal. Not to mention whatever pull you've got through the RCMP to track this asshole down. You have resources. Intel. Manpower. Likely a whole ton of files with a history on not just Simon but on everyone who is with him or you suspect might be with him right now. Jesus Christ, you've probably got even more things than that to work with, right?" Connell nodded while sipping his beer and eyeing the crowd around us, needlessly checking for eavesdroppers. There weren't any. I leaned across the table then, getting as close as I dared. "Then with all of that going for you how come you're here right now pinning all your hopes on me?"

Connell had the decency to look embarrassed despite the anger in his eyes. "You know why I'm here."

"Yeah. Because you're a shitty cop and you suck at your job."

For the first time since I'd met the lieutenant his expression went stone cold. His eyes hardened and he slowly put the beer bottle down on the table. His entire body moved in a very subtle way, going from casual to ready-to-attack with a slight shifting of his torso and positioning of arms and feet.

"Who the fuck do you think you are?

I snorted. "I think I'm the college dropout that's facing criminal charges and personal ruin who still came closer to catching the mother fucker that's been abducting people in this town for years than your entire police force."

"Nothing in our search pointed towards Simon. How could it?"

"Cathy and I found the connection to Selkirk on the first day of looking."

"Bullshit. You had Native Posse members stooge it off to you." Connell shook his head in irritation. "Besides, we looked into those girls as well, saw that they were visiting a foster mother in Selkirk. No red flags there, and no connection to their disappearance. We sent an officer to the hospital to speak with her about them just to make sure."

A puzzle piece I didn't know I had been missing clicked into place. "Son of a bitch," I muttered.

"What?"

"If you'd sent an officer to talk to Mrs. Kubrakovich about her missing girls that must've sent Simon into a panic. Goddamn, he must've sent her sliding into a coma to keep her from making a scene or drawing attention back to the hospital."

"She's in a coma?"

"She was when I visited her. Reports said it was sudden, no reason for it they could find.

Connell rubbed at his buzzed scalp in thought.

I ground my teeth in aggravation, adding one more offence to the list I was building against Simon in my head.

Connell blinked at me. "Why didn't you put any of this in your statement?"

"Oh, you mean the statement I gave you or the official statement you convinced me to give for the record?"

This time Connell's fingers tightened, almost clenching into fists. "I did that to protect you from being charged outright for being the kidnapper. Adding your connection to that gang wouldn't have helped your case by the way."

I laughed. "Connection? I was arrested the night before for getting in a fight with members of the Posse! Another one of their members shot me earlier in the year! What kind of criminal connection is that?"

"So what? You were going to tell them Simon was behind everything? That he's using his psychic powers to abduct and control people? To kill the ones he can't continue to hide or abuse? To steal their identities for some unknown reason?"

"It's not unknown."

Connell blinked, his angry tone fading as curiosity took over. "It's not? How do you..."

"Tamara." Connell blinked again, clearly confused. I sighed, my anger gone as well to be replaced with a bad taste in my mouth. The kind I always get when telling a story that probably isn't mine to tell. But since I had no one else to talk to about this... "When Simon had his... Fuck I don't know what to call it. His mental grip on Tamara some of his thoughts and feelings were there for her to see."

Connell pursed his lips, his eyes fading in thought. "Almost everyone we brought in from the hospital for questioning says they don't remember anything that happened. Like the whole night is wiped clean."

"So what? Maybe that's true. Or maybe some of them do remember things but are too messed up to know it. More likely if they do remember they don't want to say, especially not the patients. They're already members of a mental hospital after all."

Connell nodded fractionally. "That makes sense I guess." He took a swig of beer, while the fingers of his free hand drummed on the table as the tension between us faded. "What did your friend see?"

"Not a whole lot. But enough for me to make a guess." It was my turn to glance around at the crowd searching for eavesdroppers. Connell's fingers drummed a bit faster in impatience. "Everything she got from him came in frantic moments, all during... Well, while I was busting into the hospital."

"We're going to have to talk more about how you did that later."

Yeah, right.

"When things started to get hectic for Simon, Tamara thinks

he started to panic a bit. She got flashes of things and impressions of ideas. She thinks they were plans of his."

"Details, Joe. What kind of plans."

"She can't be sure. But what might've been hotel brochures. Rental car locations on a Google Maps page. A list of cities..."

Connell shook his head. "That's fascinating in a creepy sort of way. But it doesn't smack of a plan so much as a frightened response. With you busting in on his safe haven he might just have been trying to think of the next place to run."

"Maybe. But Tamara's pretty sure that he's got a specific location in mind. A route. Something that would require him to have access to a functioning credit card and series of ID's. Maybe a bunch of them."

"That's crazy. No one would take a woman's credit card from Simon."

"These aren't the droids you're looking for."

"What?"

"Seriously?" I sighed again. Seemed like I'd been doing that a lot the last few days. "Dude. Jedi Mind Trick. Trust me. They'd take the cards. They'd believe the ID he'd show them."

The light of understanding dawned in the cops' eyes. "Okay.

But why use the cards at all? Why not just..."

"Put the whammy on the clerk?" Connell nodded. "Yeah, I thought of that too. Then I figured using the cards would provide something of a legit paper trail for the vendors, especially at the car shops. Something to keep managers from asking questions for at least the duration of the rental contracts before calling the police in."

He nodded again. "Yeah. Yeah I can see that. Pad the escape time even more. Give him a head start to get out of town."

"Even out of the country if he can get to an unmanned border crossing."

Connell grimaced. "Yeah, I'm trying not to think about that."

"So what are you thinking about?"

"What?"

The frustration wanted to build up inside me again. "About Simon. About how to catch him. Do you have a trace on the IDs of the people he's abducted? Any word on local forgers trying to make doubles of the IDs? Anything?"

"This isn't an episode of CSI, Joe. Nothing like that happens fast. Not without a high level priority for a major criminal case."

For a moment I thought my eyes were going to pop out of my head. "How is an ongoing missing women's case that has been all over the news not a high priority?"

It was Connell's turn to shrug, his face slightly sheepish. "When the police have a prime suspect in mind to narrow the focus it's tough to make the higher ups take the time to follow up on old missing ID traces that failed to be fruitful when they were first put to use."

My face ended up in my palms as I leaned elbows first onto the bar table and groaned.

"This is why I hate doing people favours," I grumbled.

"What?"

"Never mind." I sat up again, temporarily shoving aside the negative thoughts with a deep breath. *Focus, dammit.* "Okay. You want my help."

Connell nodded.

"The cops are focusing in on me, probably digging through my entire life's history and finances looking for a connection to these women."

Another nod.

"What'll happen when they don't find anything?"

"Well, some of the heat'll come off you for sure. Though I imagine you'll still be under some kind of surveillance for a week at least." Connell scratched at his unshaven scalp in thought for a moment. "You'll still be on the hook for the breaking and entering, the property damage and trespassing. Never mind the..."

"Yeah yeah yeah, I'm fucked. I get that. Hopefully once we catch Simon and bring him in to the police you can work some federal cop magic and help a guy out."

"So it's we now?"

"Fuck you. Can you help me get the charges dropped or not?"

Connell's expression soured. "Joe, some of those are pretty serious charges. I don't know if anyone can..."

"Do you want my help or not?"

"Are you blackmailing me?"

"Turn about's fair play, asshole. I'm screwed and need help too. But if you can't find Simon without me then you've gotta have something to offer."

Silence. Well, no speaking anyways. It's a strip club after all.

"I'll see what I can do." Connell finally conceded with a doubtful expression. "No promises but I'll see what I can do."

Better than nothing.

I stuck out my calloused hand. Connell didn't hesitate at all before shaking it firmly.

"Well, you boys look like you're getting along better now." Shelby's voice interrupted while sliding a platter heaped high with steaming hot, buffalo sauce laden chicken wings onto the table between us. "For a while there I thought you two were going to step outside."

"The night's still young," I quipped, my small smile appearing for Shelby.

"Fighting's for boys," Connell interjected while helping himself to a drummette. "Next time we have a dispute we'll have a bench press competition to settle things."

The sudden mental image of Connell's face after watching me do high reps with his max weight made my smile much less small.

"Deal." I grabbed a wing myself and motioned it with a thankful nod towards Shelby as my stomach rumbled in approval to the aroma hitting my nose. "How's everything going tonight? The boys got things under control?"

Shelby's well-manicured fingers touched my arm fondly. "Dave and Jordan are fine. Give them a few more weeks and they'll be true pros."

"Good stuff," I mumbled between bites.

"However I think it's time you joined the twenty-first century and got yourself a cellphone, Joe." Her fingers tightened slightly on my tricep as the smile on her lips became forced humour. "The front desk isn't your personal switchboard and we don't need to keep fielding calls for you."

Chapter 44

It was Tamara.

Not that I'd doubted that. Before leaving her room at the hospital I made sure the number to the front desk at *Peelers'* was written down in case she needed anything. I couldn't be sure I was going to be at the club, but given the choice between hanging out at home with my sleeping mother, fretting over the house sale or watching women take their clothes off while gorging myself on free pub food...

Come on. What would you do?

The race across the bar wasn't as quick as it had been the other night. Shelby's place was packed to the tits (rimshot, please) and I had to weave and dodge around various frat boys, business casual buffoons and the occasional bachelorette party to make it to the front lobby.

Thankfully I managed to make it across the room without being a complete bull in a china shop. Though it was a near thing as several people received an errant shoulder bump and let out a pissed off cry behind me. The responsible portion of my mind hoped I hadn't just set off a chain reaction of stupid for Dave and Jordan to clean up in my reckless rush to the phone. The rest of my mind had dropped into tunnel vision while the tingle at the back of my neck sparked faintly, sending the now familiar rush of life and enthusiasm down my nervous system.

Front Desk Dude was there again looking like he'd never left. And unless he had several variations on the same jeans and tee shirt combo my guess was that he hadn't even changed. Yuck.

My fingers snatched the cracked white receiver from his outstretched hand and jammed it painfully fast to my ear.

"Ow. Fuck... Hello?"

"Joe?" Tamara's voice was faint and hard to hear over the driving music from inside the club. Shelby closed the door as I glanced back at her, the fingers of my free hand pressed against my opposite ear. Connell stood a few feet away with weight balanced forward on his toes looking like a coiled spring, ready for action.

"Yeah, it's me. Can you hear me, Tamara?"

"Yes. This hospital phone sucks. Or maybe it's just real loud on your end?"

"Strip club. It happens. Are you okay?"

"More or less. I've barely been able to sleep. My dreams have been awful."

I glanced over at Connell. "Dreams? Just bad dreams?"

Tamara paused. In my mind's eye I could almost picture her sitting up in that damned uncomfortable bed just like she had been earlier in the afternoon. Curled up into a ball with the phone pressed to one ear and her eyes closed. That image hit me so vividly I had to blink my eyes for a moment and shove it aside.

Focus, dumbass.

"I... I'm not sure. Things were weird for a bit and then... Then it was like a monitor opened up in my head."

"A monitor?"

"I'm not explaining this right. One minute I don't remember dreaming anything and then suddenly there were flashing lights flaring painfully in my eyes and making me wince."

I started searching on the desk for a pen and paper much to creepy Front Desk Dude's displeasure. Connell surprised me by producing a tiny notebook and mechanical pencil from one the utility pockets in his khakis. He motioned for me to continue speaking while flipping to a clear page to take notes.

"Lights? You saw lights?" Connell began to scribble in the notebook. "Like white lights? Like some sort of a beacon? Like... Like pot lights?"

"He's not going to be at IKEA, Joe. Get a grip." Tamara huffed impatiently as she gathered her thoughts. "No they were strobing. Police lights, like when you get pulled over for speeding."

"Traffic cop lights?" I parroted for Connell's benefit. "Did you see the car?"

"No, I didn't see it. Wait..." Tamara's breathing got heavy over the phone. In a less serious situation I might've made an impolite comment. See? I can be a gentleman. "Now that I think about it I can... Wow this is messed up."

"What is?"

A hint of disgust entered her voice as she continued. "Now that I'm focusing on it I can... God, this is weird. I can pull the image back up and look at it again."

I blinked. "Really? Like a YouTube video or something?"

"Kinda but without the buffering." Tamara paused again. "Okay, yes. I can see the squad car."

"What kind of car?" Connell asked after I brought him up to speed. "What jurisdiction?"

"Jurisdiction?" Tamara sounded confused.

"Is it a City of Winnipeg Police car?" I clarified.

"Oh. Sorry, I'm having a tough time thinking with this in my head. Ugh... I can almost smell Simon's sweat. Like onions and... Wait, not a Winnipeg car. RCMP."

I gave that info to Connell who continued writing. "That's great Tamara. What else can you see?"

"Oh, God."

"What?"

"Simon's panicking .Or he was panicked at the time. I can't be sure, but he seems anxious. God, that's why I'm getting this image again. Just like with you he was panicked and didn't realize he was broadcasting his thoughts as he..."

"As he what Tamara?"

"I don't know. Things are all blurry now. I can't make it... Wait, no. Okay Simon's in the car now."

"He got arrested?"

"No he's in the passenger seat next to the computers and stuff. I think he took over the cops' mind."

Shit.

I gave that info to Connell who immediately pulled out his cellphone. "I'm gonna check with the switchboard. See if anyone's failed to report in recently."

I nodded to the lieutenant as he stepped away. "That's terrific, Tamara. You're doing great."

"Don't patronize me, Joe. I'm too disgusted to even think about how I can see all this. It makes me want to throw up."

I pointedly didn't mention what else might be making her stomach sick.

"Can you see anything else? Landmarks? Street signs?"

Tamara sighed heavily. "Not really. It's dark. I'm assuming they're on a road in the middle of nowhere. There's trees all around."

"Okay, that's good. Means they're not out in farm country at least." *Not yet anyway.* "Probably means he hasn't gotten too far."

"I guess. I can't be sure of anything, Joe."

"You're already giving us more than we had before."

"We? Wait, you've been talking to someone." Tamara's voice began to panic. "Oh my God, Joe. I've been keeping your secrets for months despite everything and you can't go one day without blabbing to someone about my visions?"

I winced. Hadn't actually thought about that when I broke the news to Connell. "Yeah, sorry. It sorta got away from me..."

"It got away from you?"

"Look I'll make it up to you by finding Simon and making him pay. But in order to do that I need Connell's help."

"Connell?" Tamara paused, her voice still heated but now thoughtful. "The RCMP guy who's been giving you weird clues and hints? The one you're not sure you can trust?"

I sighed, leaning my elbows heavily onto the front desk. "Tamara, aside from you I'm not sure there's anyone I can trust. Not completely."

Tamara got strangely silent for a moment while a shuffling sound next to me caught my attention. I glanced over quickly and realized Shelby was still standing a few feet from me, a confused expression on her face that looked slightly sad for some reason.

"Okay, Joe." Tamara's voice brought me back to the moment. It was calm again, no longer panicked. In fact it sounded calmer than it had been in days. "We'll talk about trust and secrets later. Right now you need to get to work."

I laughed mirthlessly. "I'm at work. One of them anyways.."

"No I mean you gotta get yourself in gear and hit the road."

I blinked and pushed away from the front desk to peer over at Connell. He was still in conversation on his cell but saw my motion to toss his notepad over. I caught it awkwardly and grunted "You see something else?" into the receiver as I bent down to retrieve the mechanical pencil that had bounced off me chest before clattering to the floor.

"It's a big building. Chain link fence around it. I can't see much because the streetlights are very far away." I awkwardly wedged the receiver into the crook of my neck as I fumbled with the pencil. "It's not a warehouse, at least I don't think it is."

"Landmarks? Street signs?"

"No. This is off the beaten path somewhere. But wherever it is Simon's been there for a bit."

"How can you tell?"

"Two of the patients are opening the sliding gate right now. I can see them in the headlights from the police car."

My heart rate started to steadily increase and I had to take a very deep breath to keep myself from going off half cocked. Again.

"Not a warehouse. Off the beaten path. How large?"

"Pretty large. Looks like a few buildings all connected. Like some of the complexes at the university but more like a factory." Tamara gasped. "Oh, God that's it. They're at some sort of factory."

"Following the super villain hideout cliche to a tee isn't he," I mumbled while scribbling away in the notebook. "Can you see anything else?"

"Things are jumping around a little bit now. Simon's not freaking out so I'm not getting as much to work with."

"Makes sense. If he's been settled here since the other night he'd start to get comfortable."

"I have no idea what I'm seeing."

"Describe it."

"Big. Metal. Looks like huge fans. I can't see much, the lights are almost all out." Tamara made a frustrated sound. "I can't... Dammit Joe. I've lost it."

I finished writing what little she had given me down and tried not to growl in frustration. I forced a calm into my voice. "You've done great, believe me."

"I think I'm going to be sick."

"I can only imagine," I replied distractedly. Connell was off to the side motioning frantically at me to toss his notepad back. Shelby surprised me, taking the paper and pencil from my clumsy fingers and walking them over to the lieutenant, her face still unreadable. "You've got to try and get some rest."

Her voice got very quiet, I almost couldn't hear her from the driving bass in the club. "How can I rest? With everything... God..."

"You have to rest because I said so." Connell had stopped his conversation and began fiddling with his smartphone, checking the last page he had written on while thumb-typing. "Nobody's going to hurt you ever again. I promise."

The fear in her whispered reply made my blood boil. "You can't promise that, Joe."

Ain't that the truth.

"I can about Simon."

Something in the tone of my own voice scared me. The ring of sincerity.

Tamara heard it too.

"Joe?" her words were still soft. Hushed now to avoid eavesdroppers. "Joe, what are you going to do?"

Connell finished writing and looked over at me, his expression triumphant. He nodded once and motioned me over.

"Tamara, I have to go."

"Joe? Don't stop talking now. I don't want you doing something you'll regret forever. I need you to..."

"Get some rest. I'll call when I can."

I hung up on her quickly, afraid to let her say anything more. I knew what had to be done. I also knew that I couldn't let anyone talk me out of that decision even though it twisted my guts into a knot. I pushed the brief mental flashes of burned bodies and Parise being gunned down in front of me aside. I couldn't afford those thoughts. I couldn't afford distractions.

"What's up?" I asked. Shelby blinked at my tone and hopefully was ignoring the steely focus in my eyes as I walked over.

Connell's eyes were bright. "Dispatch confirmed twice for me. No one's failed to report via radio in the last twelve hours."

"So why are you smiling?"

Connell flipped his smartphone around to show me the screen. It was your standard roadmap app with a bright red beacon highlighting a spot off highway two-oh-four just east of the Red River within a ten minute drive of Selkirk..

"All RCMP vehicles are low-jacked with GPS trackers. There's been a car parked at these coordinates for the past two hours. No report of an incident. No public complaint. Just a parked car."

"Hook up spot for cops?" Shelby asked. Both Connell and I blinked and gave her a brief look. Her slight shrug did distracting things to the rest of her. "Hey. Cops have vices too."

I quirked an eyebrow questioningly at Connell.

He scowled. "If we head out to this location and find some sort of gang bang going on I promise you there will still be asses to kick."

"Depends on what's there. Hotel?"

He shook his head. "Old Manitoba Hydro plant. Still in operation but almost completely unmanned since the new dam was built in Lockport."

My heart started to pound again, feeding the surge at the back of my neck. Life. Energy. Strength. Anger. All these things filled my body, begging me to release them in a rage.

The phone at the front desk rang noisily, bringing me back to the moment.

Tamara.

Focus, Joe. He already escaped once. You won't get another chance.

Shelby hesitantly touched my arm then flinched back at the static discharge. "I... Wow, that's intense." She shook her fingers out quickly. "Joe, are you okay?"

"Never better," I muttered, eyeing the officer of the law and trying to gauge the expression on his face. "You sure about this?"

"About taking down a psychopath and a killer?" Connell's smile got winter cold. "Hell yes."

I took one last deep breath, ignoring the Front Desk Dude who was trying to get me to come back to the phone. I gave Shelby a pleading look and motioned with my head.

Her eyes got serious but she nodded. "Be careful," she said, her voice very quiet before stepping quickly away to take the phone and head off Tamara's concerns.

"Where's your car?"

"In the lot." Connell fished a set of keys out of his khakis and bounced them on his palm as he headed for the front doors. I matched his stride. "Let's roll."

I snatched away the keys mid-bounce. "I'm driving."

"The hell you are. It's my car."

"You have the map on your phone."

"So what? You can't follow a GPS?"

The night air hit me like a cold wave. It's wasn't really any cooler but my metabolism was firing so hot the summer's muggy wave felt like a splash of ice water.

"I really can't. Besides, you've been drinking."

"Two beers?"

"I don't make the laws. I just help you enforce them.

Chapter 45

With all due respect to my late, dearly departed van there was something magical about driving a truly top of the line vehicle.

No odd clicks. No struggling with the transmission. With top-notch steering control that was responsive to my every move.

And the engine speed...

I grew up on TV shows where the General Lee and K.I.T.T. were the real stars, no matter how awesome the actor's hair and chiseled features were to the female audience. And even though I may have ended up with a ride more reminiscent of B.A. Baracus' war wagon, there was something to be said for the sheer stereotypically masculine power of a muscle car's roaring as I rushed into action.

Yeah. I was enjoying myself. What of it? How often have you had the chance to drive a ninety-five Dodge Charger to a super villain's hideout?

That's what I thought.

"I don't know why you keep treating me as your personal search engine, Joe." That was Cathy on Connell's speaker phone sounding tired and aggravated. I had forgotten about her early morning flight to Calgary with Max for his fundraising golf tournament. "And why are you having me look things up? You're with that RCMP officer, why don't you have his people get more info for you or something?"

The Charger purred like a panther as I blew past a "thanks for visiting the City of Winnipeg" sign near the overpass of highway fifty-nine and the perimeter highway at a speed somewhat greater than the posted limit. It was hard not to smile as we flew along the pavement, passing other drivers without taxing the car's engine at all.

"I gotta get me one of these," I muttered, ignoring Cathy's question as I juked past an RV camper and hit the accelerator on the straightaway.

"Take it easy, Andretti," Connell winced at the sudden speed increase but replied to Cathy in my stead. "Right now we're only following up on the narrowest of leads, Ms. Greenburg. In order to open an official enquiry paperwork needs to be filed, motives need to be quantified..."

Cathy's derisive snort was something to behold, let me tell you. Even over the phone.

"So basically you've got nothing. Why are you even going to this power plant if you have so little to go on?" However, despite her annoyed tone Cathy's investigative reporter instincts were too ingrained to be ignored. "There must be something solid if you're going to risk your career affiliating yourself with a man you personally arrested in connection to the Missing Women's Case."

Connell's mouth opened and closed a few times, his eyes

visibly searching for a response to satisfy her excellent question.

Maybe it was the thrill of driving or the prospect of actually doing something productive after the last couple of misery filled days. Either way, the words that rolled out of my lips next were not part of a plan or any attempt at misdirection. It wasn't until after the words came out that I even realized who I was speaking in front of.

"Cathy, you never asked me about why I called you the night *Cowboy Shotz* burned to the ground." Connell's eyes widened slightly, as a small smirk creased one corner of his mouth. I pointedly ignored him. "Well tonight is like that night. We know things that the rest of the police don't. And since they don't know about it they can't do anything about it. But someone has to do something about it. And since no one else is available, that someone is me. Now in order to do anything I need to know what I'm walking into. So please, can you check your files and let me know if there's been any criminal activity reported at this old Hydro plant? Any mention of gang activity? Hell, anything you can find that a simple Google search wouldn't satisfy?"

The phone was silent for a long moment.

I sweetened the pot.

"Besides, if I'm right and something does happen tonight think about how far ahead of the rest of the media you'll be when the story breaks."

More silence, but now the thoughtful kind.

Then finally...

"Dammit, Joe..." Cathy's voice was gruff but eager, ready to dig into the media files I knew she had backed up on personal drives. "I'll call you back right away. Try not to get arrested. I don't want to explain to my boss why he's not getting back the bail money I begged him for because you couldn't keep your nose out of trouble for forty-eight hours."

"Thanks, Cathy. I owe you."

Her laugh was mirthless. "We're back to owing favours are we?"

Our conversation from earlier in the hospital waiting room came back to me. A slight hint of embarrassment at the memory of my indignation crept into my voice. "Yeah, I guess. But don't forget, I'm allergic to cats."

More laughter, this time genuine. "I'll call you right back."

Connell's phone switched back to GPS mode as the turn off to Birds' Hill Park whipped past us on the right.

"Now I know what the term 'drive it like you stole it' means," Connell muttered sourly.

A short laugh escaped my lips. "Yeah. Cause' you've never

opened this girl up on the highways before."

"I am an RCMP officer, Joe. I follow the law.

"Except when you side with a suspected criminal to go and track down another criminal without calling for backup."

"Trust me, if your friend Tamara's visions are correct I'll be calling for backup. I'm good, but if he's got a group of people there under his thrall I am going to be hard pressed to handle them all by myself."

I spared Connell a sharp glance. "By yourself, huh?"

"Well..."

"You're gonna tell me to wait in the car?"

"I'm already going out on a limb as it is, Joe."

"This was your idea," I reminded him as we hit a sharp bend in the road, which the beauty car took like a champ. "You wanted to help me get Simon and here you are. After we're done with him..."

"Done with him?" Connell's voice was serious. Or stressed out, it was hard to tell going by how firmly he was gripping the front dashboard while keeping one eye on the GPS map. "What do you mean?"

Conflicting emotions swirled in my guts. The Neanderthal's war cry and the scared little boy who didn't want to hurt anyone were debating loudly with each other over the knowledge of what was coming.

I kept my voice low, not trusting it to be tremble free. "You know what I mean."

"Spell it out."

My knuckles tightened on the steering wheel as the energy buzzed at the back of my neck. I forced air in through my nose in a long steadying breath. *Easy, Joe. Conserve your strength.* I didn't speak again until the tingling sensation had been pushed back and I regained full control over my involuntary vice grip.

"Say we do this. Everything goes perfect and we arrest Simon. What then?"

"The usual," Connell replied. His tone of voice was matter of fact but there was something else in his eyes. A challenge almost. "Charges laid. A trial. More time added to his sentence and then a nice, long jail term."

I barked a sour laugh. "Yeah, cause that worked so well last time."

The challenge in Connell's eyes deepened as he waited for me to continue.

"He spent what, two years in a proper jail before the system declared him medically unfit? I mean, federal psychiatrists looking to make a case study for themselves to advance their careers have done some idiotic things in the past without having to deal with a mind bending telepath like Simon." I had to take another deep breath before continuing. "So say we do this the right way. Say he's back in cuffs and back in jail." I met Connell's eyes sharply, my guts still twisting away. "How long do you think he'll stay there?"

Connell's didn't reply. But his eyes demanded more from me.

Since I seemed to be in a chatty mood I obliged him.

"Sexual predator. Liar. Identity thieving murderer. Kidnapper of men and women. Psychic powers to manipulate and override the will of anyone who gets in his way." Despite the deep yoga breathing I could feel the angry bile rising in my throat. "Tell me. Is that the sort of man you even want in jail? At least now he's only got a few mental patients, staffers and a couple of Mounties under his spell. Imagine the riot he could cause in a maximum security facility."

I ran out of words. I was also running out of control over my emotions. So I forced my eyes ahead to the road, letting the silence be washed away by the roar of eight-cylinder action and two hundred horses under the hood.

The quiet lasted for maybe a minute.

"They were right about you."

I blinked, stunned out of my conflicted navel gazing.

"What?"

"Do you think you can do it?" Connell asked, his gaze now firmly locked onto the GPS screen.

"Who was right about me?"

"Can you do it?" he repeated firmly.

"Do what? Stop Simon?" Connell nodded, his eyes not leaving the screen or giving any more information.

What the fuck?

I pushed my questions aside. At the moment they weren't the important ones.

"I don't know," I finally grumbled as the signs indicating the turn onto highway two-oh-four was rapidly approaching. My guts rolled again in fear and anticipation. "I don't know if I can stop him. I don't know if I can do what needs to be done."

Connell raised his eyes to look at me. "So why are you doing this?"

I didn't answer.

Silence reigned supreme.

Until the piercing chorus of Katy Perry's "Teenage Dream" shrilled from Connell's smartphone. Both of us jumped at the sudden chorus though Connell's expression became stony as he fumbled with the screen to answer the call.

"Really?"

"I usually have this thing on vibrate," he muttered. "My daughter must've been playing with my phone again."

"Hey man, we all have guilty pleasures."

"Fuck off."

"Excuse me?" Cathy's surprised voice cut off the pop track. "Who are you telling to fuck off? I just did a ton of..."

"Ms. Greenburg, I'm sorry. I was talking to Joe."

Cathy's voice got wry. "Oh, well carry on then. I've been meaning to tell him that since you boys called me tonight."

I smiled tightly. "Since you're in a good enough mood to give me shit why don't you tell me what you found?"

She cleared her throat and very faintly I could hear the sound of fingers on a keyboard as she gathered her notes.

"No criminal activity. No reports of squatting or vagrant behaviour. A few graffiti reports and assorted minor vandalism. A few trespassing instances. But it's basically been a skeleton crew run facility since Hydro expanded the big dam out in Lockport. I think they have maybe one or two staffers pop in over the course of a week to check in on things and make repairs as needed. Aside from that it's practically abandoned."

Connell frowned and shook his head. "So nothing out of the ordinary? I told you we shouldn't have called her, Joe. Now we've involved the media without..."

"The media would've been involved eventually, Lieutenant. We're good like that." I could practically see the smirk on Cathy's lips as I drove. "What the reports don't say outright is what's more interesting."

"How so?" I asked, while taking my foot off the accelerator as the big left turn to the two-oh-four was coming up.

Cathy's voice took on the know-it-all quality I remembered vividly from journalism class in college. It made me smile.

"About six months ago all reports stopped from this facility."

Connell's confusion was evident. "You just said there wasn't any activity"

"Come on, Lieutenant. This is a big building ten kilometres away from a small city in rural Manitoba. The graffiti and trespassing incidents of teenagers and kids breaking onto the site to explore, make out and such were steady every few weeks or so until six months ago. Suddenly all reports just stopped."

Connell mulled that over and shot me a glance. "Does that give us anything?"

I shrugged. "Maybe Simon's been scouting the place for a while. Using his Jedi stuff to keep people away?"

"What good would that do him?"

"Hold on! Simon? The Scout Stalker?" Cathy's voice climbed in volume as her excitement swelled. "You guys think Simon Pritchard is hiding out at this plant? Wait, no... You think that he's behind the kidnappings! That must be..."

"Easy Cathy, you don't want to wake up the captain."

"What?"

"You're getting too loud, don't wake up your boyfriend." I gave Connell a glance, he nodded in return. "I promise to explain more to you later. Hell, Connell might even give you an exclusive interview if you ask him nicely. I know how much you like those."

"I wouldn't count on it," he muttered.

"Wait, Joe. I need to know what you're going to do."

No you don't.

"Thank you, Cathy. I'll call when I can."

Connell cut off her next sentence with a flick of his thumb, ending the call.

Silence again.

Then.

"Joe?"

"Yeah?"

Connell appeared to struggle with the question.

"Can you stop Simon?"

The GPS voice on his phone told me what my eyes had already seen. Our turn was coming up fast on the left.

My fingers tightened on the wheel.

"I think I might be the only one who can."

I took the corner at sixty klicks and punched the Charger out of the skid by dropping it into low gear and hitting the throttle, sending us roaring down the smaller highway at top speed. According to Connell's GPS the Hydro plant was five minutes away.

Chapter 46

It was well past midnight by the time Connell and I made it to the chain link fence surrounding the old Manitoba Hydro Selkirk Generating Station. Contrary to how it often looks in the movies, it is very difficult to make your way through trees and underbrush in the pitch blackness under a countryside sky. Not that there were all that many trees in this area, Prairie Province after all. But there was enough for cover in the dark.

"Did we have to park quite so far away?" I grumbled while dumping some dirt and crap out of my left sneaker. "I'm not exactly dressed for a hike."

"Quiet," Connell hissed, his eyes gleaming in the near blackness as he scanned ahead along the fence line, his service pistol held low and safetied.

I may have grumbled some more as I hopped on one foot to get my sneaker back in place. Some subconscious part of me realized how desperately I was trying to keep my fear and anxiety in check by being smarmy and even a touch immature. Call it a self-defence mechanism. Sure, the energy at the back of my neck tingled furiously and the Neanderthal in my belly was primed to unleash hell on the deserving Simon but I couldn't get rid of that feeling of helplessness back at the hospital in Selkirk. The moments after I blew my wad and was left exhausted, out of juice and completely incapable of forming a coherent thought through the blinding headache and hunger. It had been much the same at *Cowboy Shotz* once things had really gotten hot.

As such I knew how little I could afford to let things get out of hand here. I'd been lucky before. Luck runs out. I had to be patient and conservative. People's lives depended on it.

Mine, primarily.

So I took deep, steadying breaths. I made some smart ass comments and tried to keep things light. As much as I would have preferred for Connell and the rest of the RCMP or National Guard or whomever to deal with this problem I knew what I had to do. And I knew I couldn't afford to play this one by ear.

"So, what's the plan?" I asked quietly, peering over Connell's head at the seemingly abandoned complex.

He shrugged his broad shoulders. "Front gate?"

Okay, fine. Play it by ear it is.

"Sure. I hate climbing fences."

Both of us crouched low to the ground as we skirted the chain link fence line towards the hinged gate that allowed highway access. Connell's eyes never left the building as he trotted two steps ahead of me, still managing to keep his footing despite his split attention. For once not having to be the guy looking for warning signs I wouldn't recognize even if I saw them allowed me to focus solely on managing my heart rate and keeping my footing.

We made it to the gate without a single face plant incident. Yay me.

Still crouched down Connell took a hold of the heavy steel chain and key-lock keeping the gate shut. Unlike typical Hollywood heroes neither of us were narrow shouldered enough to use the chain's extra links to force an opening wide enough for easy squeezy access.

Connell eyeballed the top of the gate speculatively. "Sure you don't want to climb?"

"The RCMP taught you to read lips but not to pick locks?" I hissed at him.

He shrugged.

I sighed and shuffled past him, taking the chain in both hands and fumbling around for a good grip as sweat began to trickle down from the brim of my black hat. Connell gave me a speculative glance. "You know magicians are full of shit when they talk about finding the weak links in chains, right?"

Ignoring him was easy. What wasn't easy was trying to access the barest fraction of the energy pooled at the back of my neck. From the very first time I noticed this sensation and the strength and life it provided me I've never been very good at holding anything back. Even when practising with it and training at the YMCA all I've ever done is show up, feel it take over my nervous system and then hang on for the ride.

What also wasn't easy was knowing that I was about to use my strength in front of Connell in a way that he couldn't explain.

But we couldn't let Simon get away again. And I couldn't afford to lose control.

So my eyes closed as I reached inward for that electrical light and very tentatively allowed it to flow.

Oddly the sensation was familiar. The tingling rolled down along my spine and followed along to my fingers and toes in a cool rush, similar to how I often felt near the end of a heavy cardio session on the track. Marathoners' call it a Runner's High I think. That pure endorphin blast that keeps them pushing forward on auto pilot even when the rest of their body is tapped out.

In my case, I knew I'd only just begun to tap the keg.

My fingers gripped at the heavy Masterlock and chain while I took a deep steadying breath. With one sharp wrench I felt the steel haft of the lock break away and part in my hands along with a sudden flash of pain.

The sound was minimal but given the quiet prairie night there was no way to be sure how far it might have travelled.

I dropped the broken lock and links to the ground and swung open the gate.

Connell's eyes were wide with questions but the one he asked wasn't what I expected.

"How's the hand?"

I blinked, glancing down at my right palm. I had a fairly shallow gash just below the weightlifting callouses. It stung but only distantly and blood began to well.

"I'm good."

Connell shook his head and checked his pistol, flipping the safety off. "Why did you bring that damned hat anyway?"

'Because I like it." I motioned forward with my chin. "Ladies first."

It was a long walk from the open gate to the main complex, slightly less than a football field but not by much. The only light came from the moon and a few of the security lights directly above every entrance, and even those really needed new bulbs. Even so we hustled at a quick step, trying to cover the distance as quickly as possible.

The complex itself consisted of two buildings that reminded me of the Faculty of Engineering on the University of Manitoba campus. Hey, just because I wasn't a student there doesn't mean I didn't visit for a kegger once or twice.

Anyways, what I mean is that clearly one of these buildings was an afterthought. My guess as we approached was that the bigger building came first. It looked more industrial with stacks reaching from the roof to the sky, major power lines running out from it presumably to the nearby dam at the Red River and with huge rolling doors that were perfect for backing supply trucks in and out.

The other building was right against the factory, likely with connecting floors. However this one was clearly more of an office layout. Three stories tall, windows at regular intervals and with a definitive front door and small parking pad for employees.

Both buildings showed signs of the graffiti complaints the Cathy mentioned in her debriefing. Garbage was strewn about the ground, crushed beer cans and plenty of cigarette butts and fast food wrappers. Again, likely the result of Selkirk teens looking for a place to party. Also a sign that whomever was supposed to be checking on this facility was either doing a shit job of it or had been convinced not to show up for a while.

The RCMP squad car was parked in deep shadow near the office building entrance.

Connell's breath got sharp. "They're here," he muttered.

I reached out towards the building much like I had at the hospital's garden shed, trying to find an energy echo or something. Unsurprisingly I got a positive response back, after all the security lights over the doors were all on.

Duh.

"Your cops are here," I replied while peering around the complex and checking the path behind us. No one was visible. "Hopefully we're not interrupting an intimate moment."

Connell gave me a sour look.

"You calling for backup?"

By his expression it was clear that he was sorely tempted. But then Connell shook his head. "I gotta be sure. If Simon's and his victims aren't here and I call in the troops..."

"Yeah, yeah. Hell to pay. Lose your job. Blah blah blah." I grimaced sourly and wiped my bloody palm on my jeans again. "Should we complete the cliche and split up once we go inside?"

He chuckled darkly.

We stepped forward.

To my surprise the front door to the office building was unlocked. It was dark as hell once we were inside though. Connell produced a pocket flashlight and did that cop thing where he pressed it against the barrel of his gun as we began to explore. I just tried to keep cool as we travelled through the pitch black hallways.

It was a tense stomach twisting search as we went from floor to floor, checking out rooms as we came across them. Old offices with dusty desks in some. Discarded papers and supplies in others. A giant board room that looked like some teenagers had gotten into it once upon a time going by the condom wrappers, empty beer bottles and picnic blankets strewn about. We gave that room a more thorough going over, just to confirm that the debris was old.

I could sense Connell's frustration as we climbed each stairwell. To be fair that might've been my own frustration as well. It was dark. I was tense. I can't be sure of everything.

What I can be sure of was the group of people we found wearing hospital smocks all huddled together in another boardroom up on the top floor.

Much like the floors previous this boardroom was in the centre of the building's layout next to the elevator shaft. It was oversized and able to accommodate a large number of employees. Unlike the other rooms, the giant table in this room had been pushed over to the far window and tipped on it's edge. Seated with their backs against the table were five of Simon's victims from the hospital. I recognized a few of them from the dogpile assault I survived back in the atrium which told me the cops had missed more than just Simon that night in all the confusion. Three of them were women, all of them different ages and I assumed all of them were patients given their emaciated and frail appearance.

All five of them also had that eerie faraway stare I remembered all too well.

Despite my best efforts the tingle at the back of my neck

flared to life. Hair rose all along my limbs and my feet twitched with the urge to fly into action.

Connell's hushed voice was triumphant as he repeated himself. "They're here."

I nodded sharply and glanced around the room. Some food stuffs and blankets were bundled up against one wall along with some discarded boxes. Supplies of some sort I guess, though I was kinda surprised to see Simon taking any care whatsoever of his human drone fleet.

"Call it in," I muttered, returning my gaze to the stunned and silent patients. Their eyes were open and appeared not to be seeing anything. But I knew better this time. "Do it now. He knows we're here."

Connell blinked at my harsh tone but didn't argue as he fished out his smartphone. He fussed with it for a few minutes, cursing softly the whole time.

"What?"

"I can't get a signal. This makes no sense, it worked the whole way up here."

The whole way up here I was practically swallowing my tongue to keep my energies in check.

Shit.

I tried a few calming breaths but knew I was too far gone. The power had surged and I was feeling it too strongly.

"Go out in the hallway. Get as far away from me as you need to until you get a signal."

Connell looked up from his phone at me, confused. "I thought you didn't want to split up?"

"I also want you to call for back up. Now go away, I'll wait here."

Connell eyed me askance, bouncing the phone in his free hand as he thought.

"Goddammit, go! I'll be fine."

He swore under his breath. "Fine. I'll be right back."

Connell disappeared out the door and his footsteps echoed along the hallway behind him.

Leaving me alone with the patients.

Not creepy at all.

My yoga breathing wasn't exactly hatha-approved or anything, but it was better than just standing still and counting to a million in order to keep my thoughts and mind focused on the task at hand. It took some doing but I managed to gain some measure of control over the tingling sensation and quell it down to a slightly less adrenaline blasting level.

For a moment I had things under control.

And then all five patients raised their heads in unison to stare at me.

I froze.

"Hello Joseph." Two simple words spoken by five voices at the same time. It made my stomach lurch.

Get it together, asshole!

"We playing hide and seek, Simon?" I think I managed to keep the emotion out of my voice. I didn't know which of the five patients to address so I gave each of them my attention. "I think we're past campfire games and stories."

Five identical smiles. Like a fucking horror show.

"You never did like games did you, Joseph? Too impatient for them as I recall. A pity." Five identical sighs. "Such a sad little boy."

My teeth ground together. "Never occurred to you that I thought you were a creep even back then, has it Simon? That I knew you were bad news and didn't want anything to do with you."

Five identical sad chuckles.

"Never occurred to me then. But now that you mention it, I think I know why we never got along." Five identical conspiratorial leaning in motions. "Too bad we'll never get a chance to fix that."

"Never too late," I quipped, trying to keep the horrified bile from rising. "Tell me where you are and we can make up for lost time."

More laughter in stereo.

"Sadly, I think we're well past that Joseph. In fact, in a few moments I think we'll be past everything."

Footsteps behind me. I breathed a quick sigh of relief as Connell came back after making his call.

I glanced over my shoulder, readying another quip to the Simon-chorus.

Words caught in my throat.

The two missing RCMP officers stepped into the boardroom with guns drawn and faraway looks in their eyes.

Seven identical voices now.

"Goodbye, Joseph. I'm sorry it has to be this way."

Both officers raised their pistols and fired.

Chapter 47

For a moment I was taken back to the instant my life changed. The strongest flash ever flooded my brain and superimposed the image of a scared sixteen year old boy who only wanted to know what had happened to his sister over my immediate view of the brainwashed police officers. That boy had also pointed a gun at me. Scars on my body were a constant reminder of that day and they buzzed at the memory.

In many ways, that was the most important day of my life.

Because without that day, I wouldn't have survived this one.

As the RCMP officers raised their pistols in automatic, muscle-memory-produced two handed grips fear sent my heart hammering, shortened my breathing and made me want to tense up.

But the energy at the back of my neck had erupted at the sight, setting my nervous system on fire and sending me fully into overdrive.

The guns roared impossibly loud in the night, echoing off the walls and in my ears. But I was in motion before the triggers had been pulled, rushing towards the officers with my head tucked low. By the time the guns went off I was executing a CFL style body tackle, taking both officers about the waist and driving them back through the boardroom's open doorway.

Things got vague for a moment.

Absently I realized that several seconds had passed. By the time I came back to myself I was seated against one wall, holding both hands to my ringing and bleeding ears. The guns had gone off directly over my head as I'd plowed into the cops and had severely messed with my equilibrium.

Plus it hurt like a motherfucker.

Blood from my ears mingled with the blood on my cut palm. It stung a bit as I wiped absently at the legs of my jeans. Both officers were unconscious on either side of me in the hallway and breathing steadily as far as I could tell. I wanted to give them a quick examination, see if I had hurt them. After a moment I gave up on the idea since I'm about the furthest thing from a doctor and stood up uneasily, the energy still pulsing strongly in my veins gave me strength but didn't do much for a pair of blown out eardrums.

Both officers' pistols were on the floor in front of me.

I ignored them and stumbled back into the boardroom, scooping my battered hat from the ground and slapping it uneasily back on my head.

Windows on the far side of the boardroom were now spiderwebbed, which gave me a sense of relief knowing that none of the patients had been hit by the stray bullets.

As I started to regain my balance and the ringing in my ears faded to a dull ache I noted the obvious change in all five of the patients. Two of the women had passed out. The third was rocking back and forth with both arms wrapped tightly around her knees, eyes wide and terrified. One of the men was laying on his side, sobbing loudly while the other was simply staring up at me in terror.

Weird.

I stopped in front of the last patient and met his eyes. He stared back at me, still frightened but seemed coherent.

"Where's Simon?" To my battered hearing my own voice sounded hollow and tinny. Like being on the far end of one of those camp phones with a can and a string.

The patient stared up at me, his mouth moving but making no sounds.

I think.

"Speak up. I can't hear you."

More mouth moving. Some faint sounds. Might have been words.

Shit.

I held up my hands. The patient stopped talking.

"Is Simon here? Nod yes or no."

A nod.

"In this building?"

Confused expression as the patient thought about it. Then a head shake.

"In the factory side?"

Nod.

The energy pulsed again, making my toes twitch and my ears ring even louder. I gritted my teeth and pushed the sensation back.

I told Connell I'd wait for him here.

Then it occurred to me how long it had been since the guns had gone off. How loud it must've been. And how Connell hadn't come rushing back.

My stomach dropped.

"How do I get to the other building?"

More words I couldn't here, this time accompanied by some vague pointing and motioning.

"Wait, stop."

He stopped.

"Downstairs?"

Head shake.

"This floor?"

Nod.

"Convenient," I muttered. "Left down the hallway?"

Another nod.

Energy continued to pulse in time with my heart beat.

About time something went right.

"Stay here. Watch the others. Help is on the way."

At least, I hoped it was as I spun all wobbly on one heel to walk out past the floored RCMP officers to take a left down the hallway.

Darkness is not your friend. It's not until you walk down a nearly pitch black hallway in the middle of the night without full use of your hearing that you can truly appreciate just how terrifying the world must be to someone without sight or sound.

So obviously I was kicking myself for not checking to see if one of the officers had been carrying a flashlight.

Eventually I stumbled my way around another corner and saw the faint red glow from an EXIT sign above what appeared to be a steel reinforced doorway. The downward slope in the floor as I approached confirmed my suspicions from outside, this building had been designed after the factory was built and this access floor was adjusted to line up with the industrial building.

Small victories. I needed small victories here.

It wasn't until after I bulled my way through the door, kicking the release handle and shoving it open wide that the thought of maybe attempting some stealth might've been in order.

I mean, just because I couldn't hear it slam into the wall as it crashed open...

Anyways.

Enough lights were on in the factory to give me a clear view of the room.

I was up on a steel catwalk that circled the whole building with a passageway that cut across the middle, an access point for the stacks and jumbo sized power lines that extended from the huge electrical turbines that took up the majority of the room on the main floor. Both turbines were dormant and layered in dust. There was a wide open space large enough for transport trucks to back in and out of, explaining the oversized rolling door I had originally seen from outside.

There were benches and work desks against the walls at various points, some still sporting tools and the like for maintaining the turbines. A few of them now had a variety of boxes on them as well. Some filled with foodstuffs, some with clothes and still another with what appeared to be license plates.

I made special note of the boxes since several of them were in the process of being loaded into the back of the six-seater passenger van parked in the middle of the room. Three beefy orderlies from the hospital still in their scrubs were doing the loading automatically, not phased by whatever noise I had made crashing through the door. Two nurses were quickly packing another box at the nearest table.

The man overseeing the ladies' work was Simon.

I knew this because he had turned to face me. His eyes wide and wild at the same time.

His hand snapped up to point at me, lips moving in a shout.

One of the orderlies came out of his trance and reached into the van.

He came back into view with a hunting rifle.

Chapter 48

Some people like to think things through before they do anything.

When I'm in my quieter moments I like to think of myself as one of those people. Someone who looks at a situation from every possible angle before making a logical, cognizant decision.

In my less quiet moments I know better.

Which is why I was vaulting over the catwalk's railing and hurtling towards the ground before the plan to do so had fully formed.

It was quite the fall. Even with energy and life flooding my limbs there was a distinct pain in my bad knee as I landed feet first on the roof of Simon's van. My two-hundred-fifty pound frame rocked the vehicle hard on impact, leaving a huge dent in the roof and spiderwebbing the windshield.

Momentum from the van's abused shocks bounced me into the air again on a funny angle. I managed to land unevenly on the concrete floor amidst a cloud of dust with a sharp exhalation of breath and more pain rocketing up the right side of my body. Damned bad knee whiplashed to the concrete as I rolled away, losing my hat somehow in the process.

Beats getting shot.

Speaking of.

I pushed up to my good knee and rubbed at my eyes to clear them of grit.

Beefy orderly with the rifle had drawn a bead on my skull.

Energy flared. Blood pumped furiously. Super-charged adrenaline raced.

All pain was forgotten.

I was on both feet and blurring across the cement floor faster than I would have ever dreamed possible, slapping the rifle barrel aside with one arm. I could feel the rifle fire but my damaged ears were too far gone for me to hear even it at this close range.

Moving too fast to slow down my shoulder collided mid-mass with the big orderly, sending his body flying backwards into one of his co-workers as I slowed to a stop. Seeing the brainwashed bodies slam heavily into each other and tumble away sent another pang of regret to my gut. Nobody here deserved to be hurt.

Nobody save for Simon.

With power surging through my veins I clenched both fists, felt the hair on my knuckles rise and turned to the source of all this misery.

Simon was backing away, both hands stretched out in front of him. Words spilled from his mouth. Pressure began to mount against the energy at the back of my skull. Simon's influence. His gift. His weapon. It clawed and scraped at my source of power, trying to gain purchase in my mind. Trying to slow my approach as I stalked across the floor towards him.

I was thankful for a moment that I couldn't hear a word Simon was saying. Never figured having a blown out set of eardrums would be a blessing. Remembering how things had gone at the hospital in Selkirk, how his very words held a weight and a power along with the mental pressure holding me down. Even though I could start to feel the outer edges of my energy beginning to leech away, knowing that all Simon could do to me was exert his gift over my mind I was confident that I had the juice to keep his filthy thoughts at bay.

Then the third beefy orderly blindsided me with an elbow to the side of my face and I was no longer thankful to be unable to hear anything.

Stars exploded in my vision as I stumbled to the ground, pain shooting up from my knee once again. My already wonky equilibrium had escalated to gyroscope levels as the room spun in my watery vision. Not sure where the final orderly was – hell, or where anything was – I used the forward motion as best I could to crawl and roll on my knees and elbows. Scrabbling desperately to get somewhat vertical and bring my hands up to a defensive posture in front of my face.

Then a knee passed my feeble guard and broke my nose in a

flood of blood, tears and pain.

All I could see were stars.

All I could feel was pain.

And then, more pressure at the base of my skull.

Why are you still fighting me, Joseph?

My already ragged breath caught in my throat.

I didn't hear those words.

At least not with my ears.

Shit.

My head began to ache in a way that was both different from the agony I was suffering from and terribly familiar. The efforts I had made to keep my energy reserves in check earlier were now completely gone as I had been burning through my inner well at a frantic pace. I had no doubt that the power sputtering from the back of my neck was the only thing even keeping me conscious as I pushed up from the floor, pain shooting up my leg and joining in with the pulsing in my brain.

Oh, I didn't know you had a bad leg Joseph.

Fire in my leg. A sickening pop behind my knee.

I screamed.

However did you injure that?

Oh, fuck it hurt.

I could feel the joint swelling underneath my hands as I rocked back and away from the orderly who had kicked viciously at the side of my knee. Trying to scoot on my ass and shoulder blades to create a bit of distance between myself and the walking Simon-bot.

Eventually I hit the wall.

It's strange. I remember you hating the boys who fought all the time. And yet, here you are. Looking to fight with me and my family.

Literally the heavy brick wall across from the rolling access door. It smacked sharply against my back and shoulders putting an end to my desperate retreat.

Didn't stop me from pushing back with my good leg, forcing myself to a seated position as Simon and his orderly approached.

My goodness you are a mess, Joseph. We can't send you home to your mother looking like that.

Blood from my broken nose had completely soaked the front of my shirt and filled my mouth with that awful iron tang. Stars had faded from my watery eyes a bit as the war continued in my head between my will and Simon's.

I placed my right foot flat on the floor and pushed carefully. The fresh pain that shot up from my knee was intense but I hoped it would take some weight if I could just get vertical.

There's a good boy. Don't let others push you around.

With my back flat against the wall and an agonized scream muffled by clenched teeth I leveraged my body upwards, sliding up the concrete for support. Grit and more scraped at my wrecked tee-shirt, tearing long lines in it the flesh of my back.

Pain.

Very good, Joseph. Stand tall.

In a world where few things made sense, where life threw you curveballs and made good choices seem like bad ones there was one constant that reminded me of who I am. One constant that narrowed my focus when I needed to block out everything else.

Pain.

It truly is a shame that few will understand what happened here today. I warned everyone though. Back when they first arrested me, when they took me away from my home. From my family. From my lovers. I warned them all that they didn't understand me.

I understand pain. We're old friends.

Not necessarily the physical kind like I was dealing with here. But pain all the same. The pain of loss after the death of my father and brother. The pain of watching my mother weaken day by day, year after year from heart disease. The pain of keeping bill collectors at bay, working sixteen hour days and three jobs at the expense of all else. The pain of running into old friends and colleagues from school and hearing about their careers, their families and the pursuit of their dreams.

I warned everyone, Joseph. I warned them what a mistake they were making by arresting me. No one understands the pain I suffered in that prison. No one understands the pain of being separated from the people who love and support them.

My heart continued to hammer in my chest as I pressed my palms flat against the wall and tested my bad leg. It flared unsteadily beneath me. I brought my gaze up to meet Simon's dark eyes. His fear was gone, though I knew that already from his creepy inner-outer monologue. An expression of smarmy self-confidence that I remembered all too vividly from my childhood was back on his face. A wide, shit-eating grin that frankly looked more than a touch mad highlighted the expression, never fading even as he spoke to me the words that only resonated in my head.

Of course when I initially warned them I wasn't able to be as persuasive as I am now. It's funny how the pain of loss sharpens the mind and focuses ones gifts, isn't it Joseph?

The orderly who'd attempted to shatter my knee was only a few yards away and slightly to my left, just in front of Simon. Behind him I could see the other two orderlies back on their feet and limping towards us.

How can anyone understand the depth of my suffering? Or understand the conflict in my head? How difficult it is to deal with the thoughts and emotions of other people. Those pathetic souls without the will to take control of their own lives. What would they do without me to control it for them? Who could understand the responsibility I have to my family?

"I understand, Simon."

Everything paused. The pressure at the back of my head. The approach of the orderlies. The nurses packing travel boxes. Simon's chatter.

All eyes were on me.

I was only going to get one shot at this.

You understand?

"Yeah."

Simon's expression became condescending, as if speaking to an infant.

No one understands me, Joseph. No one can experience life in the way that I can. Knowing people inside and out. Being able to see their hopes. Their dreams. Their suffering. Being able to experience their lives through their eyes and help them to make the decisions they could never make for themselves.

Phlegm and blood bubbled into my mouth as I chuckled darkly.

Something's funny?

"I understand just how convinced of your own bullshit you are," I spat, literally hawking the crap out of my mouth to the dusty floor in a gross stream.

Simon blinked. Silently daring me to continue.

My voice was inaudible to my ears though I heard it distinctly in my head as I stared down the man who had tormented, abused and murdered men and women for years.

"I understand how you believe you're above the rest of us. How you are better than everyone you meet." My teeth grit together briefly as I repositioned myself, trying to get both feet lined up. "Even as kids I could see that in you. Your arrogance. Your elitist attitude."

I am better, Joseph. He motioned to the people held under his thrall with arms spread wide, the smile broadening. *Is this not evidence enough that I am more than the sum of my parts. That my desires, my will cannot be held back by a society that doesn't accept what it believes to be wrong?*

The pressure increased at the back of my head. Vision went hazy for a moment as Simon's efforts increased, trying to sway my admittedly tentative grip on coherent thought. I countered by releasing every last ounce of energy I could feel tingling at my neck., removing every last mental block I had been using to keep something in reserve.

The rush of light that filled my vision was amazing.

The rush of clarity that filled my mind was even brighter.

And suddenly, I no longer felt any guilt over what I knew I had to do.

Simon's mental pressure snapped away in an instant. The agony from my knee and elsewhere faded to a manageable ache. All along my body I could feel the hair rise as electricity danced from cell to cell in a rush.

The effect on Simon was obvious. His head rocked back like someone had popped him with a sharp jab. I could see even in the darkness a trickle of blood beginning to roll out from one nostril as he stumbled away from me.

My small smile spread across blood-stained lips, showing teeth.

With a lurch I pushed away from the wall, taking heavy limping strides forward.

I'm not a lip reader. Simon's thoughts no longer echoed in my head. My ears were still blown out.

But there was no doubt that he was screaming at me to stop.

"You didn't say 'Simon Says'," I muttered grimly as the orderlies approached, unphased by what were undoubtedly the worst final words anyone could ever have muttered grimly.

Then moonlight started to fill the room. I couldn't hear it, but I could feel the electrical surge as the overhead doors began to roll upwards, exposing the dusty factory to the humid night air.

Everybody froze.

Silhouetted in the doorway were at least a dozen women of varying ages and states of health and one very broad shouldered man.

They all walked into the room in unison.

Yes, unison.

Simon's shit-eating grin came back, blood from his nose staining his too white teeth.

Connell and the women stepped forward until I could see their faces and the faraway look in their eyes.

Chapter 49

At least Connell wasn't pointing his gun at me.

Hey. Small mercies.

With the remains of my power fading by the second the last thing I wanted to do was stand frozen in place while surrounded by Simon's goon squad.

Yet as Connell and a collection of Simon's victims approached I found myself locked in position, completely unsure of my next move.

While it had made me sick to engage the orderlies and RCMP officers I was able to justify the violent actions as a necessary evil. All of them were physical folks, used to a more rough and ready occupation. I tried to convince myself that they wouldn't hesitate to do the same if the roles were reversed. Hell. If it was just Connell approaching I might have been able to knock the hell out of him with a smile on my face whether he was under Simon's thrall or not.

But those women...

Damned chivalric tendencies.

That smarmy smile across Simon's face was begging me to smash it. The pressure at the base of my skull began to war again with the sputtering energy that pulsed infrequently back there, sending barely enough juice to my limbs to keep me vertical.

Ladies. Lieutenant. If you please.

As one, the missing women of Winnipeg advanced on me with the blank eyed Connell leading the way, his pistol still held low and pointed away.

My feet twitched, sending a new shot of pain up from my abused knee. I grit my teeth together and tried frantically to keep from crying out.

Fingers grabbed at my arms, the rough and experienced at detaining people fingers of the orderlies. They trapped my hands behind me in duelling hammerlocks and hoisted me up onto my toes, sending another shot of pain up from my knee in the process.

I flexed and twisted my upper body as much as possible but had no leverage left to speak of. The sudden rush of energy had faded until it was barely there and my head had begun to pound in a very familiar way, adding to the broken nose and Simon's mental attack.

More hands grabbed at me. The ladies.

Soon I was hoisted from the ground and being carried backwards, away from the open overhead door. Like the lead singer after stage diving into the crowd I was being held up and restrained by people I no longer had the strength or even the will to fight.

I was beaten.

And Simon knew it.

Things got hazy as I fought against unconsciousness. Fatigue and pain are brutal opponents after all.

Eventually I acknowledged the cold metal pressing against my back and the new ache in my arms.

Blinking away the blackness I could see Simon standing directly before me, his eyes focused intently on mine. Behind him activity was picking up as the missing women joined in with the nurses, packing the travel items into the few remaining boxes while others began to unload the now undrivable passenger van.

The three orderlies stood to Simon's left, dead eyed and grim. Connell stood to his right, gaze distant and faraway.

An ache in my shoulders added to the agony in my head and the fire in my knee. Glancing upwards I saw my wrists duct-taped haphazardly together against what looked like the edge of some giant fan.

Awesome. Prisoner to a psychopath.

Best. Day. Ever.

Small and dirty fingers gripped at my chin, forcing my face

forward. Simon. His eyes locked again on mine from mere inches away. Fury and indignation burning in his gaze.

Even from this distance I could only hear the words in my mind.

Why are you so different, Joseph? He asked, the tone in my head ringing imperiously. Like a Roman Emperor shouting from the golden dais to his minions. Simon's eyes flashed, the pressure intensifying and causing still more pain to light up my brain.

My teeth grit together hard. Even if I cracked the enamel in my molars I refused to give him the satisfaction of more sound.

Fingers gripped tighter.

Why can I not get through to you? Sharp nails began to dig into my flesh. His dank breath assaulting my nostrils. *You aren't special. You never have been. Not like my family. Not like my people.*

More teeth gritting. No response given.

Simon's eyes got wild and he shook at my head, rapping it solidly off the metal object I was trapped against.

Why? Why are you able to thwart me?

It was a good question.

One that I wished I had the answer to.

Activity slowed behind Simon. The ladies had completed their packing and unloading. An exchange of thoughts passed between them that I didn't hear but could easily follow was happening. Connell dug out his car keys and handed them to an orderly while the two nurses began to head out the door.

New rides. Connell's charger and the cop car. At least until they made it somewhere to rent or buy a new transport.

"Bet you wish you had those credit cards, huh?" I mumbled spitefully through the fingers clenching my jaw together.

Simon didn't bother replying though his eyes glinted with fury.

A new thought hit me then as Simon's eyes changed, his focus shifting while he gave instructions to his people. Maybe not a thought, an intuition? An impression? Oh God, was I starting to pick up on Simon's thoughts in the way Tamara had? The thought made me want to throw up.

The thought? Or the plan.

What's Simon going to do to the people who won't fit in the vehicles?

My memory flashed to the sodden wood chipper at the Selkirk

Mental Hospital. I felt it resonate somehow with the pressure Simon was exerting on the back of my skull.

Shit.

Despite the lack of circulation in my numb fingers I managed to clench them against their bindings, tightening them into scarred and calloused fists.

Simon blinked suddenly, his mental pressure adjusting as he noticed the change in me.

Beat up. But not beaten.

Defiant.

I stared death at Simon, trying to bore a hole through the back of his head. Somehow deep in my body I felt the barest tingle of life, the faintest spark of energy tingling at the back of my neck. Fuelled by my anger maybe. By my pain perhaps. But certainly focused by my will.

Simon blinked again. Then his face twisted darkly. Both hands gripped my head now at the temples.

Pressure became something else.

Gravity. A steady and constant pull that refused to allow earthly beings to leave the ground and defy its power.

And yet defy I did.

Our eyes were locked and the intensity must have been visible to anyone who looked. I could almost see the waves of thought being hammered at me flowing down Simon's arms and into my skull. I could feel the vibration of my electricity pulsing away, pushing back with everything in my soul to keep his need for dominance and control at bay.

It was a war that lasted an eternity. It lasted milliseconds. We were locked in place and brawling like drunks in a tavern, flailing at each other with everything in our soul.

Why won't you submit to me? Simon's thoughts raged in my head. Spittle forming at his lips and spraying my face. *Why?*

Oh God the agony.

Time went on. Simon's assault was winning and I could feel the tingling sensation I was desperately clinging to slipping away.

I was spent.

Thoughts hit me in a flood. Regrets over bad choices. Paths not taken. Battles that I should have fought that I walked away from. Thoughts about Mom and how she'd react. Thoughts about Cathy and the horror she would feel knowing her favour set me on the path to this. Thoughts about Tamara, sitting up in her hospital bed with wide terrified eyes that were seeing something faraway, somehow staring right into mine.

All of these thoughts hit me in one of those life-flashing-before-your-eyes montages that...

Wait.

Tamara.

Sitting in her hospital bed.

That wasn't a memory flash.

That was happening now. In this moment.

Her comments about Simon's intensity. His fear and anxiety. How in those moments she was able to re-establish a connection with his thoughts.

That she could see what he saw.

And she was seeing him trying to control me.

And there was nothing I could do about it.

Simon's lips peeled back into a monstrous smile. All attempts at smarm and subterfuge were gone. He knew what I had realized. He could feel the connection Tamara had made in this moment. And now he was ready to finish off the one person to ever deny his power.

More flashes hit my brain.

My memories.

Simon's look of fear as I confronted him at the hospital, shoving him back against the wall before blowing out all the lights and computers.

In the atrium. His look of astonishment after I broke the mental connection and threw him across the room.

The absolute look of horror after grabbing the vending machine live wires, sending myself into overdrive and finding himself powerless and disconnected from all the hospital staff and patients that had been dog-piling me.

The hint of that very same fear began to glint in the very back of Simon's eyes.

My memories.

Tamara's incentive.

Simon's livid question.

Why can't I control you?

Then the image of Tamara, scared and crying in her hospital bed. But staring not into space but directly into my eyes from where she was.

She had a question of her own.

What are thoughts, Joe? At their biological core, what are they?

Simon's monstrous smile wavered as the gravitational pressure continued in my skull.

My mind flashed in a crazy way, the picture in picture memories to live action image scrolling at an impossible speed behind my eyes. Flickering like cards in the hands of a skilled illusionist, showing image after image from my memories. Somehow they scrolled faster, scrubbing through my history and showing me crystal clear images of things that I hadn't thought about in years.

The image froze in the unlikeliest of places. Mr. Skroemeda's grade nine biology class. He was standing next to a screen with a large picture of the human brain on display thanks to the overhead projector loudly humming away in front of him.

"Excellent question, Renata." Mr Skroemeda smiled in response to the unheard question before uncapping a blue marker and drawing little jagged lines across the picture of the brain. Jagged little lines that looked like lightning bolts. "At this time the scientific community has good reason to believe that thoughts are an emergent property of neurological activity. Now this activity can be electrical, but also chemical and biological and indeed the boundary between the three is not distinct. According to the experts biology is biochemistry and biochemistry is electromagnetic energy. We do not yet know precisely how or why neurological events are interpreted as thoughts. But..."

I saw a smaller version of my own hand rise into the image in my head, heard my own hormonally charged voice cracking as I asked: "So, thoughts are electricity? How does that work?"

Mr. Skroemeda shrugged with a smile. "It's an ever growing study, Joe. No one knows for certain at this point. But there's no denying that at our very core the human body acts as an imperfect electrical conductor. Our cells respond to it. Muscles twitch and grow under electrical stimulus. And under neural examination, our thoughts show up on scans as electrical impulses."

The memory dissolved.

Tamara's face no longer looked terrified.

Simon's face was turning red, sweat pouring from his brow at the effort to dominate my mind.

Thoughts are electricity.

Simon's gift is to control other people's thoughts and actions.

My gift is the ability to feel and channel electricity.

My gritted teeth showed as a wolfish smile pressed against Simon's gripping hands.

"You can't control me," I muttered.

The memory flashes made sense. Back at the atrium, gripping the live wire. The sudden rush of energy broke Simon's contact not just on me but on everyone there.

Sure, at the moment I was helpless and barely remaining conscious. I had been pushing my reserves for weeks. Testing myself. Seeing how far I could take things. Setting new records for strength, speed and endurance. Tamara had warned me of the consequences for running myself to the brink.

My personal battery was tapped out.

So what I needed was more juice.

The cold metal pressed against my back again. A subconscious nudge.

Simon and his goons had duct-taped me to a fan. No, not a fan. A turbine used to cool down the generators for an all but abandoned hydro-electric plant.

A hydro-electric plant that Cathy's reports had told me was still operational.

My smile grew wider.

Simon's eyes got manic.

Now I'm not an engineer. I don't know dick about working in a power plant. I couldn't tell you what any of the machines in this building did or how they operated.

But I also ain't a mechanic and yet I managed to fire up the truck of those fool car-jackers from a dead stop just by feeling for the power source and making a connection with it.

Now or never.

The shift between holding Simon's thoughts at bay and reaching out behind me nearly ended me in the space between one heartbeat and the next. Feeling the absence of my block, Simon's filthy thoughts filled my head like an oil stain spreading over the ocean, choking the life out of everything in its path. Suddenly I had access not just to Simon's insecurities but to his desires. His plans. His need for dominance over others to feed not just his sexual cravings but his insurmountable ego as well. Simon saw himself as more than human. He truly believed that others were beneath him. That his gifts and power placed him on a pedestal and that mere humans' attempts to contain him were only a nuisance to be humoured until the time to assume control presented itself.

That moment between heartbeats nearly ended my life as his mental grip took a hold of my will and sunk in claws.

And then I found the spark of dormant batteries used to fire up the generators and bring them to life in case there ever a need.

And holy shit, was I in need.

I reached for the spark and applied my will to it.

Never before in my life had I ever felt so alive as I did in the following moments.

People are not meant to feel that strong. That aware of themselves and their surroundings.

For the briefest of time I could make account not just of every person in the factory, I could feel the presence of living creatures for miles around. Not in a creepy way mentally, but as sheer electronic blips on my mental radar.

It was the wildest thing.

And it was more than I could possibly handle.

Behind me the lights flared on all machines. The turbines behind me fired up and sent a rush of dusty air billowing past me in a hot rush. Overhead lights flared to the brink before exploding in a shower of sparks and glass in an ever expanding wave with my body at the epicentre.

Light filled my eyes. Fire filled my brain, violently shoving Simon out. Distantly I saw his body launch back and away, his hands now gripping at his own head as he writhed on the ground.

Explosions. Heat. The smell of burned metal and rubber. All that and more assaulted my body.

Every nerve ending screamed at me. In pleasure. In pain. The taste of blood in my mouth was gone, replaced with something much more metallic.

It was amazing.

It was impossible to contain.

So I let it go.

There was a second rush of energy. The already burst lights overhead sparked and flared once more. The machines powering the plant made awful grinding noises as they too erupted in showers of sparks and glass.

Smoke began to fill the air as old wiring began to smoulder. Most of the plant was made from cement but I knew from experience that this building could still go up in flames.

It took an eon for my brain to come back to the present. It may only have been seconds, I truly couldn't tell you the difference.

When it did I was on my feet. Clear headed and filled with life. Energy flared from the back of my neck stronger than ever before. Absently I realized that my knee while still tender was holding my weight with confidence and stability. A quick check to my face and my broken nose seemed to have fused itself together, though I doubted it was a pretty look. Even the cut on the palm of my hand was rapidly fading as I stared at it, little shocks and bolts jumped from one edge of the cut to the other before my eyes looking like a damned sewing machine stitching a seam.

Around me everything was in a state of confusion.

Two of the orderlies were out cold as were over half of the missing women. There were shocked cries and sobs coming from the others. One of the nurses was rocking in the fetal position on the ground while unintelligible sounds tumbled out of her mouth. Everyone there had a shocked expression on their faces with hair in complete disarray.

The smoke intensified.

Simon was before me, pushed up to his knees. Blood was now pouring from his nose and ears.

He no longer looked like the all powerful demi-god he believed himself to be.

Reality had crashed down on him. Reducing him back to the pathetic, child-molesting bastard who used his ability to manipulate the minds of others to satisfy his every whim.

I had seen inside his head. I knew that this wouldn't stop him. Letting the police take him in, putting him back on trial and locking him away wouldn't do any good. Even locked in the deepest cell, away from everyone... Eventually people would get too close. Eventually he would find someone to manipulate. Someone to subsume and dominate.

Someone to control.

Simon was all about control.

No matter the consequences.

Power filled my very being. Clarity filled my mind.

Revulsion twisted my guts.

I knew what I had to do.

"Please." Simon's voice. No longer in my head. Now just whimpering and broken to my restored ears. Blood bubbled over his lips as he sputtered. "Please don't."

It would be so easy.

I knew it was what I needed to do.

And yet I hesitated.

From his knees, Simon saw the hesitation. His eyes blinked, faint hope returning to them. He held out his hands in a helpless gesture, as if expecting me to produce handcuffs from somewhere.

His voice gained some strength.

"I won't fight you anymore, Joseph. I will go willingly. Please just..."

The back of Simon's head exploded in a spray of blood and gore. His body flopped wetly to the ground as the gunshot echoed loudly in the confined space.

Connell was back on his feet, pistol smoking in his hand and a fierce look on his exhausted face.

We locked eyes.

Suddenly the enormity of the evening hit me and I didn't know what to do. Everyone here had seen me in action and one of them was a damned RCMP lieutenant.

The impossible level of energy bottled inside me raged, telling me to flee.

Connell lowered the pistol and nodded to Simon's corpse.

"You weren't going to do it." Not a question.

I didn't respond.

What was there to say?

In the distance carried by the quiet prairie sky came the sound of sirens.

I blinked.

Connell shrugged his broad shoulders. "I made the call. Didn't expect to run into the missing women when I did. That's when he..." Connell's voice trailed off, his face going pale at the memory.

The sirens were distant but getting closer.

I truly didn't know what to do.

Connell made the decision for me.

He walked towards the destroyed van and bent over to pick something up. He tossed it at me.

I grabbed my battered felt hat out of the air, staring at it and then him.

"You were never here." Connell made a shooing motion with his gun hand, aiming for the door. "I'll handle this, but you need to be gone."

My heart surged, the energy begging for a release feeding my limbs with anticipation.

Connell's eyes narrowed. "But don't disappear on me. We need to talk."

I grunted, firmly settling my hat in place over frazzled hair. "You gonna clear my name?"

"I will."

"Then we'll talk."

He nodded and repeated the shooing motion.

My eyes scanned the now smoke filled power plant, glancing at all of the people there. The living people who now had another chance at life. A chance to control their own lives and destiny.

I could relate.

My gaze stopped on Simon's corpse.

My stomach churned.

The sirens got louder.

I let the overwhelming energy flare from the back of my neck and gave into the urge to run, rocketing out the door in a blur and not slowing down until I passed the "Welcome to Winnipeg" sign along highway fifty-nine.

Chapter 50

"What did you say? Joe, I can barely understand you."

I made an effort to clear my throat and swallow heavily. "Are you watching the news?" I mumbled as clearly as I could through the remaining mouthful of Captain Crunch I was loudly chewing.

I finally ran out of borrowed energy once I got close to Kildonan Place mall. Thankfully the bar rush had been over for at little while so finding a cab willing to drive my sweat soaked, exhausted and blood stained self home wasn't too hard to flag down. He even kept me off the meter, accepting the last ten bucks in my pocket as payment.

After throwing the smoking remains of my old sneakers into the trash bin I managed to slip past my mother's sleeping form on the couch and stumbled downstairs without making too much noise, stripped off my ruined clothes and collapsed in my shower stall as hot water scalded my body clean. I wished it could've done the same for my mind.

The fact that I was alive seemed too much to comprehend.

So much had happened. I didn't know what was real anymore.

Then my stomach rumbled impossibly loud and sent the familiar starvation headache ablaze, reminding me of the only reality I needed to know.

Go eat something, fool.

Half an hour later I was mostly laying on the ancient couch in my mom's basement and balancing a giant mixing bowl filled with an entire box of children's cereal on my chest as the TV screen flickered in front of me. Tamara's voice was in my ear via the old school landline receiver. She sounded more exhausted than I felt.

And I felt completely exhausted.

Sugar and fat hit my stomach in equal amounts, appeasing the hunger pangs and sending relief up into my skull. A minor irritant after the rest of the agony I'd dealt with in the previous few hours.

I barely knew how to explain it.

So I kept changing the subject.

"Seriously. Cathy and her team have broken into the overnight infomercials to report on this. Turn on channel five."

Tamara sighed in my ear. "Fine, hold on."

As she put her phone down I paid more attention to what was on the screen.

Cathy was standing on the road leading into the power plant about half a football field away from the main gate. Police tape was up behind her as was a collection of cop cars, RCMP and WPS, and a few fire trucks. Firefighters were working hoses on the smouldering parts of the building in the background as Simon's victims were being tended to near an ambulance, blankets covering their shoulders and medics tending to their needs.

"Scott, this scene is like nothing I've ever witnessed before," Cathy said into her microphone while staring directly at the camera. She looked dishevelled, clearly just throwing her clothes together in a frantic rush in order to have made it to Selkirk so quickly to actually be reporting live. She shook her head in astonishment. "Police on location haven't confirmed whether or not an arrest has been made but one thing we can confirm unequivocally is that several of the people involved in the Missing Women Case have been found here at this old Hydro Plant near Selkirk, Manitoba."

"Isn't she supposed to be going to Calgary with Max in the morning?" Tamara asked in my ear.

The memory of Captain Max's cold eyes flashed briefly.

I couldn't worry about that now.

"It's still early. She might make her flight."

"It really seems extraordinary, Cathy. What amazing work by the police force to have finally tracked down some of these poor victims." The image shifted back to the studio. Scott Armstrong was the late night anchor and overnight CTV producer, usually not seen on camera past the eleven-thirty broadcast. He too was dishevelled, likely disturbed from his mid morning nap and ushered back to the set as Cathy's report was coming in. "What can you tell us about the case if anything?"

"Scott I was able to speak to a few people before being ushered out past the security line. Did you receive the footage we've sent back to studio yet?"

"I think we... Yes, we have it. Ronnie? Let's roll that footage."

Connell's face appeared with his name and title printed near the screen's edge, his expression grim as Cathy's microphone pressed near his face. "At present time we have no comment on the goings on here. Sometime tomorrow the RCMP and Winnipeg Police Service will hold a joint press conference. At that time questions will be answered."

Cathy's voice cut in. "Lieutenant Connell can you at least confirm that this raid or whatever was in relation to the ongoing Missing Women's Case being operated jointly by..."

"All of your questions will be answered tomorrow during the press conference."

"Lieutenant Connell, did the activities here at the Hydro Plant tonight cause the blackout that shorted out power to over half of the homes in the City of Selkirk just over an hour..."

"Again, questions will be answered at the press conference

tomorrow. Now if you'll excuse me."

The scene cut away to a woman. One of Simon's victims. Her shoulders were covered with a blanket and her face was dirty and pallid. Her sunken eyes were red-rimmed from crying and she seemed ready to collapse. The graphic at the bottom of the screen introduced her as Jennifer.

"It's all so strange, I don't know how any of this happened." Jennifer coughed wetly, turning away from the camera briefly. Cathy's voice quietly encouraged her to continue if she wanted. "I have no idea how long I've been away, or what I've been doing. All I know is that I am so glad he's dead."

"Who's dead? Jennifer, can you tell me who you're referring to?"

The camera angle shifted madly, spinning away. Officer Swan was visible briefly amidst the action.

"This is a police zone, what do you think you're doing?"

"We're just wanting to ask some questions and..."

"Shut that fucking camera off."

The scene cut back to a double shot of Scott in studio and Cathy on location. Scott's face went white as he stammered out an apology to whichever post three a.m. viewers might have been offended by the officers' profanity in the previous clip.

"Wow." Tamara's voice in my ear. "She really is a pitbull when on a story isn't she?"

My spoon made a scraping sound. I blinked, noting the now empty mixing bowl resting on my chest. The headache had faded but I knew more food was in order.

"Joe?"

"Yeah, still here." I turned down the volume on the TV and sat up to a better posture. "How're you feeling?"

"Tired. Really tired."

"Yeah. Me too."

"I'll bet. I have no idea how you're still awake."

So many thoughts and questions flickered through my mind.

I settled on an easy one.

"How's your head? Still getting images?"

Tamara made a disgusted noise. "From Simon? Ugh, no. Thank God for that."

"Were you... Did it hurt when he got..."

"Joe I lost all contact with him after trying to help you. Once you started up the power plant... Well, let's just say I won't be needing a curling iron for a few days."

I blinked in surprise. "Did I hurt you?"

"No, not at all. Just a bit of a shock is all."

"Are you sure? What about... You know. The baby?"

Long pause. "I think everything's okay there. I don't feel any different."

"Get the doctors to check. Please. I would never forgive myself if something happened."

Tamara's laugh was rueful. "Well since I managed to throw up just before you called I'm inclined to think that everything's still lodged safely in place."

I sighed, whether in relief or for another reason I couldn't tell you.

"So yeah," Tamara continued her voice a mystery. "Guess things got a bit weird between us, eh?"

"Yeah. I guess they did."

"I mean, women have been accused of reading a man's mind before in relationships but this was..."

"Thank you."

Tamara paused. "For what?"

My stomach rumbled again, demanding more food.

"For helping me stop Simon. For showing me how."

Tamara's voice got very quiet. "You did all the work, Joe. Hell, I was barely more than a bystander."

"Don't do that."

"Do what?"

"You help me, Tamara. Every day. Without you..." My voice trailed off, strangled by a sudden fear and teenaged level shyness that was afraid to open up. Which frankly was ridiculous after the whole mental connection from over thirty kilometres away thing.

"Joe?"

Man up or shut up asshole.

I chose shut up.

"Just thank you. You helped save a bunch of people today. Primarily me."

She didn't respond.

But my belly did. Loudly.

I stood up. "Look, I'm going to go and grab more food and check on Mom. Try to get some sleep."

Tamara found her voice again. "Yeah... Okay. I guess. But, Joe?"

"Yeah."

"Are we... Is everything... Now that I've been in your head are we going to be all right?"

I made my voice as light as possible. "You already knew I was a perve. Skimming my brain couldn't have shown you anything new."

She laughed.

It wasn't much, but it would be enough. For now.

I hung up and padded upstairs as quietly as possible in my bare feet. More thoughts, concerns and questions rattled around in my head. Or jumped in my head like little lightning bolts I suppose.

Connell. What was his deal and why was he backing me up? Or is he backing me up? What if this is some sort of long con that I can't understand? It's clear now that he not only knew I was involved in the stuff at *Cowboy Shotz* but he also suspected that there was more to me than what I was letting on. How else could anyone explain his lack of surprise to the things he had seen me do, or his immediate acceptance of Simon's telepathic abilities?

Tamara. Despite my bravado I was completely freaked out about her being in my head. I shuddered slightly while reaching into cupboard, wondering what sort of things she had seen. What sort of awful thoughts or ideas I'd had that she might have gleaned. My jealousies. My darkest thoughts. My insecurities.

Yuck.

So many questions.

I only knew one thing for sure.

If I was going to get this place ready for the open house at two p.m. I was going to need at least a little bit of sleep.

So I poured myself another mixing bowl of cereal - Honeycomb if you must know – and drowned it in a litre of milk before heading into the living room, scooping a ladle of sweet sugary goodness to my mouth as I stumbled along.

Mom always looked so peaceful when she was asleep. Propped on the couch by her pillows. Remote control within easy reach on top of her pile of the weeks' newspapers. An empty coffee mug on the floor next to her and covered in a housecoat and blankets to keep her frail body warm.

A sad version of my small smile appeared. The thought that this might be one of the last times I would see her here, in this house before moving her into her nursing facility.

Though the thought no longer made me feel guilty.

It was past time maybe to take control of my own life. To stop living it for someone else.

What better way to honour the memory of my father and brother could there be than that?

I sat down gingerly on the edge of my mother's coffee table and just stared at her as a thousand memories flashed through my head once again. Happy memories. Dinnertime with the family. Board games. Trips to the zoo. Vacations to exotic Grand Forks.

My mother's smiling face. Full of life and laughter. Even now as she slept with her eyes closed and her too pale flesh I could see the smile lines and hear her laugh.

I reached out and took her tiny hand in mine.

"I love you, Mom." I whispered, giving her icy fingers a squeeze.

She didn't stir.

Then I realized that her fingers weren't just icy.

They were stiff.

And she wasn't breathing.

Author's Note and Legal Disclaimer

June 19, 2015

The preceding work of fiction is intended solely for entertainment purposes. Any reference to actual places and businesses is used only to provide a sense of space and context for the reader and is in no way meant to take advantage of or exploit other people's properties or brands. In addition, any similarities between characters mentioned in this book and actual people is purely coincidental.

As a proud, full time resident of the City of Winnipeg it seemed only appropriate to begin my literary journey in my hometown and display pieces of it prominently as set pieces in this series. The axiom "write what you know" has been essential for me in this process and I am hopeful that this tale becomes a fun read for other citizens of Winnipeg, whether current, former or future.

If you have enjoyed this book I invite you to join the OVERDRIVE Official Facebook Page and start a conversation. I will be visiting it as often as I can to provide insights and updates for future stories and answer any questions you might have about this or anything else I might have written or done.

You can also follow me on Twitter (@OutlawAK) . Though I warn you in advance I also use this forum to talk about my upcoming Pro Wrestling dates, my workout routines and various other entertainments that make me laugh.

Thank you very much for taking a chance on my work. Writing has been a passion of mine for as long as I can remember.

Regards,

Adam Knight

Twitter - @OutlawAK

www.Facebook.com/OverdriveSeries

Made in the USA
Charleston, SC
02 June 2016